She stood

"What's the matter?" Morgan asked, returning

"Nothing. I...I..." She stumbled over the words. "I have to go and get cleaned up for the recital and dinner."

"Recital?" He arched his eyebrows. "What's that about?"

She groaned. "I didn't want to, but Daddy insisted I play. I can never say no to him."

"So you're the headliner at this recital?" Morgan asked as he stood, brushing himself off. "What do you do?"

She stood, watching Morgan, but glanced at her watch again. "The piano. I play the piano."

"Well, I'd never want to hold up the show. Can I walk the star back to the house?"

"Of course." Giddy with unfamiliar feelings, she turned and headed back at a half-run.

Morgan fell in beside her. "How long have you been playing?"

"Since I was four."

Candace called from the back porch again.

"Wow." He showed a look she thought was admiration. "A champion rider and a virtuoso on the keyboard, too?"

"Really?" She searched his eyes for amusement, a hint he was mocking her. She saw none. "Thanks, but you may be overestimating my skills."

Candace called a third time. Louder this time.

"I'm coming," Paige managed.

Morgan stopped, took her by the shoulders, and gently turned her to face him. His smile held warmth and affection. "Something tells me I'm not."

Praise for Kevin V. Symmons

"[*OUT OF THE STORM*] has great plot that steadily evolves and offers lots of twists and turns you don't see coming! Everything you would want—mystery, intrigue, suspense, and romance. This was a great read."

~RLA Reviews

~*~

"If you're looking for a paranormal tale without the usual vampires, werewolves, and zombies, [*RITE OF PASSAGE*] is the book for you!! A compelling romance between a beautiful young witch and a dashing member of the upper crust is set against the backdrop of an epic struggle between good and evil. But it's a lot more than a romance. The author has skillfully woven elements of a mystery and a thriller into a story that will keep you turning the pages. It's a great read with a surprise ending that doesn't disappoint."

~Georgia Girl Reviews

~*~

RITE OF PASSAGE was a 2013 RomCon Readers Crown Award Finalist!

~*~

"*SOLO* is a realistic life story as well as a love story. The characters are complex, often intriguingly flawed, and their journey takes them through the beauty of the arts and ugliness of domestic violence. Kevin Symmons gives the reader a rich, intricate plot and superb writing. He brings a passion for music and literature to this tale of two talented souls who will haunt readers long after the book goes back on the shelf."

~Susan Trausch, Best-selling author
and former Boston Globe columnist and feature writer

Dedication

To the two most amazing parents
a man could ever ask for...
thank you for always believing in me!

Prologue

March 2001, Massachusetts Maximum Security Correctional Facility, Walpole, Massachusetts

He sat in his cell brooding, calculating, planning. He knew who would be the first. Had worked it out years ago when freedom was only a dim possibility. He'd been at this place for twelve years. But today that was over. He stood and walked to the bars at the front, staring out at the cruel dungeon that had almost consumed him. Slowly and systematically, this place had stolen any shred of innocence and decency. As he watched his fellow prisoners in the common area, Julian smiled. In a few hours, he'd be a free man. To prove it wasn't a daydream, he turned back inside and went to the small metal table bolted to the wall. On it was his copy of the judge's order for his release.

After the last decade of hell, his lawyers had been able to find and prove the truth. *D-N-A*. Three glorious, life-saving letters. If he still believed in God, he would thank Him. Somewhere on one of those terrible nights when they'd used him, tortured him, and left him lying in a heap for the guards to discover, he had given up on the Almighty.

He opened his Bible and removed the paper. He recalled reading that hate was a far stronger emotion than love. But of course he had only been in love once.

1

The girl next door, he mused. It had begun in their childhood and grew as he became a man. And *she* would be waiting for him. His love for her kept him alive during the long dark years of despair, but it paled when compared to the depth and strength of his hate. Julian could taste his hate for the animals that had made life a living hell. It was alive and palpable like the bile that rose in his throat when he closed his eyes and recalled the nightmare he'd lived. Yes, his hate transcended every other emotion and feeling, anchoring his grip on life it had prevented him from giving up and killing himself.

He stared at the list written in his precise script. Six names—the list he'd composed in the futile hope he would someday be exonerated. Now that flicker of hope had come to fruition. He smiled again as he wet his lips and closed his eyes and envisioned how he would deal with each name, reserving a special place for the last one on the list.

****

An hour later, Julian Warren picked up his belongings at the desk.

"Good luck, Julian. I'm…" The warden's words faltered. He had come to say good-bye. The warden knew what Julian had been subjected to in the early years of his imprisonment. But whether through impotence or turning a blind eye had done little to stop it. True, this was no boys' school. The inmates truly ran the asylum. Julian studied the man's face. Had this man, like so many, taken solace in his torment assuming Julian was the monster they claimed? What was that in the warden's eyes? Regret? Long overdue and useless sympathy?

"I'm sure you are," Julian said bitterly, holding a neutral expression. He ignored the man's offered handshake.

He stepped around the warden and through the door, stopping at the gate. Sophie would be there, standing beside Julian's well-preserved Mercedes coupe. Sophie. The person he had loved his entire life. He refused to look at another. It had resulted in terrible consequences. His secret devotion to that exquisite young girl added to the mystery and stories that sprouted about him and the youthful relationship he refused to admit.

"It will help your case!" she had argued vehemently. He would not sully her or the reputation of Hamilton's first families. No, Julian naïvely clung to the belief his high-priced attorneys would have the ability to punch holes in the flimsy case the State presented.

Naïve. Yes. He had been naïve. Brushing off his misconceived notions as the gate squeaked open, he rushed outside and thought of her nestling in his arms. More importantly he thought of the faces of those on his list when they recognized him and spent their last hours suffering as he had suffered for so long…

Kevin V. Symmons

Chrysalis

PART ONE

Kevin V. Symmons

Chapter 1

June 2001. The Fuller Estate, Mattapoisett, Massachusetts

Paige Fuller sat and stared out at the long swells skidding across Buzzards Bay. How should you feel when the boy you've been secretly in love with since you were children was about to descend on you for the weekend? Great if you looked like Candy. Shaky and terrified if you wore braces, glasses, and had a mask of freckles across the bridge of your nose! Paige looked down at her careless riding clothes, thankful Morgan wasn't due till dinner. She'd have time to get cleaned up and wear something presentable.

Like it really mattered. He'd never even see her. No, Morgan Cahill, major stud and Ivy-League idol, would look past her and see Candy, her oh-so-beautiful, poised, and popular sister. But Paige wasn't jealous. Candy was a great sister, and Paige did have a lot going for her. Trouble was, when the person you wanted desperately to impress was so handsome and talented he didn't even know you existed, all the victories, trophies, and walls covered with awards meant nothing.

"Hello. Earth to Paige Fuller!" Candy touched her arm as they finished their sandwiches and sodas. "Are you in there somewhere, little sister?"

Paige sighed. "Yep." She checked her watch. "We

should probably get going. It's almost two o'clock."

"I just can't wait." Candy beamed her magazine-cover smile. "Have to be all sparkly and beautiful when the guest of honor arrives."

Eyeing her spectacular sister, Paige ran her tongue across her braces and wished they'd miraculously disappear. "C'mon. Morgan's not the guest of honor," she whispered in denial as she stuffed the leftovers of lunch into her saddlebags. "It is Daddy's special weekend, you know."

"Okay, okay. I know you're Daddy's little girl, but I see it differently." Candy laughed as she gracefully mounted Caesar, her magnificent Dutch Warmblood.

Paige bounced up into the saddle and slumped as she took Alex's reins. "Well, view it any way you want," she said dejectedly as she thought about the two endless days that stretched before her. Days that only promised more hurt and rejection. "Morgan'll be here till Sunday night and be gone as soon as he can."

"Paige Fuller, you are such a pessimist," Candy scolded. "When will you get out of this funk? Don't be so negative. He's not some mindless jock. Daddy said he was valedictorian at Roxbury Latin last year."

Paige ignored her sister and cantered across the tall grass. She closed her eyes for a moment. She knew Morgan's accomplishments. Had committed them to memory. But he'd come and look right through her, his very presence mocking her.

"Hey," Candy yelled as she caught up with Paige. "Maybe he likes sweet, brilliant, shy girls with braces and a wall full of blue ribbons from show jumping."

Paige turned and frowned at Candy. "Yeah, right," she scoffed. She urged her horse into a gallop toward home, allowing her elegant, beautiful sister to trail behind.

****

A hand-crafted wooden sign with four inch gold lettering hung from two polished brass hooks. Cedar Acres. Morgan Cahill eased his BMW 325 convertible into the Fullers' long driveway. Its engine resonated in the thick air. The car was a reward from his adoptive father for breaking the single-season Ivy League rushing record. Malcolm Cahill enjoyed rewarding the child he and his wife found in an orphanage before the child's fourth birthday. Morgan had grown accustomed to his dad's indulgences but often wondered what would happen if he failed to impress. To date, he'd had no occasion to worry.

Two perfect stone pillars flanked the entryway, each capped by an antique, multi-faceted lantern. The left-hand pillar displayed a spotless white sign with the house number and the name Fuller carved in lettering matching the Cedar Acres sign. Morgan vaguely remembered the sign from his first visit to their estate in Mattapoisett, a small town on Massachusetts's South Coast. The estate lay nestled on a dozen acres a short distance from Buzzards Bay, a turbulent expanse of water that separated it from Cape Cod by twelve miles.

The winding, gravel drive stretched before him, dappled by intermittent sunlight and flanked by massive oak, red maple, and birch trees. A warm, almost sultry breeze from the Bay did little to stem the early summer heat. Over the sound of the car's throbbing engine, the whine of cicadas greeted him.

Conflicted feelings assaulted him about spending a weekend with the Fullers. He remembered the Fuller girls, daughters of his father's oldest friend. Candace, the oldest, had been cute when they'd met years ago. Her younger sister was cute, too, but in a different way. Not sweet, accommodating, and flirtatious like Candace. No, the younger daughter had an edge. Defensive, even combative. But Morgan found that intriguing. After six years, he still remembered her. The eyes, the smile. And smart? After a couple of days he'd been blown away. Paige—that was her name—was a damn genius at eleven. But so much time had passed since that visit he had no idea what their lives were like or what the girls had grown into. Morgan wanted to please his father but had a plausible escape story on hold if the weekend turned into a disaster.

The estate was spectacular. And Fuller was a name held in high esteem in a setting where your lineage was of consequence. His father said the Fullers were direct descendants of Samuel Fuller, a signatory of the Mayflower Compact. He'd also told his son stories of their family's heroism dating from the time of King Philip's War to Vietnam. The family had achieved exalted political status. Josiah, their host for the weekend, was legendary—a no-nonsense district attorney who, for a reason his dad could not understand, had decided to step down at an early age. Yep. The Fullers were as close to royalty as a New England family could get.

The leisurely half-mile drive to the house seemed ordinary. Halfway to the imposing main house he saw the girls, walking in sunlight that filtered through the foliage, making intricate patterns on the gravel and grass. Later, he'd remember nothing—no flash of lightning or omen to indicate a star-crossed meeting that would change the course of his life—and so many others.

Faded jeans hung on the hips of the smaller girl as she led the impressive mount beside her. A loose T-shirt and riding boots completed her outfit. A black riding helmet dangled carelessly from her right hand. Next to her, impeccably dressed in breeches that clung and a white, fitted blouse walked a taller girl with effortless, flowing movements.

They walked in the middle of the driveway, talking and laughing, oblivious to his approach. Fearful of scaring the horses, Morgan eased his convertible to a stop a hundred feet behind them. The tall girl—Candace he assumed—heard him and turned, flashing an expensive smile. Morgan got out and walked toward them.

"Well, hello. Is this Morgan?" asked the girl with honey hair hanging in two perfect braids. "We heard you were coming, didn't we, Paige?"

Paige. That *was* her. She nodded, fidgeting with the reins while she studied the ground. Morgan watched her. She'd grown up. Though shorter than her sister and wearing clothing that did little to show her figure, Morgan could see it right away. She moved with the poise and fluid grace of the thoroughbred she led. Paige had become a young woman.

Candace showed him more of her flawless smile. Not an easy task. She'd done a magnificent job the first time.

But Morgan watched Paige, remembering her from their weekend years ago. She pushed her lips into a pout, avoiding his eyes. Short dark brown hair hung several inches above her slim shoulders. Her round face showed a sprinkling of freckles over her slender nose and enormous eyes.

"Yep, that's me," Morgan confessed. "I think my folks are already here."

The blonde girl nodded. "I'm Candace. But you can call me Candy. We met a few years ago," she offered, batting thick lashes. "We've heard so much about you. But then you're a *legend*."

"Thanks. I remember you, Candace," Morgan answered, blushing at her praise.

Morgan turned toward Paige, who'd favored him with a timid glance. She wore glasses that failed to hide her eyes. Fine with Morgan. They were soft, large, and brown with the silky look of velvet. Her long lashes fell as she resumed her study of the driveway.

"Hi, Paige?"

"Paige." The taller girl gave her sister a gentle nudge. Morgan understood her reticence. Who wouldn't be shy standing near the goddess with the perfect figure and the honey hair?

Paige lifted her head a second time, teasing him with the hint of a smile. "Hi. Glad you could come." Her sultry voice was in counterpoint to her sister's and her appearance. It had a sensual, hypnotic quality. "I… I remember meeting you," she added, finding his gaze.

"You look great, Paige."

She studied him suspiciously, as if she doubted his sincerity.

Morgan returned her stare, enjoying it. Paige's bashfulness hid a lovely young woman. He allowed a smile to cross his face. A gentle grin blossomed in return. Deep dimples appeared in her cheeks. She wore braces—perhaps another reason to hide your smile if you were next to Candace, the sunshine queen.

He offered his hand. She pulled off her riding glove, wiping her hand on her faded jeans before shaking. Her firm grip belied her small, warm hand, the palm calloused. This was no prima-donna. She withdrew her hand rapidly as her face flushed.

He offered Candace his hand. "Nice to see you again, too, Candace." Unlike her sister, she let her grip linger as she held his gaze with hers.

"Gotta go," Paige announced suddenly as she left the driveway, heading across a brilliant field of wildflowers and long grass swimming in the sultry breeze. Morgan saw a massive barn in the distance. "See you later," she added.

"Where are you going?" Morgan called after Paige, disappointed and confused at her abrupt departure.

"Gotta give Alex a rubdown," she answered over her shoulder, favoring him with a backward glance.

"Alex?" he asked, taking two steps after her. "Don't know much about riding, but he looks like quite a horse," Morgan called.

"He is. He's a wonderful mount," Paige offered with a look of admiration. She stroked the animal's mane affectionately as she walked. Morgan followed her with his gaze, an innocent, beguiling apparition, teasing him as she crossed the tall grass swimming in the shimmering heat.

"Don't mind Paige." Candace left her mount, letting the reins fall as she walked back and studied his car. "She's seventeen. I remember what that was like. Nice ride, by the way."

"Thanks," Morgan acknowledged, doubting Candace had any idea what it would be like to be her less glamorous sibling.

"Don't get me wrong," Candace added quickly. "She's a wonderful sister and a great kid. I think she feels awkward and..." She glanced at her sister. Her eyes were expressive, showing warmth and compassion. Morgan liked that. Candace was no shallow prom queen.

"I should go, too. Caesar needs some attention. We put them through their paces today. Especially Paige." She stared after her sister with admiration. "She's wonderful. Such a great rider. You should see her."

"Alex and Caesar?" Morgan laughed.

"Alex is short for Alexander." Candace nodded toward Paige, smiling. "We're both ancient history buffs."

She touched his arm as she turned and headed back to retrieve her mount.

He got in, started the engine, and headed toward the main house. Morgan waved to Candace. She seemed genuine. He liked that. She was also spectacular. He had no doubt she was captain of the cheerleaders, prom queen, and class president. He already knew her very well. His whole life had been spent surrounded by girls like Candace.

As he guided the BMW the last quarter mile, he touched the brake and turned for a moment, letting his eyes follow the slender figure retreating to the barn. *Paige.* Something about her touched Morgan. Something he could not understand. This shy girl with the dimples, braces, and beautiful eyes intrigued him. Yep. Prospects for the weekend had unexpectedly brightened. *Paige*—the name seemed to fit her. He mouthed her name again: *Paige.*

Chapter 2

"Oh my God," Candace swooned as she led Caesar into the barn. "Did I call that one? Is he good enough to gobble up or what?"

Paige tried to pretend she hadn't heard, determined Morgan would not overrun her heart. No one would do that. Ever again.

"What?" she asked, desperate to sound casual—to erase the excitement of seeing Morgan again and the blood pulsing in her ears when she thought of him.

"Morgan, for God's sake." Candy stood watching her, hands on her hips. "I know you pretend that guys don't exist. But I worry about you sometimes, Paige. Really!" Her gaze softened as she approached her sister. "C'mon. Even *you* have to admit he was amazing."

Of course! Paige needed no reminder. Her cheeks heated, remembering the warmth of his touch, the way his shorts and polo shirt clung to his lean, athletic body. It was all she could think about.

"He was kinda cute," Paige acknowledged, doing her best to hide a smile.

"Oh—my—God. Is the world going to end?" Her sister grinned and gave Paige a friendly push. "Did the ice princess actually say a boy might be cute?"

"Yes! Okay, he's very cute," Paige whispered. Her cheeks burned as she pushed past Candy to get a curry brush. "But c'mon, Candy. He is the son of Daddy's oldest friend." She frowned.

"So what?" Candy gave her a knowing smile and went after her own brush. "He's fair game. They are *all* fair game."

"Maybe," she said. Stopping and leaning against the wood, she removed her glasses and put them on the two-by-six that acted as a cap between the stalls. "But he'll be gone in two days and…" Paige thought of the years she'd dreamed about him after their meeting as children, the snatches of stories she'd read and heard about him.

"I think he liked you, Paige." Candy appeared behind Paige after finishing with Caesar. Candy's gentle grip turned Paige to face her.

Paige stared at the stable floor. She resisted the urge to pull away as Candace took her chin and lifted her face upward. "Stop making excuses to keep your heart locked in a box."

Paige lifted her gaze to meet her sister's.

"I know what happened. You've been using that as an excuse to pack it in, give up on the world, and spend your life with the horses and chicks. I understand." She shook her head and sighed. "Alex and Caesar never broke a heart."

Paige opened her mouth to protest. Candace held up her hand and shook her head again. "I don't want to hear it. Maybe you're right. Morgan will be gone on Sunday, but I'm telling you, sis. He was not looking at me. Not that I didn't try." Candace grinned. "He was watching you."

"But look at me." Paige let her head fall as she studied her outfit.

"Paigey, you are sweet, gentle, talented beyond all belief, and when you try, you can be the most adorable thing around!" Candy's voice rose with passion.

Paige tried to resist the building grin.

"You've got to-die-for eyes, those damn dimples I'd give anything for, and though you do your best to ignore them, boys look at you all the time. If you wanted to be, you could be downright hot!"

Paige gave her sister a nudge. "Get out. You're just trying to make me feel better."

"Yes, I am." Candace took Paige firmly by the shoulders. "But it happens to be true."

Paige threw her arms around her sister. "Thanks." She squeezed Candace.

"Okay, but here's the deal." Candace backed out of Paige's embrace and her nose wrinkled. "I'm going to take a shower, and honey, you need one, too, big time. C'mon, get out of those raunchy riding clothes, take a shower and—" Candace looked embarrassed. "You could use a toothbrush."

"Okay," Paige agreed. She took her sister's hands. "Thanks." She paused. "You really think he liked me?"

"Yes…now c'mon!" Candace ordered.

"I will, promise. Just have to finish up and put the stuff away and check on my chicks."

"All right but if you're not at the house in fifteen minutes, I'm coming back to drag you out of here!"

"Promise," Paige repeated as Candace waved.

Paige realized how lucky she was to have Candy for a sister. She'd heard about sibling rivalry. but Candy had always been her biggest supporter.

Paige looked down at her T-shirt and baggy jeans. Just the kind of outfit to send thrills through a hunky jock like Morgan. He wasn't supposed to arrive till dinner. Still, she could have worn something better. Something that fit and didn't reek of horses and the stables.

"Oh," Candy yelled as she reappeared at the stable door. "Mom said they're having drinks by the pool. We can sneak some wine." Candy winked and gave her a knowing smile. "You can do some serious flirting. I know he—liked—you."

Paige waved and nodded.

She looked at her T-shirt again, covered with dust from her ride and cleaning Alex. Paige peeled off her glove and stole a look around. She put her hand in front of her mouth and blew into it softly to check her breath. *Oh God.* She kicked the barn wondering what Morgan must have thought.

Could Candy be right? He did seem to pay attention to her. Acted disappointed when she left. Paige knew it certainly wasn't her outfit. She picked up the grooming brush as a tiny tendril of hope blossomed. By the time Morgan saw her again, she'd be a perfumed vision of loveliness.

****

Morgan arrived at the house and parked his BMW in the generous circular driveway. He surveyed the white farmhouse and the manicured lawns that surrounded it. This was what a country home should look like. A picket fence bordered much of the rambling main house situated on a small rise. The land fell away in the direction of the barn two-hundred yards inland. The wood fence was white, freshly painted. The place must have twenty-five rooms, Morgan thought as he closed the BMW's door. In the distance he could just glimpse the gray-blue of Buzzards Bay. Several large A/C condensers droned, shielded behind a low hedge as Morgan sauntered up the walk. Before he reached the door their hostess, Vera Fuller, and his mother came to meet him.

"Where have you been, Morg? We were worried. You called half an hour ago and said you'd made the turn-off. Did you have an accident?" his mother asked with concern as she looked behind him toward the BMW.

"Aliens," he whispered, glancing around furtively. "They beamed me up."

His mother swatted his shoulder as a look of amusement crossed her face.

"I'm fine, Mom, and so is the new ride." He gave her a kiss on the cheek searching her face to make sure she was all right. "Actually, I ran into Candace and Paige. I stopped and we talked for a while."

"You remember Mrs. Fuller?" his mother asked.

"Of course." He nodded as they shook hands. "Thanks for inviting us." After meeting the girls, the prospects for the weekend were definitely looking up.

"That's nice. Please call me Vera. When a handsome young man calls me Mrs. Fuller, I feel ancient." She grinned. This lady was stunning. It was obvious where her daughters got their looks from. "Did you get a word out of Paige?" she asked with a look of mild annoyance. "I swear that child would sleep in the barn if we'd let her." Vera turned to look at Morgan's mother, wearing a look of frustration. She cleared her throat and worked at showing a forced smile.

Great support system, Morgan thought. No wonder Paige seemed shy and self-conscious.

"Yes, they were both very friendly…Vera." Morgan said. He was curious and confused. Wondered why the judgmental attitude, especially in front of a stranger? Paige was quiet and bashful, not doing cocaine.

"Paige seems *very* nice," he emphasized, determined not to encourage her negativity.

"You met Candace then?" his mother asked, raising her eyebrows. "Isn't she lovely?" She smiled at Vera. "I know she remembers you, Morg!"

His mother playing matchmaker? Odd. Not her usual style. Even more odd—the Fuller girl on Morgan's mind wasn't Candace.

****

After putting his things away in one of the well-appointed guest rooms, Morgan went downstairs and found his way onto the deck overlooking the Fullers' massive swimming pool. He remembered it from their earlier visit. As he looked across the broad expanse of water, it occurred to Morgan that somebody ought to name it. He looked in the direction of the barn since neither of the girls had appeared at the house.

He spotted his dad and their host, Josiah Fuller. As always when he appeared, the conversation turned to sports—the Red Sox elusive World Series quest, the Patriots' chances for that Super Bowl, the Celtics, the Bruins, etc. Because of Morgan's athletic accomplishments, people assumed that was all he cared about. He couldn't remember the last time anyone had asked him about his feelings or dreams.

He let it go. *Stop being so damned self-centered,* he scolded himself. He owed his parents so much. They'd adopted him before his fourth birthday, shortly after their infant son had died. Morgan had been the recipient of their love and generosity—indulged and pampered as a child of privilege.

"Where are the girls?" Morgan asked, trying to sound casual.

"Think I saw Candace heading upstairs," Josiah said looking toward the barn. "It'll take her the rest of the afternoon to get ready." He chuckled. "But if I know my youngest, she's at the barn playing groom and nursemaid to the horses, chicks, ducks, and anything that whinnies, clucks, or walks on four legs."

Josiah's face reflected his amusement.

Although glad one of the Fullers was a Paige advocate, he puzzled over why.

"Thanks." Morgan smiled, held up his soda, and headed toward the house, adding, "Thought I'd look around this amazing place of yours."

"Sure, son." Josiah nodded affably. "Maybe you can take a walk to the barn and round up Paige."

Now *that* sounded like a plan. He walked through the massive house to the front porch, looking at the barn, wondering if she might be there.

Morgan found his mother and Vera Fuller sitting on two oversized Adirondack rockers sipping iced tea. After a few minutes of polite conversation, he asked if he could have another soda.

"Of course, dear. You know where the kitchen is. Ask Lizbeth. She's our cook." Vera swatted lazily at a horsefly as she waved in that direction.

The breeze from the Bay had fallen away, and the afternoon had become steamy. But Morgan's mind was not on the weather. He walked into the kitchen, smiling at the two people working slavishly over trays of *hors d'ouvres*.

"You Lizbeth?" he asked.

The woman wiped her brow and nodded. "That's me, dear." She smiled warmly.

"Hi. I'm Morgan." He gave her a casual wave. "All right if I take a soda?"

"Help yourself." The massive middle-aged woman pointed toward one of the two large stainless steel refrigerators.

"Thanks," he said. He took another, letting himself out the door to the back porch.

Morgan crossed the distance to the barn. He tried convincing himself his visit was casual, just something to kill time. He knew better. He wanted to see the shy cute girl who'd been knocking around in his head for the last hour.

And Paige *was* cute. Damn cute! And in the space of a few minutes she'd awakened something in Morgan. Something new and exciting. He could listen to her soft, smooth voice all day. There were her great eyes and those dimples and... *Snap out of it, Romeo. You just met her, and you'll be on your way home in forty-eight hours. You may never see her again.* His disappointment at that thought surprised him.

As he approached the barn, still confused by this intense and immediate attraction for Paige, his cell phone rang.

"Hey, man." *Damn!* It was his buddy Josh and from the sound of his speech, his friend hadn't been drinking iced tea. Josh was the organizer, the fixer, the guy who put together parties and acted as the matchmaker.

"Hi, Josh." Morgan looked toward the barn

knowing the purpose of his friend's call. Morgan had told his friends about the family get-together and asked them to let him know what was happening in case he wanted to bail. He'd even developed a cover story with his parents.

"You told me to call you." His friend paused. "Well, man, you are not going to believe this. You remember Madison, the babe from Vassar? The one who hung around you like a puppy-dog after the Yale game? The one with the l-o-n-g blonde hair who looked like a swimsuit model?"

"Yeah, I do," Morgan answered tentatively. "So what?"

"Well, we are thirty minutes away at Ben's house over in Falmouth. Right near Old Silver Beach and she is here and all she's talking about is you, you lucky son of a bitch. If she looked good in jeans and a sweater, you cannot imagine her in a string bikini." His friend howled from delight and too much drink.

"Well," Morgan said looking toward the barn again. "I'm not sure…"

"Morg, are you friggin' crazy," his friend interrupted. "This woman wants to jump your bones. Get your skinny ass over here."

Taking a last look at the barn he turned. As he did, the sound of the barn door caught his attention. When he looked back, Paige stood frozen. She made a quick attempt to brush off her T-shirt and jeans.

"Hi," she said softly, giving him a look that held both shock and surprise. "I…I didn't expect to see you till dinner."

Her cheeks flushed. So did his.

"Hi, Paige," Morgan responded, finding her eyes.

"Hey, man. C'mon. Get over here. Pronto! The party's just getting underway," Josh insisted.

Morgan watched Paige. She stood, fumbling with her clothes and her hair. But he didn't care. Her outfit and the telltale evidence of grooming the horses were irrelevant. He only saw the girl who'd bewitched him in the space of an afternoon.

"Sorry, Josh. Gotta go," Morgan said without hesitation, whispering into his phone as he closed it.

He approached her, retrieving the can of soda from his pocket and offered it to her.

Paige took it, adding a quiet, "Thanks."

"Now, if you got a few minutes, I'd like a tour of this magnificent place you call a barn."

She watched his eyes for a moment, searching them. "I really should get cleaned up for dinner." Paige fidgeted with her hair again, tugging at her outfit, trying to hide a smile. She failed. It morphed into a grin.

"Your dad and Candace say you're the expert here, and I know nothing about horses or riding. C'mon, please. Show me around?" he asked, hoping she wouldn't vanish again.

"O…okay." She nodded as they headed toward the barn. "I didn't know you were interested in riding."

"Let's just say it's a newly acquired taste," Morgan said.

Chapter 3

Paige swallowed deeply and sneaked a look at her outfit again, hoping that like Cinderella, her fairy godmother would change her soiled, funky riding clothes into a ball gown. No luck. It must have been her godmother's day off.

"You do know that Candy went to get cleaned up and—"

"Yep, I know," Morgan assured her. "I came looking for you. Rumor has it that you're the resident talent when it comes to this equestrian thing. And this is quite a place. Figured if I bribed you with a cold drink I *just* might get an up-close and personal tour."

Had he really come to see her? Could Candy be right?

"Well." Paige cleared her throat and in her most confident voice began, "These are the stalls where we keep our horses. We used to have eight, but there are only six right now. Two Arabians, two Dutch Warmbloods, and two Friesians. The Arabians are great for jumping and fancy show stuff. They're exquisite. Alex—Alexander and Caesar are Dutch Warmbloods." She gestured in the direction of their stalls. She tried to keep it simple knowing she desperately needed a shower and a toothbrush. But to her delight and confusion Morgan wasn't keeping his distance, placating her, or giving her that polite, glossed-over look. Just the opposite. He stood right next to her, a thoughtful expression on his face, hanging on her every word.

"The Friesians are new," Paige continued. "But they're wonderful. The perfect mix," she said as if instructing one of her riding students. She nodded. "The strength of a quarter horse but the agility and maneuverability of much smaller mounts. During the Crusades knights rode them because…"

She saw him watching her and stopped mid-sentence. "Am I boring you?" she asked.

Was he hiding a smile?

"Oh God—no. Absolutely not. I'm just taking it all in." He gestured around the massive stable. "This place. It's just so amazing." He shook his head.

Paige stopped. "What is it?"

"Oh, nothing."

"Please," she asked. "What are you thinking?"

"Nothing, Paige." He cleared his throat and looked uncomfortable. "Well okay. I was just thinking about some inner city kids I worked with last summer and wondered how they'd love to spend a day here."

Should she ask him about them? She was about to when she remembered her braces and her bad breath. She took a step back and put her hand over her mouth.

"How 'bout we go outside and find some sun. It is a little dark in here." Morgan pointed toward the back door before she had the chance to say anything else.

"I know. I'm really sorry," she whispered. "It's not exactly the sweetest smelling place." Paige put her hand over her mouth again.

He laughed loudly. "It's not a problem, Paige. This is like perfume compared to two-a-days in August."

"Two-a-days?"

"C'mon." He took her hand loosely, and they walked into the warm, moist late afternoon sunshine.

She sneaked a look, blushing as his grip tightened. Was this really happening?

He headed for her favorite oak tree—the one with the three-foot trunk that stood fifty feet from the barn door. The sanctuary where she could think her innermost thoughts.

"What are two-a-days?" she asked again.

"Oh, yeah." Morgan sat down and patted the ground. She sat next to him. "I'll make you a deal." He guided her to a spot on the ground. "I'll tell you"—he gently took her hand and removed it from her mouth—"if you stop doing that."

She sighed and smiled in spite of herself. Might as well enjoy this surreal situation. Paige was sure she'd been committed and was in a drug-induced never-never land.

He found her eyes again. "I like it when you smile." His face flushed as he looked straight ahead. "It's just that—well—you don't do it often enough."

She guessed her face must be crimson. Probably bright red. It felt that way—sitting under her favorite oak tree with the boy she'd been in love with since she was eleven, holding her hand and telling her he liked her smile.

"Okay." Her hand dropped as she found a spot next to him. Paige let herself slide a few inches closer. Morgan released her grip. She saw the dirt under her nails and brushed a stray piece of straw from her T-shirt, still conscious that the sour fragrance of the stable must be on her clothes. But…what the heck?

"You never told me about two-a-days?" she asked.

"Oh—right." Morgan leaned against the large oak and smiled. "Before we begin football season we go to training camp at a place in New Hampshire. The first week we go through two workouts every day. At the end of the day believe me our locker room would make your stable smell like a perfume counter." He chuckled.

She giggled. "Well I doubt that," Paige said as she leaned against the massive tree trunk close to Morgan. She closed her eyes and sighed. This had to be a delusion. Or maybe she'd died and gone to heaven.

"That's so much nicer," he whispered, inching closer. "Paige," he began softly and took her hand again.

"*Paige!*"

She sat up straight startled as Candy's voice carried across the lawn. The spell was broken. Paige looked at her watch. *Oh, God!* She'd promised Candace to be back at the house in fifteen minutes. It was five p.m. Forty-five minutes had passed since her sister had left her to finish up.

She stood abruptly.

"What's the matter?" Morgan asked, frowning.

"Nothing. I…I…" She stumbled over the words. "I have to go and get cleaned up for the recital and dinner."

"Recital?" He arched his eyebrows. "What's that about?"

She groaned. "I didn't want to, but Daddy insisted I play. I can never say no to him."

"So you're the headliner at this recital?" Morgan asked as he stood, brushing himself off. "What do you do?"

She stood, watching Morgan, but glanced at her watch again. "The piano. I play the piano."

"Well, I'd never want to hold up the show. Can I walk the star back to the house?"

"Of course." Giddy with unfamiliar feelings, she turned and headed back in a half-run.

Morgan fell in beside her. "How long have you been playing?"

"Since I was four."

Candace called from the back porch again.

"Wow." He showed a look she thought was admiration. "A champion rider and a virtuoso on the keyboard, too?"

"Really?" She searched his eyes for amusement, a hint he was mocking her. She saw none. "Thanks, but you may be overestimating my skills."

Candace called a third time. Louder this time.

"I'm coming," Paige managed.

Morgan stopped, took her by the shoulders, and gently turned her to face him. His smile held warmth and affection. "Something tells me I'm not."

****

Morgan sat on the thick chair in his room, staring at his cell phone, trying to figure out why he couldn't get Paige out of his mind. There was something about her, something he'd never felt before. This shy, sweet girl had consumed him, filling his thoughts like a sorceress.

From his chair he could see the dresser. It held a picture of the Fuller family taken years earlier. As he was about to walk over and look at it more closely his cell phone rang. He checked the caller I.D. Josh again.

He sighed and answered, "Hi. What's happening?"

"You're missing quite a show, dude!" His friend's words were deliberate. Josh tried to sound sober. Morgan knew better. "Wine, women, and song, man!" His friend broke into unsteady laughter.

"Is Ben around?" Morgan asked, seeking more rational counsel.

Ben and Morgan had been best friends since their first year at Roxbury Latin School, one of Greater Boston's premier private schools. Ben was the real deal—the one Morgan talked to about things that mattered.

"Yeah…I…I think I can find him," Josh slurred. Listening to the background noise Morgan imagined Josh stumbling around looking for Ben.

"Hey, man, what's happenin?" Morgan recognized his best friend's authoritative baritone. As expected, Ben sounded more coherent than Josh.

"Hi. I'm still in Mattapoisett with my folks. Josh keeps me updated," Morgan told his friend.

Ben chuckled loudly. "Yeah, Josh is having a hell of a good time. I give him till eight before we lose him," Ben told him. "I'm going inside. Too noisy out here."

Morgan heard the sound of music and laughter, someone squealing. The noise faded as his friend found a sheltered spot.

"What's happenin'?" Ben asked.

"I wasn't sure about this thing," Morgan began. "Figured it might be a real drag—" He hesitated.

"I remember you said that. I'm guessing there's a 'but' coming?"

"Well, the place is spectacular, and—I met this girl. Daughter of my dad's oldest friend."

"Okay. There's a story there. So, what's she like?"

"Nice. Real nice," Morgan told his friend. "I know I talked about coming over to join you guys, but I'm gonna hang here."

"You want to give me the particulars?" Ben asked.

"Maybe later." Morgan knew that describing Paige wouldn't do her justice, and he still wasn't sure what she thought about him. He thought she liked him, but they'd had only two conversations—an hour together? It was possible she was just being polite. All Morgan knew was that when he was with her he felt different. Relaxed and at peace. Free in a way he'd never known. The words sounded heavy but there it was.

"So, we'll talk later. Remember. I want every detail," Ben teased, adding, "What's her name?"

"Paige, P-a-i-g-e," Morgan spelled quietly as he pictured her face.

"Paige," Ben said. "I like it. And if you found something about her to like, she must be special."

Morgan sat contemplating his friend's words.

"Morg? You there?" Ben asked.

"Yeah. Right here." He paused. "She is, Ben. Special. Real special."

"Sounds like she's made quite an impression. Good enough for me, bro. Have a great time."

"See ya, Ben. You, too."

Morgan closed his phone and walked to the window. In the distance he could see the oak tree where they'd sat. He turned and headed to the bathroom to get cleaned up, stopping to stare at the picture of Paige as a kid, one with her family and one alone. He remembered the day they met. He picked it up. All arms and legs with the same enormous eyes and freckles that dominated her face and those dimples carved in her cheeks. She was cute even then. Very cute. He hadn't realized how much till he saw the picture again. Morgan smiled. "Special," he whispered to himself as he replaced the picture gently. "Really special."

Morgan could tell Ben all about Paige. Because Ben was not only his best friend, he was the only person who knew that Morgan, big-time jock with ice water in his veins and everything under control, was not what he appeared.

Chapter 4

While the Fullers and their guests prepared for an evening of celebration at their opulent estate on Buzzards Bay, forty miles to the north in the wealthy suburb of Hamilton, Julian and Sophie were sequestered in the well-equipped gymnasium in the basement of his estate's main house. Since his release, Sophie had moved into Julian's ancestral home.

Julian strained and grunted under the watchful eye of a first-rate martial arts instructor. A few weeks earlier Julian's initial attempt to exact retribution on the first victim of his long awaited vendetta had almost ended in catastrophe. He realized that despite spending several months strengthening his wiry physique his diminutive stature simply could not overpower and subdue many of the larger men that comprised his list of targets. They might be in a sad state of physical condition, but it was simple physics. Without some serious training in the principles of self-defense, judo, and basic martial arts, a 260-pound man could simply overpower a 160-pound adversary no matter what the level of condition of the smaller man.

Only pure luck, clumsiness, and drunkenness on the part of his target had saved him from ending his holy quest for justice on its first attempt. So now, both Julian and Sophie had employed the services of a reclusive, world-class Sensei to train them. The fact that both had now devoted two months to a routine of slavish conditioning was in their favor. So after eight weeks of long daily workouts both had made themselves into formidable foes. No longer simply fit, they had trained themselves into virtual human weapons.

"I don't think I've seen anyone quite so dedicated. You two have mastered the skills and disciplines as if your lives depended on them." The instructor nodded in obvious admiration.

"Let me try it with you," Julian invited quietly.

"You must remember, sir that I've spent my life at this and while you are superior in skills and conditioning to my other students, I don't think that would be fair…"

Twenty minutes later the Sensei held up his arms in mock surrender. While Julian had not defeated him, they had fought to a virtual draw. And only a slip on the sweat dampened mat allowed the instructor to prevail.

Sophie watched from the edge of the workout area. "Bravo, dear!" she cheered like a high school girl at a pep rally. "This calls for Champagne!"

They made their way upstairs where a bottle of vintage Dom Pérignon sat cooling.

After Julian opened the bottle and poured three flutes, they sipped the sumptuous liquid and sat in front of the fire. Julian excused himself and returned, tiptoeing behind the couch where their instructor sat.

"I have something for you, Roland," he said teasing with a delicious smile as he pulled a syringe from behind his back and deftly thrust it into the man's carotid. A foolish grin passed across his chiseled features as his head slumped and small bubbles emerged from his thin lips.

"Au revoir, mon ami," Sophie whispered as she put her slender fingers to his neck, checking his pulse. "I believe he's succumbed to all this excitement, my dear." She beamed in Julian's direction.

"Yes, he did seem rather high-strung." He shook his head in mock regret. "But then I fear no one will note his passing, will they?"

"No, he was a completely solitary man who lived for his craft. And now, poor dear, he's passed along that craft to you and I, *mon cher.*"

They sat contentedly while they finished the 750 ml bottle of exquisite Champagne.

Finally, Julian stood and looked at the man. He sat, fierce warrior's eyes still open as a tiny river of spittle drained from his open mouth.

"I'll go down and light the furnace. Let's give it a few minutes to warm up then we can deposit the poor fellow inside."

"And then, dearest I think I feel the need for a long leisurely soak in the whirlpool."

Just imagining the way she would tease and provoke him aroused Julian to a frenzy.

"Well then. The sooner the better! We have work to do later this evening!"

They both giggled like children.

Chapter 5

"Dear Diary, I cannot believe it! *Morgan arrived at the house this afternoon, then came to the stables to see me. I felt like Cinderella minus the ball gown. And I know I was a complete ditz—clumsy, goofy, etc. But* he *didn't seem to care! Every time I see him, my legs turn to jelly and I get this crazy, hollow feeling in my stomach—part terror, part excitement. But I don't know. I'm just a skinny high-school girl with braces and glasses. What would he see in me? I mean, he didn't even notice Candy. All I know is* I *can't wait to see him tonight. Is it possible...could he* really *like me? And if he does when I tell him what I have to it'll hurt him...and break my heart!"*

Paige sat at her dressing table, looking in the three-sided mirror. Her large room had all the earmarks of her mother's creation. Plush wallpaper and lace window treatments decorated the walls, while her queen-sized, four-poster bed sported a thick matching spread. Fashionable, overstuffed chairs and a couch covered in pink-and-white-flowered fabric covering robust heavy walnut frames decorated the room's spacious interior.

Paige appreciated her mother's efforts, but as she surveyed the room from the dressing table she smiled. Paige had asserted herself in her subtle way and taken control. Her boots, riding clothes, jeans, and other outfits sat on and around the massive chair in the corner and covered her oversized heavy walnut desk and dresser. Coordinated prints that had once hung in perfect alignment had been replaced by an asymmetrical collection of awards, ribbons, and photos of Paige on horseback, receiving awards, or at her piano. Every conceivable nook and surface was covered—consumed with Paige's belongings, awards, and memorabilia.

She fixed her gaze on the two worn volumes that lay side by side on her dresser. Paige's favorites—*Jane Eyre* and *Pride and Prejudice*. She'd read each a dozen times, wondering when her Mr. Rochester or Darcy might miraculously appear, wondering as she stared in the mirror if he finally had. Behind the books stood rows of trophies, awards, and certificates—silent witness to Paige's many accomplishments. Yes, the room might be cluttered but never dirty. Paige saw to that.

She continued her gaze into the three-sided mirror on her vanity. Paige closed her eyes, thinking about the evening and her next meeting with Morgan. Having washed her hair twice, she brushed it vigorously, putting it to her nose to make sure it was completely clean. It was so short she wasn't sure what to do with it.

Her hair wasn't the only thing on her mind. Her closet overflowed with expensive clothes. Another motherly attempt on Vera's part to fashion her into a clone of Candy and herself! Elegant clothing and *haute couture* wasn't Paige's thing. No. She opted for something simple but flattering, something to erase the image of those stinky, loose-fitting riding clothes she'd greeted him in. Paige would show Morgan she wasn't the scrawny kid he'd met six years ago. Determined to look grown-up, she pondered the three outfits displayed on her bed.

A tap sounded on the doorframe. "Go with the long navy skirt and the fitted white silk blouse. You look awesome in them."

"Hi," Paige said as Candace stepped in and closed the door behind her. "You'll never believe it but—"

"He came to the barn. I know." Her sister rolled her enormous gray-blue eyes. "What happened?"

"What do you think happened? You know I was filthy and needed a toothbrush big time, but he didn't care." Paige shook her head and shrugged.

"Wow." Candy's eyes grew wider. "So what did you guys do?" She flashed a mischievous smile.

"Nothing really. He brought me a soda, and I showed him the barn, then we walked out and sat under the oak tree and just talked and…" Paige looked down, fidgeting with the brush on her dressing table.

"And—oh come on, Paige. You're driving me crazy." Candy looked like a balloon about to burst.

"Well, he kind of—held my hand and we sat really close." Paige met her sister's eyes in the mirror as a smile spread across her face.

"Oh my God!" Candy squealed, putting her hand over her mouth.

"Yeah. It all happened so fast."

Candy focused on Paige's reflection as she narrowed her eyes. "He didn't try to—to kiss you, did he?"

"No, thank goodness." Paige shook her head.

Candace laughed softly and nodded, closing her eyes. "Yeah, that would not have been good. You needed a serious cleanup."

"So what do you think?" Paige asked, turning her dressing chair to look at her sister.

"Well, I may be way off base." Candy narrowed her eyes. "But since he went to the barn to connect with you and held your hand, I'll repeat what I said before. He likes you, little sister." She raised her eyebrows.

Paige perked up. "Really? I—I don't know what to think." She gestured toward her image in the mirror. "I mean, look at me."

"Of course." Candy nodded with a mock frown, raising her voice. "We all agree you're hideous beyond human comprehension and a social pariah, but maybe Morgan's *learning impaired*!"

Paige stared, shaking her head.

Candace put on her best look of disapproval. "You know it's really getting tough being your sister," she began. "Jesus, Paige, look at yourself. I mean really look." She stood behind her sister holding her head so Paige was forced to see her image. "I told you this afternoon. Forget what happened last year! You've got scars from the accident, and your first crush moved away. You're cute. And as for that figure you're always hiding under extra large T-shirts and baggy jeans. You've grown up, Paige. Guys look at you all the time."

"You're just trying to make me feel better," Paige protested.

"That's right, I am. 'Cause you're my little sister and I love you. But what I said was true. Paige, you have so much going for you. I mean look at this stuff." Candy turned, gesturing toward the large oak desk and the dresser covered with awards. Candace finished with a loud, "You're amazing."

"Okay, okay. I believe you. I'm perfect." A shy grin crossed Paige's face. "Of course the rest of the world may not see it that way."

"Honey, I know nothing about Morgan. He's here for the weekend. That may be the end of the story. All we know about him is that he seems nice and he likes you. That's my point, Paige. Boys see something in you they like—if you give them half a chance."

"Okay." Paige agreed, despite knowing that when it came to Morgan, the story would never be over. She stood and went to the bed, shed her robe, and put on the outfit her sister had suggested, adding a special lightweight undergarment to hide the scars on her back and stomach.

"What about my hair? I just got it cut. And it's so short I don't know what to do with it." Paige glared in the mirror.

Candy stood for a minute, concentrating. She pulled Paige's thick hair up and back from her forehead on one side holding it in place with a jeweled barrette, then pushed the hair on the other side behind Paige's ear.

Paige studied her reflection. Perfection!

She stood and went to the bed, picked up the skirt, and put it on. Then she slipped into the silky fitted white top.

"Can you help me again—with the zipper? Please?" Paige held her hands in mock prayer.

Candace gave her a faux scowl. "You are a nuisance!"

They both giggled.

"There. You're sure you can find the foyer without my help?" She gave Paige a friendly push.

"I'll try." Paige nodded.

When she'd put on the top and the long skirt, Candace steered Paige to the full-length mirror and spun her around wearing an I-told-you-so smile. "Not bad," she whispered as she headed for the door. "Now, sister dear, I believe you're scheduled to perform this evening?"

Paige stood, looking at her reflection as she spun around twice like a ballerina. Her lips curled into a smile. Candy was right. Paige liked what she saw.

****

The Fullers had invited neighbors and friends to help celebrate Josiah's fiftieth birthday and his retirement from the Barnstable County District Attorney's Office. After twenty years as southeastern Massachusetts's toughest prosecutor, he was leaving office.

Morgan rushed down the stairs into the spacious foyer dressed in a lightweight blazer, beige cotton slacks, and a colorful summer necktie. He couldn't wait to see Paige. The sound of animated conversation and laughter emerged from the great room at the rear of the house. By the time he reached the massive wood-framed entry arch, the party had begun. Drinks and *hors d'ouvres* were being served to a crowd of about twenty.

Surveying the room, Morgan spotted Candace pinned in the far corner, being ogled by an older man in a poorly-fitting suit. Her admirer looked glassy-eyed and swayed as he spoke. The little man leered as he hung over the Fullers' eldest daughter in her silky cocktail dress. She spotted Morgan and rolled her eyes, pleading for relief. Fortunately, Josiah had seen the situation and approached the man, taking his arm, and none too gently steering him away from Candace. Morgan's dad joked that Josiah guarded his daughters like they were the crown jewels.

"Thank God," she said, grinning as Morgan approached.

"Tough to be *sooo* beautiful," he teased. "But you do look great, Candace."

She gave him a playful shove and looked him up and down with a coy smile. "You should know, handsome."

Candace's black dress hugged her figure. She looked spectacular, but Morgan was impatient. He turned, searching the room for Paige.

Candace touched his arm lightly and cleared her throat. "Looking for someone special?"

He swore she hid a smile as she followed his gaze.

"Just checking out the guests." He tried to sound casual.

"I hear you paid my sister a visit at the stables." Her large blue eyes held a playful sparkle.

Morgan nodded as his stomach tightened. "Why? Did she say something?"

"Hmmm. Can't remember exactly. About what?" Candace asked with a pretense of innocence as she waved to some of the new arrivals. The crowd had swelled to thirty.

"I don't know. Anything," he answered with uncharacteristic self-consciousness.

Just as Candace shrugged, her glance fixed on the front door. "Oh shit," she whispered under her breath as her eyes narrowed.

Morgan followed her stare. Three people entered the foyer: a middle-aged couple who nodded to several of the other guests and a tall, spectacular redhead with short hair pushed behind sculpted ears. She wore a floor-length print skirt and a sheer yellow top that complemented it and fit as if painted on. She paid only passing attention to those greeting her companions—her parents Morgan assumed. She looked around, distracted, as if searching for someone.

"What's wrong?" Morgan whispered to Candace.

As he did, the redhead fixed cat-like green eyes on them and approached with a purpose.

"I can't believe my mother invited them—and her." The look on Candy's face left no doubt. These two were not friends.

Just as she spoke, Paige entered the room. Dressed in a long navy skirt and fitted, silky white top, her appearance spiked Morgan's heart rate. Her dark hair shone, arranged in a way that gave her a completely different look. His breath caught in his throat. Morgan waved.

Paige beamed a warm smile at him. She waved back and wound toward him through the crush of guests. Paige was halfway across the great room when the spectacular redhead materialized in front of him.

"Why, my goodness." The girl fluttered her dark-shadowed emerald eyes. If there was a contest for the most perfect white teeth, this girl and Candace would be in a dead heat. "You must be Morgan Cahill. I've heard and read so much about you." She held out her hand.

Morgan shot a look toward Candace. Her frozen half-smile held icicles.

Morgan took the young woman's hand and shook it. As he did he looked toward Paige. She stood stock-still, a look of shock on her face.

"Morgan, this is Monique Burke." Candace squeezed as much contempt as she could into the polite introduction.

"I can't tell you how much I've wanted to meet you," Monique gushed, surrounding Morgan's hand with hers.

While he shook Monique's hand, Morgan watched, concerned and mystified as Paige's expression morphed into disappointment. Paige stared at them, still frozen in place. After a long moment, she turned and headed toward her father. Mr. Fuller stood at the entrance to the large study where the recital was to be held.

"Hello, Monique," Morgan offered weakly. The animosity between Candace and Monique was palpable. It left him searching for a hiding place.

Desperation to see Paige coursed through him. But she'd run away. Vanished—again. Monique's appearance had created obvious and unexpected tension.

Candace took Morgan's arm and pulled him free of Monique's grip. "Time for the recital to begin. Paige will want us to sit up front, Morgan."

As they left Monique called after him, "Very nice to meet you, Morgan. Save me a seat. I'd love to join you for dinner."

"What was that about?" Morgan asked as he looked back at Monique. "And why did Paige run off?"

"It's a long story. Let's just say that Monique's not my favorite person—or Paige's," she fumed. "You could say she's a legend in her own right." Candace looked back, venom in her narrowed eyes. "But unlike you it has nothing to do with her accomplishments!"

Chapter 6

Paige headed toward the study, stopping before the broad oak archway. Her stomach churned, and she squeezed her eyes shut. Tugging at the seams in her blouse, she straightened her skirt and fidgeted with her barrette as she scanned the crowd. This could not happen. Not with Morgan.

After an icy stare in Monique's direction, Paige waited while her father crossed the small space that separated them. He took her arm, escorting her toward the study. The air conditioning hummed, working overtime as it fought the thick air, but the doors were open and tiny beads of sweat emerged on Paige's forehead as a trickle worked its way down her back.

"Sorry, honey," he whispered and shrugged as he shot a look at Monique. "I know how you feel about her and asked your mother to leave them off the guest list. But you know that Mrs. Burke and your mother go back to high school. She just can't believe that her best friend's daughter could have done anything to hurt you."

"It's okay, Daddy." Paige touched his arm and managed a smile. "I can't spend the rest of my life angry and in hiding," Paige said, surprising herself. Candy was right. Time to move on. Morgan's appearance and unexpected attention had brought out her long-dormant streak of confidence and stubbornness. Paige had heard it said you can't repair history. A bad chapter had been written. Time to let it go.

She and her father stopped near the doorway, making conversation with friends and neighbors as they headed into the large study that doubled as the music room. Paige smiled politely, scanning the room for Morgan and trying not to think about the redheaded nemesis that was obviously on the prowl for him.

When they reached the door, Josiah tapped his wine glass. The crowd quieted and turned toward him.

"Good evening and welcome. Our daughter Paige"—he cleared his throat and gestured in her direction—"winner, for the third consecutive year, of the South Coast Music Festival, has agreed to honor us with a selection from Peter Ilyich Tchaikovsky."

The gathered guests smiled and applauded politely before heading inside.

Paige moved quickly, taking a seat at the magnificent Steinway sitting near the French doors that opened onto the patio. She looked down at the keyboard, flexing her fingers and placing them on the keys. Exhaling deeply, she tried to relax as she heard the perfect harmonics when she lightly fingered several chords. She straightened, determined nothing would ruin her performance. Paige focused on the Steinway's gleaming keys. There would be no disappointing her father, her champion, and greatest supporter.

She glanced at the friendly faces. It was a small crowd compared to most she'd performed before. Morgan now sat in front of her next to Candy. That made this otherwise effortless performance special. No sign of Monique. Good!

She breathed deeply, finding Morgan's eyes for a second, then exhaled slowly as her father approached and asked, "Ready?"

Paige nodded and cleared her throat as her dad took a seat next to Candy.

"Thank you all for coming to help my father celebrate a special birthday and meaningful occasion in his life." Paige grinned, paused, and took another breath. "Though I would never tell his age."

Expectant eyes turned her way as Paige's comments drew muffled laughter and applause.

"I'd like to play something special this evening—a brief excerpt from Tchaikovsky's *Romeo and Juliet Overture*."

As she spoke Paige stole another look at Morgan. Her shoulders relaxed as she flexed her fingers a second time. She could see Morgan watching. Their eyes met, longer this time. Paige hid a smile, turned, and put her fingers on the keyboard, beginning with a series of rapid arpeggios, showing off. Enjoying every moment.

She stopped, looked up then closed her eyes as she launched into the overture. Her fingers flew across the keys. She'd been playing this piece for a decade but as she thought about Morgan the title held a deeper meaning.

****

Time flew. When Paige's performance was over Morgan sat spellbound. It was the most amazing thing he'd ever seen. The music was haunting. But it was Paige—her emotion, her energy, and skill that held him captive. He'd been to concerts, but watching Paige's fingers fly effortlessly and with such precision across the keys was something to behold, like a skilled surgeon performing a procedure.

"Hey, you with us?" Candace touched his shoulder as he sat, mute and completely transfixed.

"Ah—yeah. Sure." Morgan nodded as she broke the spell.

Paige stood by the piano, surrounded by a wall of guests. They'd given her a standing ovation. Her father hovered nearby, beaming.

"Daddy's girl," Candace said quietly with a generous smile, "Always was. So be *very* careful, my friend." A brief pause. "'Fraid I'm just a Vera clone."

Paige looked at him plaintively.

Morgan raised his eyebrows and gestured. Her lips curled upward as she blushed. She did her best to break free and join him, but the tight circle of admirers held her captive.

Suddenly, Morgan felt a tug on his sleeve. "Well. You look like a man in search of a dinner partner." Monique Burke showed another glimpse of her expensive smile.

"Actually, he has one," Candace said icily.

"Oh—" Monique's expression froze, her face a mixture of frustration and anger. Ms. Burke didn't enjoy rejection.

Morgan reluctantly abandoned his quest and followed Candace out of the study and down the long hallway. Oriental rugs covered the thick, dark flooring. A row of somber-looking portraits lined the walls as they found the generous dining room. Two long, adjoining tables were set for the forty guests. Each was dominated by a blazing, fresh cut floral centerpiece from the Fuller gardens.

Morgan slowed and turned, frustrated, searching

the hallway for Paige.

"Believe me. She wants to be with you," Candace assured him. "But Daddy's so proud of Paige. He dotes on her. Guards her like a princess. And Paige is funny. When she gets in the spotlight she blossoms. Opens like a butterfly emerging from its cocoon."

"Why, that's downright poetic, Ms. Fuller," Morgan acknowledged.

"She loves it. The competition and the spotlight," Candace said thoughtfully. "And you, Mr. Cahill, can thank me."

"Why?" Morgan raised his eyebrows.

She searched the room with a mock scowl and whispered, "I rescued you from the conniving clutches of Monique Burke."

Morgan laughed.

Candace gestured toward two empty seats and Morgan sat, still hoping to find Paige in the confusion.

Candace must have sensed his frustration. "Look, better to lose Paige for a few minutes than to—" She stopped in mid-sentence. Monique stood opposite them. How had she managed it? Candace's jaw dropped. Somehow the redhead had managed to sneak around the long table and find a seat opposite them under cover of the grandiose floral centerpiece.

"Well, this is just perfect." Monique wore the look of the hunter. Morgan felt like the prey. "Just the man I want to get to know better." Monique's oval eyes narrowed as her gaze turned toward Candace. "And one of my dearest childhood friends."

Monique made no attempt to hide the look on her face as she stared at Candace. Morgan knew the look well. It was the look of victory.

Chapter 7

Dinner passed in slow motion, a painful test of wills. As he watched the subtle loathing play out between Candace and Monique he sat helpless—ignorant of the reason behind it but witness to their obvious and passionate dislike.

Morgan tried not to check his watch repeatedly as delicious but painfully slow courses were served. When he did, elapsed time from salad to coffee was just over an hour and thirty minutes. Three lifetimes had passed for him watching these two beauties lobbing not-so-subtle barbs across the table like rivals at a tennis match.

Monique did her best to tease and tempt Morgan, ignoring Candace and her attempts to interfere. The wine flowed freely. Morgan and his parents weren't drinkers. His mother was strongly medicated, and he found himself in training for one athletic season or another, but Candace took full advantage of her parents' indulgence, fueled by her battle with Monique. As he sat captive, Morgan wondered about his decision to leave and join his friends.

Morgan wanted to see Paige, talk with her, to tell her she was incredible, and just look at her again. But she'd arrived too late and sat with her father—far away and almost out of sight. His seat put him in an awkward position—unable to move or get up easily since the servers hovered behind and around him constantly. When he was able to sneak a look in her direction, Paige looked hurt. She wore a pout, avoiding his eyes.

About nine-thirty, Vera stood and tapped her wine glass. She offered a toast to her husband, revealing his age to good-natured cheers and raucous laughter. Morgan saw it as an opportunity to escape. Excusing himself, he rushed through the warm, crowded kitchen, nodding to Lizbeth, the plump, good-natured cook, and out to the flagstone apron surrounding the massive swimming pool.

He exhaled deeply and walked slowly to the far side, leaning against the fence. He'd always loved the night sky, but as he looked up for consolation he found none. The house lights muted the dim belt of the Milky Way overhead. Morgan stood and stared blankly into the darkness, confused and angry as someone called his name from the back porch. He squinted and made out a slender figure in a silky black dress. Candace.

"Okay if I join you?" she asked with a tentative wave. Her speech sounded slurred.

"Sure," he nodded. "I just had to get away from—" He stopped in mid-sentence, not sure how to finish the thought.

She slipped out of her four-inch heels and weaved her way to join him.

"Sorry you had to witness that," she said, shaking her head. "I wouldn't blame you if you got in your Beamer and bailed."

He managed a weak smile. "You guys sure don't like each other. What gives?"

She perched on a low wall that bordered the pool and sighed. It was Candace's turn. She studied the inky sky.

After a few moments she turned to him. "I'm not sure if I should tell you or leave that to Paige."

"Paige? I saw the way she looked at your *friend*." He shook his head, adding, "What's Paige have to do with this?"

"She was the victim," Candace said with a burp.

"Victim?" Morgan had no idea what she was rambling on about. But his curiosity piqued.

Candace sighed and sat silently for a moment. Then she met his gaze and offered, "I'd love to sit here with you, but maybe you can go inside and find her."

"Sounds like a plan," Morgan agreed and stood, heading back to the dining room, hoping to find Paige and salvage some of the evening. As Candace stood and tagged along she stumbled.

Morgan studied her, realizing Candace was hammered. Under other circumstances he might have found that funny, but he was on a mission. He took her hand and helped her, guiding her through the kitchen, nodding to Lizbeth again and back to the dining room. By the time they returned only a few guests remained. Candy took a half-empty glass of wine and swallowed it in one gulp. Her eyes had an unfocused glassy look.

"Maybe you should give it a rest, Candy," Morgan suggested, trying not to sound judgmental.

She shrugged. "Bravo!"

Morgan must have looked confused.

"You finally called me Candy." She giggled. "I guess Paige is gone," she added, stifling a yawn.

Morgan blew out a long breath, frustrated. Paige was sweet, innocent, and vulnerable. Maybe too innocent and too vulnerable? Something was obviously going on here. Something he'd fallen into the middle of. But damn it, Morgan hadn't felt like this about a girl in—well, he wasn't sure he'd ever felt like this about a girl. Not so quickly and with such conviction. He could not get her out of his head! He hoped desperately he hadn't lost something special for reasons beyond his control.

"Would you be a gentleman and see a la-dy to her room?" Candace asked with a silly smile, another giggle, and a hiccup.

"Sure, why not?" He nodded with resignation.

She took his arm, and they headed toward the long circular stairway.

Candy asked if he thought he had a chance in the NFL draft.

"Hardly any Ivy League players get drafted," he told her.

Candace nodded and narrowed her eyes, volunteering, "Paige may go to the Rolex."

"The Rolex?"

"Yeah. Sort a like the Super Bowl of equestrian events. Her specialty is show jumping." Candace closed her eyes in admiration. "I mean I'm good at stuff—field hockey and softball." She hiccupped again. "But Paige is like world-class. At a whole different level—like you."

Candace held Morgan's arm to steady her as they walked slowly through the foyer and up the staircase. When they arrived at the endless upstairs hallway, Candace pushed her thumb to the right.

"I'm at the end down this way," she managed with difficulty.

She clung to him and swerved toward a large six-panel door. When they reached their destination, she gave him a sloppy grin. "Thanks, Morg." She did her best to focus. "You know. I was right. I told Paige you were a good guy."

That gave him some temporary solace.

Candace looked up at him with those wide, pale eyes. Morgan was sure those eyes had brought more than a few guys to their knees.

"Yep! I knew it from the first." She nodded vigorously. Her speech had gone from slurred to erratic.

Morgan opened the door and gently nudged her inside. "Goodnight, Candy. Thanks for trying to help. Get some sleep. I'll see you tomorrow."

"Hmmm. Wait a minute." She stared up at him. "Not getting away that easy." Reaching up, she pulled his face clumsily toward her, giving him a wet kiss on the cheek.

He turned and began to close the door. Candace put her foot out as she stuck her head into the hall, whispering loudly, "Try the stables."

"Huh? What about them?" His confusion must have shown.

"Paige," Candace said with the look of a conspirator. "She goes there sometimes when she's down or upset. To think. Kinda like her special place." She waved, raised her eyebrows, and smiled another silly smile as she closed the door.

The stables? He looked at his watch. No. It was too late. He'd have to change and it was dark. It was probably infested with mosquitoes, and he had no flashlight. There was no way he was going there. No way at all.

Chapter 8

Paige wore jeans and a sweatshirt again, having taken refuge at her sanctuary. She lay under the massive oak where they'd sat that afternoon, out from its branches so she could catch the dizzying display overhead. The moon had set a few minutes before, and the lights by the pool were turned off. Paige traced the constellations with her finger, trying to put Morgan out of her mind—like that could ever happen!

She questioned herself again. Even if Monique hadn't appeared, what would Morgan see in a tongue-tied high-school girl with braces and glasses? She'd been a fool, letting Candy talk her into this fantasy, thinking he might be interested in her. He was just being nice, polite to his dad's oldest friend. Nothing more. Tears filled her eyes and overflowed, trickling down her cheeks. Pent-up frustration from being near him after dreaming about him for so long. End of story.

Paige swatted angrily at the squadron of mosquitoes hovering around her, thinking she should have remembered the insect repellent when she'd plotted her escape.

"Leave me alone," she complained, waving her hand at the squadron of insects in the damp air. "I have enough on my mind without you."

Something moved behind Paige. Her heart raced as she swallowed. Who'd be here this late at night? She kept her eyes fixed on the night sky and searched for her flashlight, not sure what to do. She took a firm grip and tensed, ready to move when…

"Really?" a soft baritone behind her asked. "Like what?"

Morgan? Paige turned her head toward him for an instant, then back toward the sky. It was him. No. She had to be back in her room, lying in bed, dreaming.

"Hi," she stuttered, sitting up hastily.

"How come a cute, talented girl like you is out here talking to herself at"—he paused—"Eleven-twenty at night?"

Cute? Talented? Had she finally gone over the edge? He sounded concerned. She sneaked another look. He'd changed into gym shorts, a T-shirt, and sneakers. She looked back, then away again, still not trusting her senses.

"How'd you find me?" she asked, ignoring his question.

"A good friend."

"Okay." She nodded. "Why'd you come looking? I figured that maybe you and—" She stopped in mid-sentence, not sure how to finish.

He shook his head and chuckled softly as he sat down next to her.

"I have no interest in her, Paige. She's not my type. Yours either, I hear. But you ran away, just disappeared…again. You know that could get to be an annoying habit." He showed a tentative smile. But it looked shy, almost questioning. Paige found it hard to think of Morgan as shy or unsure. But her eyes told a different story. She remembered his comment about being a jock.

"Candy had a little too much wine," he added. "Probably asleep by now, but she said you might be here."

"I wasn't worried," she lied. Her words sounded hollow, defensive. "And I didn't run away. I just—" Paige stumbled over her words, trying to sound haughty and aloof. Suddenly, Morgan's words sank in. "Candy? She told you I might be here?"

"Yep. Gotta tell ya. You've got one pretty cool sister. She really cares about you."

Paige swallowed again and nodded in the dim light. "I know."

Paige wasn't imagining this. He'd come looking for her. Twice. Candy had been right all along. He did like her. "We should get back before we get eaten alive," Paige suggested, knowing it was the last thing she wanted. She waved her hand at the cluster of mosquitoes.

"Got the answer to that." He held up a can of insect repellent. "Spotted it in the kitchen on my way out. May I, Ms. Fuller?"

She giggled and nodded, closing her eyes as she took off her glasses. Morgan gave her a quick spray.

"Let me know if you need more."

"I will."

"You were awesome on the piano."

"Thanks," she whispered. This was something out of her wildest fantasies. Paige turned and looked at him, glad he couldn't see her blushing. Her face must be bright red.

"Never heard anyone play like that," he added.

"Just takes practice," she assured him.

"Humility is great, Paige. But can you admit you're

good at something?"

"Okay, I'm great," she whispered. "And…I'm really glad you liked it." She was. Very glad. She'd picked that piece knowing he'd be there, never thinking in her wildest fantasies they'd be sitting here talking about it.

They lay back side by side, neither speaking for a time.

Morgan broke the silence. "Paige, I was wondering—"

"Yes?" She cleared her throat not sure what was coming.

He sighed. "Can we try again? Please? You know, start over. I'd *really* like to be friends."

Paige sat, mouth falling open. "Ah…yeah. Sure," she said. *Brilliant response, Paige!*

"Great." He slid a few inches closer. "So what are you gonna be? Olympic equestrian, soloist at the BSO? Brain surgeon? Candy told me you're top of the class in everything."

Paige never hesitated. "Nothing that grand."

"Okay, hmmm. I can't begin to guess. If we're really gonna be friends maybe you could share."

Paige edged a few precious inches closer. She couldn't be sure but thought she caught him smile. "I'm gonna study biology then become a veterinarian."

"No kidding. That's really cool." He nodded as he turned toward her.

"How about you?"

He shook his head. "You'd never believe me."

"What happened to our friendship?" she said, gaining confidence.

He turned so he could face her and rested on his

arm. His breath feathered over her face. "Astronomy."

"Yeah right," she said with a giggle, stopping at his serious expression. He looked…almost hurt by her reaction. "You're not kidding?"

"Scout's honor," he whispered holding up three fingers as he lay on his back again.

"Sorry," she was embarrassed. "Didn't…didn't mean to make fun. Just couldn't see you as an astronomer."

"Astrophysicist, actually. I want to study deep space from the space station."

She sat silently still not sure he was serious.

"It's okay. 'Cause I run the football and can throw a fastball everybody thinks I'm a jock." His words held no bitterness just simple resignation. "That all I care about is sports."

Paige swallowed deeply and summoning her courage she reached for his hand. Finding it she took it and held it letting their fingers intertwine.

She sighed deeply. "Morgan."

"Yep."

"I didn't mean it like that. I never thought you were just a jock. Guess I just saw you running some big corporation or being a whiz on Wall Street. You know. Something like that." Paige swallowed, adding, "I…I think you could do anything you put your mind to."

"Thanks." He laughed softly. "Well I am kind of an adrenaline junkie, and there's a lot more rush doing a space-walk than running a hedge fund." He paused. "And that's really cool about you being a vet. I mean you have so much experience and you're such a great rider."

"That's true," Paige agreed. "But I want to do

more. There are strains of parasites and infections that..." She stopped, realizing she'd taken a detour into veterinary nerd-land.

"That what?" he asked, turning toward her again.

"I don't think you came here to listen to me go off on tropical parasitic infestations," she whispered.

He squeezed her hand and found her eyes in the distant light that shone from the house. "Can you understand I'll listen to anything you want to talk about? Okay?"

"Deal." She nodded.

Chapter 9

Having just checked his watch, Julian searched the deserted Brockton Street as he waited patiently at the door. Sophie had dropped him at the corner of this shabby neighborhood on Warren Avenue where he would deal with the second name on his list. Dark clothing would help keep him anonymous. The June weather had turned chilly and damp. He could not hide his excitement as he licked his lips. His damp hand twitched then came to rest on the nine millimeter Walther PPK in his pocket.

Small, slender, and quiet, his face was unmemorable. He faded into the crowd. Unremarkable. That was the word the young district attorney had used at his trial. It may well have contributed to his conviction for the vile things they accused him of in 1989. He was an everyman, a chameleon who blended into the crowd. That, his lack of friends, and his passionate devotion to his underage neighbor that remained hidden during his trial certainly added weight to the prosecution's case and jaundiced the jury of his peers against him.

No matter. That was in the past. Ancient history. This was the present.

After ringing the doorbell three times, a rotund, scruffy man appeared at the door. When he opened it a crack the smell of whiskey on his fetid breath drifted out through the six-inch opening.

Julian pulled the baseball hat over his face and approached the door closely.

"What the hell do you want?" the man inside said in a throaty bass. "You know what time it is?"

"Sorry but this is an emergency," Julian whispered.

"What kind of emergency? What are you talkin' about?" the man inside demanded.

Julian stepped back and thrust his foot forward with all his force. An act he'd rehearsed often in the last two months of his training. Using his newly acquired skills, he kicked at the door, knocking the tired chain off and sending the dazed occupant reeling back onto the floor as splinters of shattered wood and worn paint chips landed on top of him.

Julian followed his forceful kick inside as he drew the pistol and pointed it at his victim. "Actually, old friend, I misspoke. The emergency has yet to happen. But it's about to."

Standing over the fat man on the floor, Julian pulled off his hat and turned his face revealing a scar from one corner of his right eye to the line of his jaw.

"Remember me?" he asked quietly as he threw a fierce kick to the man's groin.

A weak scream followed as the pathetic creature assumed the fetal position holding up one hand in self-defense.

Two, he thought as he felt the satisfaction. He watched as the recognition turned to terror in his victim's eyes…

Chapter 10

Paige and Morgan remained, lying quietly near the oak for a time. The mosquitoes buzzed around them but had yet to attack.

"Okay, look up at the sky," Morgan said. "What's your favorite?"

"Favorite?" Paige asked curiously.

He pointed to the Milky Way. "Your favorite constellation?"

"Orion, I think," Paige answered thoughtfully after a moment. "'Cause of its constancy. I can always find it. Anywhere. Anytime I look up," she explained.

"Great choice. Mine too. Have you ever seen M-42, the Ring Nebula? It's incredible."

"Once. When I was in junior high, we went on a field trip to the Weston Observatory. And you're right. It *was* incredible."

"Most people don't appreciate the night sky," he said, turning to look at her again. "What are you looking at?"

"You." He sounded almost irritated. "Really, is it so hard to believe I like looking at you?" he asked quietly.

"I guess not," she said, picking up her glasses with her free hand and stuffing them clumsily in her pocket.

"Do you know you have the most incredible voice?" he asked, still watching her.

"Really. You like my voice?" Paige asked.

"I love hearing you talk and laugh and—" He stopped mid-sentence. "It's amazing. Except like I said this afternoon. You don't laugh enough."

"Thanks." She'd never been told she had an amazing voice, but any praise from Morgan was fine with her.

"So, what are you doing tomorrow? Riding again?" he asked. "Candy tells me you're a wonderful rider."

Was this for real? Morgan lay a few inches away holding her hand. She closed her eyes, feeling the warmth from his body, smelling the fragrance of his after-shave as he continued throwing compliments her way.

"Probably," she answered. "My folks are having a pool party, but I'm not much for swimming, so I'll probably go riding."

He was silent for a minute. She could hear him breathing, feel those amazing eyes fixed on her. "Could I ask you a favor?"

Oh God! Was the other shoe was about to drop? "What?" she asked guardedly, suddenly terrified her fantasy was about to evaporate.

"Well, remember when we talked about riding this afternoon?"

Paige hesitated. "I think so."

"Well since you're such a good rider, I was wondering…Could I tag along?"

"I'm sorry. What did you say?" Paige managed in shock. Was he teasing her? "You want to go riding—with me?"

"I'd like to try. But I want to go with someone who's really good. Candy told me you teach at the local riding stable and said you're amazing," he explained. "I'd like to learn from the best."

"You're serious?" She reeled in surprise and pleasure.

"Maybe I'm being pushy. I mean if it's not convenient?"

"No," she cut him off. "I mean yes. I'd…I'd love to take you riding." Paige hoped her voice didn't sound too excited even though her stomach was doing gymnastics.

"Great. What time is good for you?"

"How about nine?" Paige said. "Unless that's too early?"

"No, that's great and oh, I don't have any riding clothes. Would jeans and sneakers be okay?"

"Jeans are great. But let me find you a pair of Daddy's old boots. You should have something to help you grip the stirrups. But don't worry. We won't be doing any jumps the first time out." She giggled, still trying to come to grips with all this. "What size shoe do you wear?"

"Thanks. That's good to know." He smiled at her. "And I wear size eleven."

"I can find something that'll work," Paige promised him. And she would. If she had to drive to the local riding apparel store at six a.m.

"Sounds awesome. I'm looking forward to it." He extended his hand. "It is getting late, and I'm not sure the bugs know this stuff is called insect *repellent*." He laughed. "Maybe we should be getting back."

She sat up, still holding his hand. It felt strong, warm, and electric. Goose bumps emerged on her arm as he pulled her easily to her feet. Even after she stood, he held her hand, fingers still weaved into hers as they headed back to the main house. Morgan asked about her riding, school, how she liked living on their farm.

Paige found herself talking, sharing, and laughing in a way she never had with anyone but Candy.

"What's it like to be a football star at Harvard?' she asked.

"Not what it's cracked up to be," he said with that uncharacteristic shyness Paige still found both unexpected and intriguing. "Maybe I could tell you sometime."

Paige stopped and nodded as she turned toward him. "I'd love to hear about that, Morgan. You can tell me anything."

Blood rushed to her cheeks as they headed toward the house again, neither making any attempt to release their grip.

It was only a quarter mile, but as they grew close, Paige slowed. Morgan followed her lead. They climbed the porch steps very slowly, went inside through the empty kitchen and up the darkened staircase to the long upstairs hall. Morgan followed her. When they reached her door, Morgan took her other hand in his, bent and kissed Paige softly on the cheek, giving her a hug. The goose bumps multiplied, joined by what could have been electricity tingling up her arm. She'd heard the word swoon. Suddenly, she knew what it meant. As he backed away, his lips came temptingly close to hers. Paige closed her eyes, but he pulled away. She touched her lips instinctively then smiled. Part of her was disappointed, another part glad, even flattered he hadn't tried to take advantage of her too quickly.

"Good night, Paige. Thank you. I had a really great

time." He touched her cheek gently. "I'm really looking forward to tomorrow." He turned and started walking, glancing back as he headed to his door.

She stood, following his graceful departure. Her breath came in large gulps. "Me, too, Morgan," she managed in a whisper as she waved. *Me, too!* She repeated to herself as she sighed and went inside.

Oh my God! Paige thought as she looked in the mirror, hugged herself, then walked to her bed. She picked up her diary, collapsing onto it as she giggled softly while her smile grew from ear to ear.

Diary, I don't know where to begin! I've had the most wonderful day I can remember. EVER! Morgan likes me...really likes me. He found me at the stables AGAIN, and we lay next to each other, held hands AGAIN, and asked me to take him riding. He's so much more than I could ever have hoped for...kind, thoughtful, funny, handsome (of course) and in his own way, kind of shy. I have to get up early, see Liz to get a picnic lunch and Diary...I know I won't sleep a wink tonight.

Paige closed the cover, still beaming as she lay in her clothes, shut her eyes and sighed, picturing his face and wishing for morning…

Kevin V. Symmons

Chapter 11

Morgan fell into a restless sleep after tossing half
the night. *Paige!* She was the most irritating and
amazing girl he'd ever known. His fascination with her
mystified and astonished him.

But Paige shared the attraction. Morgan was sure
of that. She said and did things that caught him off-
guard. Things that none of the prom queens and
cheerleaders he'd spent his life with would understand.
Things *he* didn't understand. Her picture should be next
to "dichotomy" in the dictionary. At times she was so
modest, so shy, stumbling over her words and
punctuating their conversations with that soft,
infectious giggle. But there was the way she played the
piano, her fierce look of determination. She attacked it
like something drove her. And Candy said she was just
as driven in the saddle. He'd seen that in the stable.
Nope! Twelve hours and Morgan was hooked. He was
her willing and compliant captive.

Morgan thought of Jennifer, the girl he'd dated his
senior year at Roxbury Latin, at least until he'd
discovered her in someone else's backseat with her top
off. But Jennifer never aroused him the way Paige had
in less than a day.

Plain adorable. Would his friends use that phrase?
Of course not. His football buddies would think he'd
lost it. Hot, babe, fox were crude words—rough and

demeaning he knew, but they were the ones his jock friends applied to the groupies that clung to them. Paige might not inspire those adjectives. Thank God! Morgan didn't care. He'd spent nineteen years surrounded by hot and found it wanting. He was ready for gentle, shy…and adorable!

****

He awoke to muted sounds of activity below, realizing he'd passed a peaceful night. None of the strange dreams that troubled him periodically. Maybe he could thank Paige for that. Sunlight peeked from behind the thick sheer curtains on the oversized windows across from his bed. It must be early. Morgan thought his dad and Mr. Fuller would be up. They had golf plans. Morgan had never found magic in chasing a defenseless white ball. No adrenaline rush there.

He yawned and stretched, catching a glimpse of a large family picture with a young Paige on the dresser. He grinned. Morgan loved the shy innocence that cloaked her like a shroud. Loved everything about her. *Love?* Morgan smiled as he lounged lazily under the thick quilt listening to the gentle purr of the A/C. He'd used that word a lot when Paige came to mind, he thought as he stole a look at the clock on his night table: 8:03 a.m. *Damn!* He'd been so pre-occupied daydreaming about her he'd forgotten to set the alarm clock. He jumped up, threw the covers off, and scrambled into the bathroom to shower and get cleaned up for their riding date.

He stood, letting the hot water wash over him. Morgan had no doubt. Paige liked him a lot. She'd given him so many signals—seemed so nervous around him: fumbling, fidgeting, and giggling. He'd enjoyed every minute with her. Morgan wanted to know more about her. But he'd take it very slowly. He saw the hurt look when he sat with Monique. Another sign of her feelings for him. But maybe a warning, too. Determined not to frighten her off, he planned on treading carefully.

He could understand Paige having self-doubts after spending her life in the company of girls like Candy and Monique. Monique was the quintessential babe— beautiful, full of herself, and completely self-serving. But he recalled his dad's warning about stereotypes. *They're all false, Morg, including this one.* Candy was living proof: beautiful, charming, and still a caring person. She looked after Paige like a mother hen guarding one of her chicks.

As he finished dressing, Morgan caught a glimpse of the family pictures on the dresser. He saw one that had been pushed behind the others, Morgan stopped. Something caught his eye. In this photograph Candy was not much older than a toddler. But standing with the look of his father was a tall, lean boy of about twelve wearing Josiah's arm around his shoulder and a broad smile. But where was Paige? She and Candy were only a year apart, but she was missing from the photo.

When he looked at another picture, this one prominently displayed, Paige stood between Candy and the boy. But something struck Morgan that he had never noticed before. All the Fullers were tall, light-haired with fair skin, and had blue eyes. Paige had none of those traits.

Morgan searched his memory but came up with nothing. There'd been no older brother or mention of one when they visited the Fullers six years ago. And why no Paige in the earlier picture? The Fullers were a very close family. He found it hard to comprehend their taking a picture without their youngest daughter. He checked his watch. No time to worry about it now. He'd ask his dad about it later.

Morgan took a last look in the oversized mirror next to the dresser, smoothed the collar of his polo shirt, and nodded, satisfied with what he saw. He left his room, hurried along the endless upstairs hallway, and headed down the back staircase to the breakfast room off the kitchen, hoping Paige would still be there.

****

"Morning, Dad." Morgan checked his watch as he sat down surveying the breakfast spread Lizbeth had laid out for her guests. "I feel invincible this morning!"

"Morg." His father turned toward him. "Got an appointment?" he asked with a smile, nodding at his watch,

"Actually I do. Going riding this morning."

"You, riding? Really?" Malcolm's half-smile grew into a grin as he shook his head. "Just be careful. Training camp is in less than two months."

"Yes, sir," he told his father with a mock salute. "I know. You do remember I'm doing my community service thing—spending six weeks as a camp counselor in Maine? That's probably more dangerous."

"I do. Not a criticism," Malcolm assured Morgan, sliding closer to his son. "By the way, what happened to you last night? Your mother and I were a little worried that…" Malcolm stopped in mid-sentence, seeing Lizbeth come in from the kitchen.

Morgan held up his hand and shrugged. "Nothing. I took a walk out back and ran into Paige. That's where

71

we came up with this riding thing." Morgan couldn't suppress his excitement. "And so far, I am having a great time!" Morgan said as Lizbeth delivered a stack of pancakes and a dish of steaming scrambled eggs. "How's Mom doing with this?" he whispered, looking around.

"She's holding up pretty well. Had to take an extra Valium once or twice but other than that, she's hanging in there just fine." His father sighed and shrugged.

"That's good." Morgan gave his father a nod and a pat on the shoulder. He looked away and buttered a large piece of home-baked wheat toast, giving the plump cook a warm smile. Morgan spread some fresh grape jelly onto his toast, closing his eyes in delight. "Great stuff, Lizbeth."

"Glad you like it," she acknowledged.

Josiah Fuller appeared from the hallway carrying a pair of low riding boots and thick socks.

"Morning, Malcolm, Morgan. I'm supposed to deliver these per head of the Fuller stables and livestock division." He smiled broadly and placed the riding boots and socks on the floor. "Don't worry, son. The socks are new," he added with a look of amusement.

They all laughed as Josiah lifted some pancakes and eggs onto his plate.

He looked at Morgan as he poured a generous stream of maple syrup over his pancakes. "So. Paige tells me you two are going riding this morning."

Morgan nodded with a grin. "Yes, sir. I hear Paige is quite a rider."

"The best I've ever seen," Josiah said with obvious admiration. He found Malcolm's eyes. "And I've already lectured her. No showing off for our handsome guest here." He gave Morgan a gentle slap on the shoulder. "I know Paige. They'll be fine."

"Well." Morgan took off his sneakers and socks, replacing both with what Josiah had delivered. "Thanks. They fit great." He nodded at Josiah, then stood as he gobbled down a second piece of Lizbeth's thick, sweet toast, stopping to put his sneakers on the stairs. "We who are about to die"—he gave an exaggerated bow—"salute you."

****

Candy's cell sat on her dresser, buzzing like angry hornets. She threw one of the decorative pillows from her bed but missed. Her swollen head buzzed with the annoying phone. Her tongue and mouth were filled with a sour funky taste. Morning breath on steroids…yuck!

"Hold on," she whispered, recalling memories of the disastrous dinner party, that bitch Monique, and all the wine she'd had to drink. She remembered giving Morgan the hint about Paige and the stable. She hoped he'd manned up and taken it.

Candace fell out of bed onto the floor. The room spun crazily for a few seconds. The phone stopped ringing as she sat against the side of her bed waiting for the room to come to rest. She managed to get her equilibrium by holding onto her bed, standing up, and weaving to her phone. It blinked and buzzed, telling her there was a message.

She opened it and saw the number: her best friend and confidant, Naomi. She was about to hit redial when a violent urge catapulted her into the bathroom. Naomi wanted the scoop on Morgan's much anticipated arrival. Her friend's curiosity would have to wait a few minutes.

****

"Hey, Naomi," Candace whispered into her phone when she returned to her bedroom. "Sorry I missed you. Not a hundred percent this morning."

"I'm guessing you snuck some vino at the party?" Naomi laughed out loud.

"Hey, not so loud," Candace said, holding her head. "And yeah. More than a little, but no sneaking was involved. It was there for the taking."

"Okay, Fuller, enough small talk. Next you'll describe the salad and the centerpieces. I need some details and some dirt—the lowdown on your visiting hunk." It was a command.

"Not much to tell. He's major league. Got here about two o'clock then *veni, vidi, vici*—he came, he saw, and man did he conquer." Candy fought to control the nausea.

"Yeah, I kinda figured that. So, c'mon. Did you two hook up?"

Candace sat on the floor next to her bed, queasy. "No, he's got a thing for Paige."

Her friend was silent for a minute, finally asking, "Paige?"

"Yes, Naomi. You know—my sweet, adorable younger sister. Paige." Candace threw back defensively.

"Okay, don't bite my f-ing head off. Paige is great but aren't you pissed?"

"Actually, no," Candace admitted. "He's great—a genuine hunk but…"

"But what? This I have to hear." Naomi sounded like a bubble about to burst. Candace's roiling stomach overcame the urge to grin. She could almost see her friend's face.

"I'm okay with it." She paused. "We didn't really connect like that. He and Paige did. So yeah, he would have been great for the trophy shelf but hell, he's got it *sooo* bad for little sister. And I know she's always had a secret thing for him, so it was love at first sight!"

"Wow, that's cool," Naomi agreed. "Glad you're okay with it."

Candace bolted for her bathroom, yelling back at the phone as she found her target, "Gotta go. Keep you up to date on Romeo and—"

When she came out a few minutes later, she looked out the window facing the stables. And there, walking toward it was Morgan. It looked like he was wearing a pair of riding boots. Candace laughed out loud as she sat on the bed.

"Well, what do you know?" she whispered as she lay back and pulled the comforter up around her, wondering. Yes, okay. She was happy for Paige. Little sister was due some good karma, but Candy couldn't help wondering what it would have been like if Morgan had chosen her.

****

Paige had saddled the horses she and Morgan would ride. She gave Morgan Aphrodite, a gentle, older mount and their best saddle—the Antarès. It cost a lot of money. Thousands, Candy had told her. The soft leather felt like a seat in a high-end luxury sedan. Paige wanted him to have the best. She chose one of the more utilitarian, everyday models for herself. She tightened the girth, checked everything twice—the stirrup lengths and the tack—bits, bridles, and reins. Since that horrible afternoon a year ago, she also checked under the saddle seat to guarantee the billets were perfect.

Confident everything was in order, Paige headed outside and finished her morning chores, throwing handfuls of feed into the chicken coop hidden behind the stables and the ducks outside their fence. She smiled and clucked at her collection of fowl, brushing her hands lightly on her best breeches when she'd finished. Paige put the feedbag inside the barn, checking her watch as she did.

Damn! She was running late—very late. Too much time spent putting on her best riding clothes, fixing her hair. Paige had added a hint of lipstick and makeup, a splash of perfume, and brushed her teeth—twice.

She reclaimed the fresh-picked bouquet from a shelf in the stables, having chosen it with care earlier that morning. Then she rushed behind the giant oak, and headed toward the grove on the stream. Her heart raced, pounding in her ears. This day was special. Paige had the chance to spend it with Morgan or as much of it as she could steal from her family. She'd dreamed about this for years, never imagining those dreams would actually come true.

But there was another task—a mission—she needed to complete before she met Morgan. The day had another connotation, more solemn and dramatic than her special riding date with Morgan. It was an anniversary, but not one you celebrated with candles and a cake.

She followed the small path to the stream and the memorial. Robbie's memorial. Not a headstone, but a small monument she'd insisted on buying with the money she'd earned from the riding lessons she taught.

She took the old flowers from the small vase fixed

to the front of the stone, kneeled, and replaced them with the violets, marigolds, and early day lilies she'd chosen from the back garden.

Paige swallowed deeply and closed her eyes, offering prayers of thanks and petitions for forgiveness, as she always did. She desperately fought the dark visions from that day ten years ago—*water rushing over and above her, panic, Candy's screams nearby, then strong arms—Robbie's arms—pulling her from beneath the water and throwing her to shore. Relief as she lay gasping safe on the bank...until he slipped and fell, hitting his head on the sharp outcropping...* As the tears grew and filled her eyes, she removed her glasses and stifled a sob.

She'd insisted the date be inscribed though it cost her an extra month in lesson revenues. Her father volunteered to pay. Paige would have none of it. It was her cross to bear.

June 11, 1991. From a sister who loved you deeply and with all her heart, it read. *Robert Ellison Fuller. Sleep with the angels, Brother. Thank you for my life.*

"Paige." Oh God. She heard Morgan calling from the barn.

She stood and smoothed her clothing.

"Paige?"

She swiped a hand across her eyes and cheeks, replacing her glasses. She didn't want him to find her. Not here. Not until he knew the story. Suddenly she heard him coming through the thicket. Paige had cut her timetable too close.

Chapter 12

Cedar Junction, Massachusetts Maximum Security Prison, Walpole

Ezra Wilson stood outside the hearing room. The monthly parole board hearing had convened an hour earlier. He'd patiently waited his turn. Until he saw that news story, Ezra had been an average prisoner—a stereotype. Embittered, angry, and anxious, just waiting for his chance to settle the score with society for putting him here. He'd been in his mid-twenties when sentenced for fifteen to twenty-five years for the second-degree murder of Jo Ann Murphy, the junkie bitch he'd lived with.

But he'd changed. Everyone had taken note, the guards, his fellow prisoners, even Warden Litwack. Strange how something like catching a local sportscast could change your life, but it had for Ezra. Not all at once. First, he had to make sure. But he did his homework, scrutinizing every paper he could get his hands on. Using the library computers. Then one day, he hit the jackpot. The local news had a feature on the latest phenom on the Boston sports scene. A freshman from Harvard breaking every record in the books. This kid stood a chance to make the pros.

The stories that filled the local sports pages detailed his fortuitous adoption at age four by a wealthy

Boston family. Pictures of the boy could have been a young Ezra. And interviews with his parents about the boy's adoption left Ezra ninety-percent positive that Morgan Cahill was Elias—the child that had been placed under state care after his sentencing. The timeline was perfect. Now he had a second reason to want out of this hell hole. Ezra had no illusions about redemption. He'd been a bad dude. Done every shitty thing a man could do. His one rationalization might be that Jo Ann had been something out of a nightmare. A creature created by the devil. And on the night in question she came at Ezra with a kitchen knife. But they were street trash and in 1985 the country wanted no part of anyone who dealt or used drugs. End of story.

The one redeeming thing in his life had been Elias, his little boy. Ezra had always hoped the kid would have the chances he never did, and if the stories in the papers and on TV were right, it had turned out just that way—no thanks to Ezra.

Ezra asked permission to use the lavatory while he waited his turn with the parole board. He went in, used the urinal, then went to the sink and the stainless steel mirror bolted securely to the wall. He opened his shirt pocket and retrieved the newspaper picture of the kid from Harvard. Ezra studied the picture then looked at his own reflection, smoothing a loose strand of dark hair with his hand, smiling at the picture he'd placed on the shelf. He stood looking at himself twenty years ago.

He could never be a part of the kid's life, even assuming the kid was his but maybe, just maybe somehow, in some way he could do something to make up for the pain and fear he must have caused his son.

He heard the door open and hastily stuffed the wrinkled piece of paper back in his shirt pocket.

"They're ready for you, Ezra," the guard told him.

"Comin' right up." He smiled affably and nodded at the guard.

He left the toilet, cleared his throat, and swallowed deeply, standing in front of the door to the hearing room.

"Go ahead," the guard said with a nod. "And good luck. You've earned it."

The door opened and he went inside wondering if this would be the year he could finally find the terrified little boy he'd left when they dragged him away. Closure. He'd heard the word so often. Ezra hoped, had even gone into the chapel and prayed that the next chapter of what had been a useless and violent life would bring closure—for him and that three-year-old who may have grown into a man to be proud of.

Chapter 13

Morgan hurried to the stables, feeling like a child on Christmas morning. Smiling broadly, he pictured the way she'd looked at dinner last night, all made up and dressed like a model. She was way beyond cute, but his attraction for Paige was more than face and figure. In less than a day, she'd bewitched him. And he could not have been happier. Morgan closed his eyes and pictured her. He could hear her voice and that wonderful giggle that bubbled up and overflowed. He loved everything about her.

After arriving at the stables, he poked his head inside, and called her name, checking his watch when she didn't answer. Early, he sat on the bench outside to wait. She could still be at the house. The morning sun beat down on his shoulders through his cotton shirt. The warmth settled over Morgan. He closed his eyes for a moment, thinking about the vivid dreams that haunted him. They came in different forms and shapes but they never failed to terrify him and leave him clutching the air, gasping for breath…

Bright flashes of light, noises so loud he screamed desperately, wanting them to stop. He sobbed then heard voices, loud angry voices. More loud noises and flashes of white light. He was running, running to get away, from what he didn't know or understand. Morgan screamed louder, begging for help, but something or someone grabbed him and picked him up violently. He was crying, heaving in sobs that shook his whole body, crying, begging. Suddenly he flew through the air in slow motion, spinning, coming to rest on something. Something underneath him felt warm and moved in short spurts. Then it stopped. Morgan held out his arms and tried to stand but slipped in the wet fluid that surrounded him. He looked at his hands. They were covered in something dark and sticky. Very dark and very sticky...

Morgan shook his head. Sometimes the dreams came three nights in a row. Then they'd leave him alone for a month. They had to have some meaning, but it always stayed beyond his grasp. He'd had nightmares since he was a child, especially when he first came to the Cahills'. His mother told him that. But nothing she could tell him would explain what he saw in the nightmares.

He'd wanted to tell his parents about them, but they'd given him so much love and support he couldn't bring himself to do it. That kind of total unconditional love could be frightening. The last thing they needed was an adopted son who needed psychoanalysis. Especially one they thought of as perfect.

He'd read books and even asked his psych professor casually about his dreams. But Morgan couldn't push it. He thought it made him sound a little wacky. And he didn't want anything that might threaten his eligibility for football. So he'd kept the dreams to himself and lived with them, letting them hang over him like a specter.

Lately, they seemed to come more often, and they'd turned Morgan inward. He kept to himself and avoided sharing his thoughts, even with Ben. His dad's travel and being at Harvard had helped, but he knew he couldn't shut out the people who loved him forever. There'd be a moment of truth. There had to be. He couldn't spend his waking hours afraid of going to sleep. Certain what he saw and heard had some relevance in his life, he hoped someday it might reveal itself like a flash of lightning.

But suddenly and without warning Morgan had found something—someone new and exciting. Since meeting Paige his emotional freeze began to thaw. Something in her, about her, seemed to release him from the constant fear of failure he harbored secretly but carried like a cross. He had no idea how or why, any more than he knew how or why the dreams began or how to decipher them.

Enough introspection. He stood, checked his watch, and strode to the stable entrance, knocked on the outside wall, and walked inside, calling Paige's name softly.

Still no answer. He checked his watch. Almost nine and there was no sign of Paige. He began to wonder. Had he misunderstood her? Could there be something about Paige he didn't know? Was she too good to be true? *No!* He shook his head in denial. He wouldn't accept that. Paige may be complex, but she was genuine and she liked him—very much. He knew it the moment she looked at him. And he'd never met anyone so special. He'd told Ben that last night. Morgan never doubted that. Paige would never disappoint him.

Morgan looked around the barn through the long slivers of morning sunlight. "Paige." Still no answer. The horses stood saddled patiently in their stalls, waiting for a rider. Morgan checked his watch again and saw it was nine o'clock. Maybe something had happened.

He decided to try out back by the large oak. Walking through the stable and out back into the sunlight, he stopped, struck by the noisy clucking of a large flock of chickens in a coop and ducks roaming around the coop. They pecked away, bumping each other while they ate. Morgan grinned as he watched. He hadn't seen the coop the day before tucked away behind the corner of the stables.

As he reached the tree he thought of as their oak he saw movement—a flash of white in the thicket beyond. When he stopped he heard the faint sound of water in the distance. Odd, he hadn't heard it before but then his mind had been totally focused on Paige.

As Morgan looked behind the larger trunk he spotted a small well-worn path in the direction he'd seen movement coming from.

"Paige?" he called a third time.

"Be right there," she managed after several seconds. Paige sounded different—halting, even sad. Not the musical voice he loved.

Concern edged into alarm. Especially when another minute passed and Paige hadn't appeared. Something was wrong. He stepped behind the oak and began walking along the path. It made a sharp turn to the left, toward the sound where Paige's voice had come from. As he made the turn Morgan heard the sound of rushing water growing louder.

"Paige? Where are…?" He stopped in mid-sentence as she ran into him. Her face was flushed and her cheeks were damp.

Paige made a desperate effort to brush away the traces of tears. She swallowed a deep sob and backed away, closing her eyes.

"I am so sorry. I…I come here sometimes," she stuttered like the Paige from their first meeting—shy, vulnerable, withdrawn. "To the river," she added, nodding toward the water sound. "But I took too much time getting ready this morning, so I was late and—"

As she stumbled over her words, Paige put her hand to her face. The tears refused to stop.

"Here," Morgan whispered as he stepped forward and drew a handkerchief, handing it to her. She sniffed and nodded in acceptance. He approached Paige and took her face, gently lifting it toward his. Her eyes were red and swollen.

"Paige," he said softly and opened his arms.

For a moment Paige stood biting her lip, frozen. She took a tentative step. Morgan closed the small distance and took her in his arms, holding her as her soft hair pressed against his shirt. Suddenly she joined the embrace, surrounding him with her arms as she melted into him. Her body pressed against his as she pulled him to her. Morgan sheltered her more tightly as he caressed her back.

"Shhh, it's all right," he whispered.

She stood shaking.

For the first time in his life, Morgan knew how it felt to be in love. He wanted to stand like this forever, protecting Paige, surrounding her with his arms, telling her everything would be all right as long as they were together. Lifting his eyes, Morgan saw a small opening. Beyond it laid a perfectly manicured plot of grass a few feet from the small stream.

In front of a small oak was a stone.

When he released Paige, she turned toward it, taking his hand silently as she dried her tears on his hanky and led him the few yards to the spot.

In front of the memorial sat a new bouquet of freshly picked flowers standing in a small vase.

Robert Ellison Fuller

Morgan looked at the date: ten years ago to the day.

"Robbie was my older brother," Paige whispered, sniffling as she squeezed his hand.

Suddenly Morgan remembered—the picture on the dresser, a distant conversation, and a graveyard when he was a child…

Paige drew him toward the stream.

"He drowned here." She pointed to the bank, pushing aside a tear. "Saving my life."

Chapter 14

They sat side by side on the bank of the small stream, staring silently as the sparkling water sped by. Morgan gripped her hand, having weaved his fingers between and around hers. His touch set her afire. Her attraction to him was more than physical. Much more. His wonderful sense of humor, and his surprising and disarming shy side, deepened her crush. His actions showed he cared very much for her. Being close to Morgan comforted Paige—enveloped her in safety—at peace in a way she'd never experienced. Eric's hurtful desertion, Monique Burke's venom and jealousy, and the terrible and painful recollection of that hot August day a year ago seemed far away, almost non-existent when he held her hand or surrounded her with his strong, gentle embrace. But being close to Morgan certainly sent shivers down her spine. The word *swoon* popped into her head again as he caressed her hand affectionately.

"You want to talk about it?" he whispered as he turned. "Tell me what happened?" When he looked at her, Paige thought he could see inside her—where she lived, what she thought. Those hypnotic blue eyes quelled her fears. And Morgan could see her dreams. She had no doubt.

Paige sighed and shrugged. She longed to share every fear and feeling with him but dodged his question. It was too soon. "We should probably get back. The horses will think they've been abandoned."

She managed a smile as she started to stand. He tightened his grip.

"Morgan?" She looked at him. "We should get back."

"Okay." He released her with reluctance. "But please. I'd like to hear the story."

Paige stood and nodded. "When we stop for our picnic," she promised him.

"Picnic?" Pleased surprise laced his words. "Wow. I figured you'd take me out, lead me around the pasture a couple of times, and ditch me so you could get in some serious riding."

Paige found it difficult to comprehend. That he thought she'd do anything to be apart from him? Paige giggled self-consciously, afraid her desire might make her dizzy.

"'Fraid not." Paige's smile grew. "You're stuck with me."

He stood and faced her. She watched the strong face she saw in her dreams. Taking both her hands in his, Morgan pulled her toward him. When she grew close, Morgan took her in his arms again, gently.

"Hmmm," he whispered. "Being stuck with you." Morgan paused thoughtfully. "Now that's an idea I like," he whispered as he caressed her back again.

She flushed and snuggled against his chest, consumed by conflict. Despite the anniversary of Robbie's death, Paige felt lightheaded as she pushed into Morgan. Her trophies, awards, everything she'd ever won or achieved dwarfed when compared with the warmth and excitement of Morgan's embrace. Who could ever want anything else?

"I like it, too," she agreed, closing her eyes as she nestled against him. "But if we're really gonna be good friends then you have to share something with me, too."

"Promise. Anything you want to hear." He gave her a squeeze and they separated, turning back toward the path and the stables.

Inside the stable Paige introduced Morgan to Aphrodite—the older mount that would be his equine companion for the day. When he showed a frown, she explained that the gentle mount he'd be riding had been Candy's once. And her sister had a flair for romance and melodrama.

He laughed good-naturedly. "Is it okay if I pat her?"

Paige nodded. "Of course. Talk to her quietly and pat her. Horses love that."

She found his hand and they did it together. Paige had no idea what Aphrodite felt, but her hand heated with awareness. The inferno raced along her arm. She took a deep breath and lifted her hand. "Look. She liked it. She likes *you*." Paige laughed out loud, putting her hand over her mouth. She knew she sounded so silly, like a little girl. But she was so happy she didn't care.

Morgan took his hand from the mare and took hers from her lips. "Remember our deal?"

She must have looked curious.

"Please. Do not hide your smile." Morgan stopped, face flushing. "I love it when you do."

Had he used the word love? Paige's face burned. "Deal," she whispered.

"Now." Paige took a deep breath, resuming her tutelage. "Horses are measured in hands."

"Hands?"

"Yep." She lifted hers and held it sideways. "The average hand is about four inches wide. Aphrodite is fifteen hands high at the shoulder." She pointed to the raised area on the gentle mare.

"Can't you just say she's sixty inches or five feet tall?" He looked puzzled.

"Everything has its own vernacular. You know, a private lingo. Is a fullback really four times deeper in the backfield than the quarterback? Is the free safety really free and a strong side safety really stronger?"

His eyes grew round in amazement.

Paige grinned at him.

Morgan looked impressed. "Touché. You know your football."

Embarrassed, Paige couldn't admit that she'd learned about football from reading about him in the papers. "Well, we do play football—even down here," she offered with pride. "Division four champs last two years."

Morgan held up his hands. "Peace, Ms. Fuller, I'm convinced. Now, tell me more."

Paige explained the importance of using your seat and legs in controlling a horse. "We call them physical aids. Balance is the key. The Mongols and the Plains Indians could control and turn a horse without ever using the reins. You use your center of gravity as a running back, don't you?"

Morgan nodded.

"It's the same idea here." She took his reins and led Alex from his stall. She handed Aphrodite's reins to Morgan, and they took the two horses outside. She half-turned the stirrup toward her, put her hand up over the center of the saddle, while holding the outside skirt for security, then pulled herself up and slid into the saddle as she mounted Alex.

He nodded in admiration. "You make it look easy."

She gave a quick demonstration. Morgan continued watching her, paying close attention and imitating her moves as he stood next to her. "Okay. I may fall off a few times, but I'm ready to give it a try."

"You'll be fine," Paige reassured him as she slipped off Alex and went inside, coming out with her helmet. It was state of the art, high-impact plastic and black in color. No crazy colors or exotic designs for her. She was a traditionalist.

Paige had picked a new helmet off the shelf that looked about Morgan's size and handed it to him.

"Can you give me a hand?" he asked. Like bottomless pools, his eyes reflected a deep, vivid blue. She closed the small distance between them as she stood inches from him, placing the helmet on his head and fastening the strap.

Morgan put his arms around her as she finished. "What would you say if I said we should stay like this all day?"

Her smile emerged and grew. "I'd say you'd be missing a great picnic in a very special place. I hope you'll love it as much as I do."

His arms fell away and he nodded, taking a step backward. "I surrender. Sounds like a plan to me."

****

An hour later they rode casually along a roundabout trail toward Buzzards Bay. Paige and Alex took the lead. The sultry heat fit her mood. They rode through the warm, thick air, sheltered from a high cloudless sky by slender oaks and white pines.

Paige had taken the long way round to get to her favorite spot, a small bluff that overlooked Buzzards Bay to the west. She'd stood atop it so often, staring at the endless gray-blue waves driven on prevailing winds over the long fetch from the Jersey Shore. Paige had lost track of the hours she'd spent dreaming as the swells crashed on the sand below. Today, she would show Morgan, hoping he'd find it as breathtaking and hypnotic as she did.

The day before she and Candy had taken the same roundabout trail. Knowing he'd be coming that day, Paige had fantasized about Morgan as she stood on the low bluff, never letting herself dream she'd be riding to her favorite spot with him.

"Hey," he called, interrupting her daydream. "Is this helmet supposed to keep slipping?"

She turned toward him, trying not to smile. He'd been teasing her since they left the stables. First about the stirrups and saddle. Now it was his helmet.

"Okay," she answered and reined Alex in, waiting for him to catch up. "I think I get the idea. You want to stop?"

He grew a broad smile and nodded. "I thought you'd never get it. You know this riding thing is hard on the backside if you're not used to it."

Paige grinned as she dismounted, waiting for him to do the same. Actually he'd mastered the whole thing very well. No surprise. She figured Morgan could master whatever came his way. Sure enough, Morgan pulled back gently on both reins and Aphrodite came to a slow stop. He was about to get down when Paige told him to stop.

She twisted Alex's reins around a nearby tree and approached Morgan. Standing, hands on hips, she surveyed him. Paige checked the stirrups and the saddle. Everything was perfect, but he enjoyed teasing her. And she enjoyed giving it right back.

"Okay, Mr. Cahill. Nice try, but the stirrups and the saddle are fine." She showed him a mock smile. "Should I hold your hand while you dismount?"

"I'd love to hold your hand, but I think I can manage this." He slid his foot from the right stirrup and slipped down from the saddle, pulling his other foot out and landing on the ground in front of her like he'd been doing it for years.

"Did I pass, teacher?" He laughed.

Paige stood back and folded her arms. "Had to show off, didn't you?"

"I wanted to impress you." He tilted his head as he approached her. He was handsome and had what Candy would call a to-die-for body—lean, tight, toned. His arms and shoulders didn't bulge with muscle, but one look at Morgan left no doubt he was an athlete. And the way he moved aroused Paige in ways she could never understand or explain, at least not in polite terms. His movements were downright erotic—like the motion of a thoroughbred, so fluid and effortless he seemed to appear in front of her as if by magic.

"Hey, teach," he whispered, taking her hands in his. "How 'bout we sit in the shade over there and have a drink?"

"Okay," Paige agreed. She took off her helmet and riding gloves, leaving them by the tree where the horses stood. He followed her lead. Perspiration formed on her forehead and trickled down her back. But Paige knew what she felt was more than the oppressive humidity.

Backing away Paige went to her saddle bags to retrieve some Gatorade. "Hope you like lemon-lime. Didn't have a chance to ask," she asked, waiting for him to join her.

As they left the horses, he put his arm loosely around Paige's shoulder, nodding. "Yep, lemon-lime's my favorite."

Part of Paige still believed she was asleep somewhere. That all this was a dream. It had to be didn't it? She put her arm around Morgan, giving his narrow waist a pinch as they reached the shade.

"Hey," he protested. "What was that for?"

She gave him a big grin and sat down, patting the ground.

"Wanted to make sure you were real," she whispered.

They sat, shoulders touching.

Paige had died and gone to heaven.

Curiosity crossed his face. He turned toward her and nodded. "I know what you mean." He laughed softly. "Yesterday at this time I was in our condo in Boston and…" He shook his head.

"C'mon. You can't do that to me." Paige punched him lightly in the ribs.

"If I confess something—promise you won't be mad?"

"Okay," she nodded, wondering what the big confession could be.

"Promise?"

"Damn it, Morgan, tell me!" she demanded. "Is there something I should—?" Paige stopped in mid-sentence. A sudden twinge of doubt re-emerged as the gymnasts worked overtime in her stomach again.

"Well," he began. "The way things have turned out I can't believe I even thought about this." He paused. "I was trying to figure some way to bail on this weekend." He shook his head. "Can you imagine us not meeting?"

Paige laughed softly. She found his hand again and squeezed it, leaning against the massive tree trunk.

"Okay. Your turn. What's so funny?" he asked as he leaned back, putting his arm around her.

"Nothing." Paige leaned into the crook of his shoulder as his hand squeezed her arm. She closed her eyes. "Now can I tell *you* something?"

"Sure. We promised to share secrets," he agreed, but his voice had an uncertain quality. Paige put her hand over his, letting her fingers surround it. She still found it surreal that Morgan had doubts, too.

"I am really glad you didn't," she whispered as she closed her eyes.

****

They mounted the horses and headed toward their destination. Slowly the smell of the ocean replaced the fragrant pine in the air as they crested a sudden rise. Thin patches of scrub grass sparsely populated the cliff. It fell away to a rocky beach one-hundred feet below. Before them spread the most magnificent view Morgan had ever seen. The whole of Buzzards Bay lay, spread out in front and below them as far as the eye could see. He reined in Aphrodite and sat in awe.

He felt Paige's stare and turned. She gestured toward the water with her hand and watched him with a shy curiosity. She shrugged and asked, "Well, what do you think?"

He took a deep breath and swallowed. "It's

beautiful, Paige. I've never seen anything like this."

She dismounted. "C'mon. Let's leave the horses in the shade and have some lunch." But as she began walking toward the small stand of trees, she turned and hesitated, asking, "Would you mind if we sat and just watched the ocean for a while?"

He nodded, feeling as he had all morning. Something had taken hold of him. Being with Paige had transformed him in a way he couldn't explain. "Your wish is my command!"

She tied the horses loosely. He waited, watching her approach, as he marveled, recalling the shy, quiet girl he'd met yesterday afternoon. Today Paige looked spectacular in her riding clothes while her flawless skin seemed to glisten in the damp sunlight, contrasting with her dark, thick hair. As she approached the heady mix of perfume mingled with the damp sensuous fragrance of her body. It was intoxicating.

When she closed the final few steps, Morgan extended his hand and took hers. He stared at Paige, unable to take his eyes away.

"What is it?" she whispered over the murmur of the surf.

"I told you last night, I like looking at you," he said, knowing there was so much more he wanted to tell her. "You look—" He stopped, at a loss for words.

She waited, anticipation and uncertainty crossing her face. After a clumsy silence, she shrugged. "Please, Morgan. What do you want to say?" she asked. "You can tell me anything."

"I know." Morgan shrugged. Of course he could. He could confess his life was a drama staged for everyone else...his parents, coaches, friends, teachers, even his rivals. And being with her, in this special place was like a dream, an oasis, a private sanctuary in a reality he'd never thought possible.

And yet somehow she knew. Morgan sensed it.

"It's all right. I think I understand." Paige held his gaze. "I love it when you look at me like that. No one else ever has." She touched his face, brushing an errant lock of hair from his forehead. "But you're holding something back."

Paige was a sorceress. She'd bewitched him, looking deep into his soul.

They turned and walked hand in hand to the edge of the small cliff before sitting in the soft sand and sparse grass. "Do you remember last night? When you asked me what it was like, being a Harvard jock?"

Paige nodded. Her gaze fixed on him. "Of course."

"Sometimes—" He looked away. He'd never shared this with anyone. Never. Not even Ben. "It's like being on a tightrope. Relief when you get to the other side but frightening when you're in the middle without a net."

She touched his lips, nodding very slowly, repeating, "I understand."

They'd formed a connection. An immutable bond. This morning Morgan had sensed her grief like it was his. Now, Paige did the same. He knew it last night when they lay next to each other. He needed no dialogue, no long explanations nor did she. They need only look in each other's eyes.

He wanted to take her, kiss her, and tell her he loved her deeply, trusted her more than he could ever have imagined.

Morgan thought she wanted it just as much, hoped

Paige ached for the intimacy that awaited. But her eyes showed doubt and fear. He felt that too. Once begun they couldn't stop. She let her hand fall away.

"Well." She flushed, took a step back, and cleared her throat. "How about lunch?"

****

The damp breeze from the southwest had picked up as it did in early afternoon. Paige sat, leaning against another thick oak in a small stand of trees fifty feet from the cliff. Her eyes were fixed on the distant horizon. Morgan's slow, rhythmic breathing lulled her. His head rested in her lap.

Some corner of her brain still teased Paige, telling her this was some massive delusion. That she'd finally gone over the edge. But when she looked at him, snoring softly after sharing his secrets, Paige had no doubt it was real.

Paige wanted to move but hesitated, afraid to interrupt his peaceful sleep. Thanks to Lizbeth they'd feasted on sandwiches, fruit, and brownies, then talked endlessly. In her seventeen years she'd never revealed so much of herself to anyone—not even Candy. She spoke openly about the tragedy and guilt she felt over Robbie's death; Eric, the serious high-school crush who'd abandoned her, breaking her heart; and of course, Monique Burke, whom Paige blamed for Eric's defection and her possible connection with the accident at last summer's jumping competition. An accident that could have crippled Paige.

Morgan followed suit, slowly at first then sharing, opening up about his frightening dreams and his constant need to be the best, the brightest, the one his peers and teammates looked up to. It was an honest and sobering look at his life. One completely different than she would ever have imagined. Paige was bright and talented, someone everybody respected and looked up to, but she had never been popular or considered beautiful. Now, she would never look at being glamorous or one of the in-crowd in the same way again.

She touched his cheek, letting her hand drift down and across his strong chin, already showing a hint of whiskers. She brushed aside a bit of perspiration from his forehead. Suddenly, he let out a small cry and moved as his eyes opened.

"Shhh…" Paige soothed. "Everything's all right."

"Sorry," he said self-consciously. "I was having a—"

Paige put her hand to his lips. "I know." And looking in his eyes she saw he did.

"Didn't mean to conk out on you," he apologized, making no attempt to sit up. "Can I stay here forever?" he asked, finding her hand.

"Fine with me." She put her other hand on his chest, feeling its rhythmic rise and fall.

He looked at his watch. "Two o'clock." Morgan shook his head. "Won't they be sending out search parties?"

Suddenly something caught Paige's attention. "Shhh," she whispered as she pointed to a nearby branch where a butterfly was emerging from its cocoon. "In all my years in these woods I've never seen that before. A chrysalis opening."

Morgan watched then turned back to find her eyes as the beautiful creature flew gracefully away. "What do you suppose that butterfly feels?"

Paige shrugged. "I don't know. Happy at suddenly being free and so exquisite but..." She stopped and bit her lip as she thought more deeply about his question.

"But what?" he asked.

"Think about this. Your whole life you've been a prisoner in that cocoon. Then as if by a miracle you're suddenly set free and discover you're beautiful." She wondered if he saw the parallel. But of course he wouldn't because he'd always been the butterfly never the moth.

"I think," he paused. "I'd be terrified, but I'd be happy."

"How so?"

"Because she's been beautiful since the day she was born. Beautiful and talented and special. But it took an action, some intervention—maybe a miracle before she realized her full potential. Just how really precious she was."

Paige sat dumbfounded. He really *could* read her thoughts—see inside her. He must have. That was exactly what she was thinking. He was the catalyst, the intervention that had freed her, and now she knew she could never love anyone or anything the way she loved Morgan.

She smiled and bent. Giving in to temptation, she found his lips. The kiss was hesitant and gentle, but she had never known anything could be so sweet, so exciting. Paige sighed deeply and pulled away quickly, terrified of getting lost in the strength of her feelings for him.

She could see he sensed her want and the fear that went with it. Morgan let it go, let her go.

Both sighed deeply as Paige looked away and

found Buzzards Bay. "I…I feel bad I'm keeping you from the pool party." Paige kept her eyes on the horizon, afraid that finding his might light the fire both knew was poised to ignite. But she also knew that their magical time together had to end.

She knew he wanted her just as much but he let it go and groaned as he sat up. "You make a nice pillow," he offered.

Her face flushed. "It was my pleasure."

Small talk, she thought. They'd shared so much. So many truths and confessions and yet they still had so much left unspoken. The busy words they said sounded hollow, empty. Where did you go after baring your soul; what was the etiquette when you wanted to stay in this spot with the person you loved forever? *Help me, Jane and Elizabeth*, she thought, calling on her favorite fictional heroines.

Morgan scratched his head. "Hey, I have a great idea."

"Okay." She shrugged. "I'm all ears, but we really should get back."

They stood and brushed themselves off, picking up the remains of their lunch and stuffing them in Paige's saddlebags.

"What's going on tonight?" Morgan asked as he put them over his shoulder and wrapped his arm around her waist.

"Daddy said they're planning a cookout," Paige volunteered. "Why?"

"I have a friend in Falmouth. He's down here for the weekend."

"Okay and…?"

"Well, maybe—" Morgan hesitated. "He could

come over and meet Candy. We could double with them. You know, go somewhere after the cookout. Maybe out for an ice cream or to town."

"He's your friend?"

"Yep. Best buds since junior high. Is Candy going with someone?"

Paige shook her head. "Not really."

He turned her to face him. "Look. I have a totally selfish motive." He smiled. "I figure that after being gone all day they might get a little suspicious if we disappear again."

He had a point. They'd gone from being strangers to intimacy in a day. Paige wanted to spend every minute she could with Morgan. But if they started playing Romeo and Juliet in front of the whole party or vanishing again it might raise questions. Tomorrow, next week, and next month were things they had to talk about. This was no weekend fling for Paige, and she hoped Morgan felt the same.

"When we get back I'll ask her. I don't think Candy's ever gone on a blind date." Paige searched her memory. "But I think she'd be okay with it if he's your friend."

As they began the return trip, a cruel reality set in. Because Paige had a revelation to deliver. Something important she'd kept from him, knowing it might destroy their magical weekend.

She felt his gaze on her. "Is everything okay?"

"Why? What's the problem?" she asked defensively, sniffling as she turned, knowing she could never hide anything from him.

He reined in his horse. "Because you're crying, Paige."

Chapter 15

Candy had fallen asleep on one of the chaise lounges that surrounded their mammoth swimming pool. Partly to work on her tan, partly to lose the wine hangover that had nagged her all day. She smiled, remembering the pool seemed so grand when she and Paige were growing up they dubbed it "Lake Fuller."

The growing sound of people and the buzz of animated conversation and laughter forced Candy back to reality. She sat up and squinted at the sun overhead. Errant clouds had begun to thicken and encroach on the western horizon as they made their way in from the shore, but the afternoon still held a balmy feel.

Candace relaxed as she heard her dad's throaty laughter. His swagger and robust sense of humor was infectious. She could hear him teasing Mr. Cahill about their golf game. In everything he did, Josiah was a fierce competitor. He prided himself on being club champion, or had until his breakneck schedule no longer permitted him the time to be a scratch golfer, whatever that was.

"So. Are you feeling better, young lady?" he asked quietly as he sat down on the lounge next to her. Candy saw right through his attempt to be stern but played along.

"Much better, Daddy. Thanks." And she was. Turning over, Candace rested on her arm, shading her eyes from the hazy sun overhead.

He scanned the small group of guests and gave her a scolding look. "I really wish you'd be more careful. We've offered you girls wine at dinner since you were children but I think you got…"

Candace held up her hand. "I know. I'm sorry." She paused. "Believe me, I've paid the price," she added, shaking her head slowly.

He watched her closely, then showed the forgiving smile she and Paige knew signaled his lectures in the social graces were over. "Good. Lesson learned. You know what's going to happen soon. I can't have you girls parading around like out-of-control sorority groupies."

"Lesson learned, *Daddy,*" Candace repeated. "I told you." She sighed, thinking about his new adventure and what it would mean to them. The families of congressmen would be under far more scrutiny, but despite her dad's confidence it wasn't *a fait accompli,* thank God. And as much as Candy loved him and knew he had monumental political ambitions, she sometimes wished his plan would fall apart.

As they finished talking, Morgan's dad walked up with a soda in hand. "Afternoon, Candy."

"Hi, Mr. Cahill." Candace squinted and gave him a nod and half-wave.

"Have you seen Morgan or my wife?" he asked, scanning the pool area and grounds beyond. Half a dozen people sat on the broad apron surrounding the sixty by twenty-five foot body of water. A handful of others stood at a redwood bar nestled under a canopy. The makeshift assembly extended clumsily from the house. Her father had it assembled and placed there for the weekend's festivities.

"No." She shook her head and checked her watch, which read 3:10. "Haven't seen your wife and I guess Paige and Morgan aren't back yet."

Candace stood and stretched lazily. As if on cue, she saw two figures walk into the barn. She couldn't be sure at first but yes, they held the reins with one hand and each other's with their free hand.

Romeo and Juliet have returned, she wanted to say and applaud but thought better of it.

"I see them going into the barn," she volunteered and pointed.

"Hmmm," said Morgan's dad. "Must have been quite a ride."

Candace hid a smile.

"Well, they didn't starve," Candace offered smugly. "Lizbeth told me she gave them a good lunch."

"As long as they had a good time," said Mr. Cahill with a shrug as he turned. "See you later, Candy. That water looks mighty tempting. I want to check on Mary Jane."

"Sounds like a plan to me," her father agreed, as he joined his friend heading toward the back porch. Suddenly, one of the servants materialized wearing a sober face. She whispered something in her dad's ear and ran off.

His demeanor suffered an immediate metamorphosis.

"Give me a minute. Got an important call." Her dad gestured toward the house. "Catch you all in a little while."

Candy saw concern and something else. Something she'd seldom seen on her dad's face. Something that could have been worry.

"Daddy." She stood and walked toward him. "Is…is everything all right?"

"Fine," he said, manufacturing a smile. "Everything's fine, honey."

Candy wasn't buying it.

"I'll catch up with you all a little later." He nodded to her and Malcolm, who'd seemed to notice the change, too.

"Sure, Joe. Go do your business and we'll see you down here later." Malcolm patted her father on the back.

Both men headed back into the house, her father almost at a run, out stepping Mr. Cahill by two strides.

Candace was curious, even worried, but she'd play detective and find out what was happening. She knew where she was headed first. To Paige's room. This she had to hear about in person!

****

"What about the horses?" Morgan asked when Alex and Aphrodite had been put in their stalls and the saddles removed. "Don't they need some kind of care— combing, brushing, a rubdown, something?"

"Don't worry." Paige held his hand, casually swinging it back and forth. "I'll take care of it."

"But it's so hot." He checked his watch. "And it's only 3:15. Could we go for a swim first and then come back? And then you can ask Candy about tonight."

"It's okay." She stopped moving his hand and squeezed it. "I told you. I'm not much of a swimmer."

Her eyes hid something. Paige had shared so much. But she'd gone dark on him again, dodging his question when he asked about the sudden unexplained tears or why she'd grown so quiet. Morgan wouldn't push. He already cared for her—very much. And Morgan knew, despite her frequent flashes of humor and intimacy there was a fragile, private girl inside Paige. He was afraid of frightening her away. So he closed the space between them and put his arms around her slender waist.

"Look. It's okay. I don't mind. If you don't swim, I won't swim." He had no idea where this relationship was heading, but Morgan wanted to spend every moment he could with Paige.

"Morgan!" she said angrily. "Go for a swim. I'll change into something cool and take care of these guys. I enjoy it. Now go!" she ordered.

Paige frowned. She could be as stubborn as he could.

He shook his head, insisting, "Then we'll both get changed and do—it—together!"

"No," she threw back just as insistently. "I told you—"

As he put his hand to her lips, she pushed them together. She looked ready to burst when he bent toward her. Carefully removing her glasses, Morgan put them on a nearby shelf.

"What are you doing?" she whispered, trying hard to sound restrained and angry. But her eyes betrayed her. They looked soft and inviting.

He stood, silently removing his helmet. Then reached up and unbuckled hers.

"Morgan, what are you doing?" she repeated breathlessly as the helmets fell to the stable floor. A smile teased the corners of her lips. Her breathing quickened and she closed her eyes in anticipation.

"This," Morgan said when he was very close. Taking her face in his hands, he found her lips, doing what he'd wanted to since he'd first seen her.

Suddenly, he heard a nervous cough. Someone behind them.

Morgan pulled away from her quickly, embarrassed and frustrated.

Paige put her hand over her mouth, watching him. She made a comical face, looking self-conscious and amused while she broke his embrace.

She cleared her throat and gave the newcomer a shy half-wave. "Hi, Sam."

Morgan did an about-face, taking in the stranger.

"Sam." She took a few steps toward the man. "This is Morgan."

Tall and wiry with dark-olive skin, Sam wore well-used overalls and a faded gray T-shirt. Despite his thin physique, Sam looked to be in magnificent shape for a man Morgan guessed to be late fifties, maybe more. His embarrassment showed through his bright smile as he looked back and forth between them, knowing he'd invaded a private moment.

"Pleasure to meet you, Mr. Morgan." The man held out his hand.

"Morgan's fine," he assured the older man.

"Thanks." He nodded, then turned toward Paige. "Looks like you give 'em quite a workout today, Miss Paige."

"We took it easy on 'em, Sam," she said, adding, "It's so hot out there." She went back to give Alex an affectionate pat. The horse made a sound Morgan swore was laughter.

Sam walked over and put his hand on Aphrodite.

"Why don't you young folks go have some fun? Let me take care of this lady and her friend here." His toothy smile showed gaps as it sparkled in the shadows. Morgan looked at him and noticed something in his expression when he looked at Paige. Something hard to read—affection, sadness...regret? His eyes held more than Morgan would have expected from a handyman or groom.

The weekend had become much more than Morgan anticipated, but there was something not quite right.

Paige seemed about to protest, but Morgan looked at Sam then walked to her side and took her hand, gently directing her toward the large double door that led toward the house. She ran back to get her glasses then fell into step next to him.

"Thanks. That'd be great, Sam." Morgan nodded at the older man as he took Paige's glasses. Her breeches were very tight so Morgan stuffed them in his pocket.

"No, I told you," she said balling her hands into fists as she looked daggers at Morgan.

Sam shook his head giving them a warm smile. He was having none of it.

"No, Miss Paige. I insist! Ain't seen Alex or his friend for days." He looked toward Morgan and shooed them toward the door. "Now you go on. I'll see you later."

Paige nodded but wore a look of angry resignation. She avoided Morgan's grip as she headed to the stable entrance.

"What's the matter?" he asked as they emerged into dappled sunlight.

"I'm not a child," she whispered though clenched teeth. "I can make my own decisions."

Morgan looked toward the house a quarter mile away. Satisfied no one was watching he took Paige's hand and gently pulled her toward the corner of the barn, then behind it.

"Trust me," he whispered, searching her face as he broke into a smile. "I know you're not a child."

"Morgan," she protested. "What do you think you're—?"

"Shhh," he said as he backed her against the side of the barn and put his hand to her lips, letting it drift over her cheek, onto and down her collarbone. She sighed and closed her eyes. He took her chin softly and turned her face to him as he drew close.

Her eyes opened and met his. A soft smile played at the corner of her lips. "What—are—you doing?" she repeated, trying to stifle a grin.

"This." He leaned into her and found her lips. They were even softer and sweeter than he'd imagined. He pressed closer, unsure whether to continue. Suddenly Paige surrounded him with her arms. Her hands stroked his back as she pulled him close.

Her subtle perfume mingled sensuously with the musky fragrance of her damp hair and body. He closed his eyes, letting his imagination run wild as he played over her full lips and her mouth, teasing both with his tongue.

For a split second she hesitated.

Had he gone too far?

The doubt evaporated as she followed his lead playing hungrily over his lips and opening her mouth to find his. Arousal coursed through him.

"Yes, oh yes, Morgan," she whispered between kisses. Her sultry voice was a hypnotic, tempting siren's song.

Morgan was in another world, tasting the sweetness beyond her lips. He opened his eyes for a moment. Paige followed his lead. They moved apart momentarily, reluctantly—breathing heavily, lost in the fever consuming them. She turned her head when he approached again.

"No," she said breathlessly. "If we don't stop now, we…we may not be able to."

She was right. Morgan had never wanted anyone so much, never dreamt he could feel like this. He wanted her now. Here against the stable wall like something out of a Tennessee Williams play. But she was right. Morgan turned her face to his and nodded reluctantly, leaning his forehead against hers.

"I know," he admitted, backing away slowly.

"Oh, Morgan," Paige said softly as she hung her head, pulled away, and ran past him. As she did her hands rubbed her eyes. He caught a glimpse of tears again.

"Paige," he called and started to follow. But she quickly ran around to the front of the house. Probably to avoid the crowd in the pool area.

Morgan wouldn't be put off. He cared too much for this sweet, shy girl who'd bewitched and mystified him.

As he stood, deciding what to do, Morgan heard something behind him. The sound of heavy breathing was joined by the smell of cigarette smoke. Morgan turned to find Sam's eyes following Paige's sudden exit.

"Go after her, Mr. Morgan," the man said with quiet conviction.

Morgan must have looked confused.

"Been working with Mr. Fuller and his brood since he was my company commander in the Rangers. They're special folks. And Miss Paige, she's the most special of 'em all."

Morgan caught that look he'd seen before. The one that said sadness, regret, something he could only guess at.

"I will, Sam." Morgan nodded. Sam was a stable hand. But it was obvious he cared for Paige. Deeply. He'd probably watched her grow up. But Sam wasn't leering. Morgan saw kindness, compassion, and something else—an emotion he couldn't read.

"Go find her," Sam repeated softly, adding, "please."

"I will. I promise," Morgan repeated. He felt Paige's glasses in his pocket. He'd find her, return them, check out whether she'd talked to Candy about Ben, and try to find out what he'd done to bring her tears.

He smiled and headed toward the noisy crowd around the pool. Morgan needed no prodding, no added incentive to find the girl he loved.

Chapter 16

Paige made her way to a side door by her father's study and peeked inside. Seeing no one, she opened the large French doors and entered. The room was cool and still—quieter than the rest of the house.

She leaned her back in a hidden corner against the bookcase and shook her head. *Oh God!* What must Morgan think? She cared so much for him and every sign, every action, everything he did told her he felt the same way! *So how did she react?* Instead of doing back flips and cheering, she broke into tears. Because Paige had a secret. Something she had to tell him but couldn't find the words.

There was noise in the hallway. Greetings from her mother as she welcomed neighbors and friends. She heard the name Cahill through the thick oak doors. Morgan's mother must be with Vera, being introduced to the guests.

Suddenly as she was about to leave someone threw open the double doors from the pool. Her father strode in. Hidden in the small nook and shielded by afternoon shadows she was out of his line of sight.

A dark, angry expression twisted her father's features. Paige couldn't recall ever seeing him like this. Jaw set, his balled fists completed the picture.

He reached the desk and grabbed the phone that had apparently been awaiting him.

"What is it?" His words sounded cold, sober…
frightening.

"Who are you talking about?"

He listened for a long minute, swallowing as he
turned and focused on the group at the pool, roughly
pulling the sheer curtains across the broad windows.

"Yes. Of course I remember the case. How did this
happen?" He spat angry words into the receiver. Then
he was silent, focusing as he concentrated on what the
speaker said.

"They found new evidence?" He paused and
inhaled deeply. "If that happened the man may deserve
to be free. Especially with all the advances in DNA
technology. Why are you calling me? I was the District
Attorney for God's sake not the judge and jury. If I
recall he had some heavyweight legal talent…"

He remained quiet again as he listened.

"Mistakes happen!" He grew a bitter smirk. "It's
not a perfect system. We do the best we can. I'm still
not sure why you're calling me."

He stood, listening again as he looked out the
double doors toward the pool area.

"I see. You say two inmates from his cell block?"
His expression turned thoughtful. "Well, that is strange.
If you find out anything else, anything substantive let
me know. Until then I won't hide in the basement." His
words sounded casual. Almost flippant. But when Paige
sneaked a look at his face concern belied his tone.

He took a deep breath, did his best to put on a
pleasant face, and pulled back the sheer curtains,
opened the doors, and headed outside, waving at
someone and sending a jovial greeting as if nothing had
happened.

Paige stood frozen, shaking as beads of sweat ran off her forehead and down her back. She swallowed deeply, then sneaked back across the office. Laughter and voices echoed from outside. But they sounded hollow, empty to her. Her imagination ran amok, but she seldom saw the hard driven side of her father. She walked across the large wood-paneled room and found the window that overlooked the pool. Paige scanned the apron and the small bar her dad had set up. No Candy. Paige wasn't sure what any of this meant. And how much to tell her big sister. She'd been in heaven at the way she and Morgan had connected. Another part continued to sink deeper into despair knowing what she had to tell him—something that could blow their blossoming romance out of the water like a torpedo. And now, a confusing secret conversation—like something out of a TV thriller. She listened at the side door that led to the kitchen and the back hallway, sneaked out on tiptoes and seeing that Lizbeth and everyone else was consumed by the pool party she ran up the back stairs suddenly feeling like the weight of the world had descended on her.

****

Candace sat on the edge of her sister's cluttered sofa, waiting for Paige. She had to hear all the details and more important how Romeo reacted when Juliet had dropped her bombshell. She wanted this to work so much for Paige. Yes, she would have loved to connect with Morgan despite her flip comments and denials to Naomi, but Candace had a debt she owed her younger sister. If that meant keeping hands off Morgan it was the price she was willing to pay. And by the looks of it she would have come in a distant second in this race.

Not a familiar position when it came to boys.

She heard the doorknob twist and held her breath as Paige skulked into her room. Her sister turned and pressed her back against the door as she closed her eyes. Even from her seat on the sofa, Candace could see the damp tracks on her sister's flushed cheeks.

Paige sighed and opened her eyes, taking a step into the room.

"Oh my God." Paige froze as she put her hands to her face. "You frightened me," she whispered.

Candace stood, not sure how to approach her. "How…how did it go?" she managed clumsily.

"With Morgan? Wonderful," Paige said, staring at her as she wiped the remains of the tears from her cheeks, drying her hands on her breeches.

"That's great. But what else would I be asking about?" Candace forced a smile.

"I…I don't know what I meant. Guess I'm just confused by everything that's happened. Just something I heard downstairs."

Paige's answer confused Candy. If things were so great, why was Paige crying? "Nice clothes," Candace gestured toward Paige's sleek new riding outfit trying to cheer her up. "What did you hear? Something about Morgan?"

Paige bit her lip, looking at Candace then shook her head. "No. Nothing about Morgan and thanks," Paige said, her mouth twisting into a forced smile. "Been saving the outfit for a special occasion," she added with a brittle laugh.

"Paige? Can you stop the double talk?" Candace stood, repeating pointedly, "How—did—it—go?"

"He's the most—" Paige slumped on her dressing

table chair. "The most amazing boy I've ever known, ever been with."

Candace found her sister's eyes and studied them. "You didn't tell him, did you?"

Paige sighed and closed her eyes. "No." She shook her head in resignation.

"Why?"

Paige nodded. "I just couldn't, Candy." She bit her lip again. "We had such an incredible day. I just couldn't spoil it."

Candace stood and crossed to Paige. She took her sister's hands and led her to the overstuffed couch, patting the spot next to her.

"Okay, we have a lot of catching up to do."

Paige stared into space, her face a mask—a curious mix of joy and regret. "All right." She nodded.

"Let's start with last night." Candace began. "I'll tell you what he said and what I saw and then you can fill in the blanks and tell me about today."

"Okay," Paige repeated with a sigh.

"But I gotta tell you Paige."

She turned toward Candace, waiting for her sister's pronouncement.

"That boy has it bad for you. Never seen case of love at first sight like this." Candace smiled and gently patted her back.

"I know." A sad smile crossed Paige's face. "I have it even worse for him."

Chapter 17

Morgan hurried across the stable yard and reached the path to the house. Laughing guests and the clinking of glasses played a backdrop to his confusion. They were having a good time. Morgan wasn't in the mood.

He didn't feel like laughing. He'd just spent an incredible day with the most…the most extraordinary girl he'd ever known. Morgan had shared his secrets and fears with Paige and she'd done the same with him. A giant weight had been lifted off his back. He recalled Camu's *Myth of Sisyphus*. But Morgan had succeeded and finally reached the peak. Or so he thought.

He wanted to believe the tears had been brought on by happiness. Joy that they were so much in sync, so perfect for each other. But that didn't ring true. Morgan had always been intuitive. He had a sense about people and events. And something didn't ring true. But based on the strength of her emotions that something was important, and Paige kept it a secret because of how it would affect them.

He reached the back steps. The giant weight had returned—on steroids.

"Hey, son."

Morgan looked up and saw his dad standing on the back steps that lead to the kitchen, looking as if he'd been waiting for Morgan.

"Hi, Dad." Morgan stood, looking around.

"I saw you coming. Sit down for a minute." His father took a seat and patted the step. "Like to hear about your day."

Morgan wanted to find Paige. He needed to know why she was in tears.

"C'mon, son. Spare your old man a few minutes." He raised his eyebrows and gave Morgan a warm smile.

"Okay," Morgan agreed reluctantly. "How's Mom doing with all this activity?"

"Holding up pretty well." His father pushed his lips together. "I wish we could get her out more. I think it would be good for her."

"I think you're right. But the doctor told us she has to want it. If we force it on her…" He let the words die.

"You're right," his dad agreed and moved on. Too often they avoided discussing his mother's condition, as if ignoring it would make it go away while both knew it wouldn't. "Now, on a more cheerful note, did you and Paige have a good time?"

"Yep," Morgan answered.

His father turned, his stare weighing heavily. "Unless I'm mistaken, there's something you're not telling me."

Morgan sighed and faced his father. "You're right, Dad. We had a great day but—"

"Share with me. Like you used to. I know something…something's kept you away from us." Malcolm put his hand on Morgan's shoulder. "We used to talk everything out but lately?" He shrugged. "We'd like to feel part of your life again, Morg."

Morgan studied his father. He might have been mistaken, but Morgan thought his father's eyes held tears. He tried to hide a smile, but his dad saw.

"What's so funny?" Malcolm asked defensively.

"Nothing, Dad. Sorry." Morgan shook his head. "It's seems I'm bringing everyone to tears this afternoon."

His father's face flushed. For a split second he looked hurt.

"Sorry, Dad," Morgan offered quietly, staring straight ahead. "Paige took off from the stables in tears after we got back."

"Really. That is odd." His father paused. "Well, maybe not." He nodded slowly as his face took on a knowing look. "Did she tell you anything? About the fall? What she was doing?"

Morgan turned toward him again. "The fall? No. Why?" Morgan was suddenly on high alert. "What could she tell me?"

"You really like her, don't you?"

"Yes, sir. More than I've ever liked anyone." He shook his head. "More than I ever thought I could. And I've only known her for a day."

"Well. Joe thought she'd share this with you. Maybe I'm overstepping here. I hate to be the one to deliver this news." Malcolm exhaled deeply. "I guess if I want you to share with me, I have to do the same."

****

"You two had quite a day." Candy patted Paige's knee. She took Paige's chin in hand and turned her face so she could find her sister's eyes.

Paige pushed her lips together tightly and nodded.

"Paige," Candy whispered.

"Yes," she said, looking at Candy.

"I know this sounds like something out of a drugstore romance novel, but I wasn't kidding before. I think Morgan's in love with you."

"But we've only known each other for a day," Paige protested.

"I saw the way he reacted last night when he was looking for you, the way he watched you and asked about you and—"

Paige closed her eyes as she absorbed Candy's words. Morgan in love with her? It was the most exciting and terrifying thing she'd ever heard.

"It can happen in a flash," Candy went on. "Which is why it's so important you tell him."

"Okay. I will. Promise." Paige crossed her heart and took a deep breath. "What do you think about going out with his friend?"

Candy put on a mock frown. "The things I do for my baby sister."

"Then you'll go?"

Candy nodded. "Sure. Sounds like fun as long as you and Romeo control yourselves. Besides any friend of Morgan's is bound to be a super-hunk, right?"

Paige brimmed with excitement. The true confessions thing had done her a world of good. "We'll try," she said, putting her hand over her mouth as she thought of their minutes behind the stable. The thing she'd overheard in her dad's office still spooked her, but he'd been a tough law and order type, maybe sometimes you had to get nasty. She'd never seen that side of him before but her dad would never do anything mean or dishonest. Paige knew that. And she was so consumed with Morgan it forced everything else to the back of her mind.

"But here's the deal." Candy's voice brought her back. "I like Morgan, too, and I don't want him to get his heart broken. So you have to tell him—tonight. Or I will."

Paige looked up at the soft knock.

Candy stood and looked at Paige who nodded. Candy crossed the room, opening the door.

"Hi," Candy said with a nervous laugh. "Paige. Someone to see you."

Paige stood, smoothed her riding clothes, wiped her palms on her breeches, and headed to the door. She peered around Candy.

Morgan stood in the doorway holding her glasses. "Thought you might need these. Can I come in or—"

Candy gave him no chance to finish. "Paige is right here."

"Hi," Morgan said, flexing his fingers nervously.

"Hi," Paige said.

Candy looked back and forth between them. "I suggest you guys go for a walk or something. Mom and Dad are pretty cool, but I don't think they'd go for you two hanging out in here alone." She arched her eyebrows and grinned. "Especially the way you look at each other. I'm afraid I may burst into flames if I get between you."

"That's fine with me," he agreed as Candy eased by him.

"See you tonight," she called back to Morgan. "Can't wait to meet your friend."

Morgan heeded the warning and stood in the hallway a foot outside Paige's door. "I just wanted to make sure you were…you know, all right."

"I am," she whispered, adding, "as long as I'm with you."

He stood watching her, moving closer and smiling

as he leaned against the doorframe. "Candy's right. And since Sam's taken Alex and Aphrodite off our hands, we should probably spend some time at the cookout."

Paige came close to the door and looked into the hallway. Seeing no one around she extended her hand. He took it, letting his fingers weave into hers as the now familiar goose bumps worked up her forearm.

"I think that's a good idea. Besides, I could really use a shower again." She shook her head but smiled.

"Not for me you don't." His face grew red. "I don't want to leave you, even for a minute."

She nodded, tilting her head. "I know, Morg. But tell you what. Why don't you call Ben and set the date up. For about seven thirty? No, wait. Better idea. I'll ask Daddy if he can come for the cookout. I'm sure he'd be good with that."

"Great." Morgan looked at his watch. "I'll bet he'd love to come, and I know he'll like Candy. They have a lot in common, just like us."

Amazement flooded over Paige. If anyone had suggested yesterday that she and Morgan Cahill had a lot in common, Paige would have advised they be committed.

"What's so funny?" he asked.

"Nothing. Just something I was thinking about."

Morgan looked at his watch. "It's a quarter after four. How about we meet by the pool in thirty minutes?"

"Can we make it forty-five minutes? And if you want to go swimming that's okay."

"I told you, Miss Fuller. You don't swim, I don't swim."

"All right. Be a martyr." She shook her head

stubbornly and gave him a push. "Do you think we have to do everything together?"

"No, Paige. We don't." He let go of her hand and took her by the shoulders. "For instance you can't come to training camp with me."

"Of course not."

He stood for a moment and took a deep breath as he found her eyes. "And we both know I can't go to Australia with you."

Paige swallowed and backed away as his arms released her. She watched Morgan. He betrayed no emotion.

"How…how did you know?"

"It's not important."

"Yes it is. Please tell me." Relief, anger, and sadness hit her all at once.

"My dad told me. Or let's say he figured it out."

Paige stood frozen, filled with disappointment, staring into the depth of his deep blue eyes.

"Earth to Paige Fuller," Morgan whispered. "It's okay. Really."

Part of her was frustrated. Bad enough she was leaving for her senior year. She wanted to be the one to tell him. "You mean you don't care?" she asked, searching his face for a signal, some sign of what he was feeling.

"Are you crazy? Of course I care. Don't be ridiculous. After what's happened between us this weekend. You're all I think about, the one I want to be with all the time but—"

There was noise on the stairs. The housekeeper was coming up with a vacuum.

Morgan snatched her hand quickly and squeezed it.

"I care very much. But you had no idea this would happen. Neither did I."

She managed a smile.

"Maybe someday I'll have to leave. You'll be disappointed. But we'll get through that, too."

Paige's eyes overflowed again with happy tears.

"My dad told me something a long time ago. I'd never paid much attention to it till now but, then I hadn't met you."

She looked up at him as she brushed the tears from her cheeks. "Can you share?"

Morgan found her eyes. His were full of understanding and affection. The smile that followed showed warmth. "He always told me, 'When you want to hear God laugh, tell Him your plans.'"

Kevin V. Symmons

Chapter 18

Julian sat in the solarium of his family's stately Hamilton estate. Once, in another lifetime, it had been a happy, nurturing place, full of warmth, sunlight, intoxicating fragrances, and love. More than anything, love. A place where he and his beautiful young Sophie would hide away from prying eyes, whiling away long wintry afternoons huddled in each other's arms in front of the massive granite fireplace.

While sitting lost in daydreams of those glorious times, a hushed sound signaled Sophie was attempting to approach and surprise him. Julian let her play out the masquerade then suddenly turned, took her slender wrist, and pulled her next to him as he smiled. She returned his smile in a provocative way.

"They suspected nothing," she said smugly.

"No." He shook his head. "The papers and the news say they're baffled. We fooled them completely, and no one made any connection between number one and this repulsive creature."

"Not a difficult task considering the cretins we're dealing with." She raised an eyebrow.

He took the pictures from his pocket. "What would they have said if they'd seen these?"

She took them from his hand, letting her fingers linger while she did.

He lifted his eyes to meet hers. "You know it was

you. You, darling, that kept me from…"

"Shhh," she whispered, taking him tightly in her arms. "Don't speak of those dark times. We'll repay the debt they owe you and then spend our lives far away from here."

Backing away she studied the pictures again as she had last night when he'd shown them to her. "Tell me again. Please. Did he scream?"

Julian shook his head thoughtfully. "For a few delightful moments, but not after I hung him by the chain," he said matter-of-factly.

"*Quel dommage!*" She beamed a conspiratorial smile. "But of course it would have been so much more pleasurable had he screamed longer."

"Yes, darling, but it would have attracted his neighbors. Even in that rat-infested gulag there would be someone who might have come to investigate."

"Of course, Julian. You know best." She took his hand, caressing it fondly. "We can't be greedy or overanxious." She showed him her perfect smile. The one he saw when he closed his eyes. The one that let him keep his sanity during all those endless terrifying nights surrounded by the fearful beasts that'd tormented him.

"No, of course we can't," he assured her. "We'll have to leave number three for a while."

"Yes, dearest. We'll leave him for a while," she agreed as she found his lips. As she melted into his sinewy frame, he reveled. Despite the abuse he'd suffered he still became magnificently aroused at the mere touch of her hand.

"Remember the line from that Star Trek movie? The one we both celebrated watching right here?"

She grinned temptingly as her thin lips found his cheek then slid to his nose. "Of course. The Romulan parable! 'Revenge is a dish best eaten cold.'"

He pulled her slender body against him, feeling her nipples hard and erect beneath her sheer silk blouse.

"We'll make them all wait and do this slowly with exquisite precision. And…" He smirked, stopping in mid-sentence.

"You know how much I hate it when you tease me, darling."

"I'll leave that thought, but I have an idea germinating. It coalesced last night while I waited for you to come home."

"Are you going to share this stroke of genius?" She nibbled on his ear while she deftly unbuttoned his shirt.

"Let's say that it occurred to me that for our last victim—the key one whose doorstep we can lay the real blame at…"

"Yes," she whispered as her fingers worked down his shirt front.

"If we were to take someone he loves very much and promise to make their last days an agonizing hell unless he acquiesces and surrenders to us then we'll have him."

"But who do you have in mind as bait?"

"I've done some research, and he's especially fond of his youngest daughter. She's a sweet little thing. Quite adorable and very talented I'm told. I think he'd do anything to save her."

"And?" She shrugged.

"I'll show you a picture of her. An innocent child that should do the job nicely." Julian took out a photo and gave it to her. "Took this at a riding stable." He fingered the picture fondly. "She's quite the equestrian I'm told."

"She is adorable." Sophie studied the photo.

"Not when we get done with her." He smiled and contemplated his plan. "We'll take her, get the father, and then enjoy her as a bonus. Yes, dearest," he continued. "As a matter of fact I'm going to their estate tomorrow to check it out."

"Can't I come along…in disguise?" she asked with a giggle.

"No, but I'll show you the pictures when I get home."

Sophie rubbed her hands together and grinned. "My goodness, Julian." You are *such* a naughty boy." Her grin grew into a throaty laugh.

Chapter 19

"So," Candy said in her best come-hither voice. "You're Ben, Morgan's friend."

He turned around and broke into a coy smile. "Unless there's someone else here I don't know about."

She laughed and he joined her. "Okay. Let's try that again. I'm Candace Fuller. Candy to you, Ben."

She looked him over trying not to be too obvious. Six two, broad shoulders, curly dark hair that hung nicely over his forehead and a physique that looked to-die-for in his shorts and the loose sports shirt that clung to his massive shoulders. *Not bad, Candy. Not bad at all!*

"Sorry, I can come across as a wise guy when I first meet people." He looked toward the pool and blushed. "You may not believe this, but I'm really kind of shy."

Candy watched his face. He looked embarrassed. She liked him—right away. She held out her hand. "Nice to meet you, Ben," adding as she pointed, "any friend of Romeo's there is a friend of mine."

Ben shifted his gaze to the broad back lawn and the badminton net where Paige and Morgan were clumsily batting the shuttlecock back and forth.

"Well, he is pretty good on a football field." Ben grinned. "I guess racket sports aren't his thing."

Candy took note of his spectacular smile. *This guy*

could be a model! "Or Paige's either. She's amazing on a horse and at the keyboard, but this is the first time's Daddy's ever put up the net."

"So, where do you go to school?" he asked as they walked over to the fence.

"Just graduated from Tabor Academy. And I'll be a freshman at Columbia this fall. I want to study poly-sci."

"Tabor's great," he said with a look of approval. "Got some friends over in Falmouth that went there. And Columbia Poly-sci. That's amazing. Great choice!" Ben enthused. "Me, too. Hope to go to The Law School or The Kennedy School of Government when I'm done with my undergrad work."

"Well, you have to meet my dad. He was the DA for Barnstable County for twenty-five years." She gestured toward her father, holding court at the bar.

"Of course. You're *that* Fuller. Josiah is your dad." Ben nodded in admiration. "He handled some really big cases."

"That's right." Candy tried to hide her amazement. Imagine a hunky jock like Ben being a legal groupie.

He smiled, turning his attention to her again. "I saw him interviewed on TV during that case where the girl was found in the dunes in Wellfleet. Oh, sorry," Ben said, blushing again. "Not exactly stimulating first date conversation."

"It's okay. My dad's kind of a local hero. I'm used to it."

"So, you just graduated? What were you into at Tabor?"

"Oh, different things. Cheerleading, softball, chorus, student government." She found herself lost in his hypnotic brown eyes. The more Candy looked at Ben the more she liked him. Maybe not like Romeo and Juliet fumbling around on the lawn and falling all over each other, but Ben seemed like a great guy, and he sure was easy on the eyes. "Paige is the real heavyweight," she volunteered. "A champion or virtuoso at everything, certified genius…a disgusting younger sister."

Candy laughed and Ben joined her, adding, "I know the feeling. Hard keeping up with Captain America there." He nodded in Morgan's direction.

"Hey, maybe they have that in the Olympics," he yelled at Morgan when they reached the fence.

"Ben, how are ya, my man?" Morgan called and waved. He ducked as the birdie zoomed by his head.

"Great!" Ben answered as Morgan ran around the net and teased Paige, pretending to bat her on the head while she squealed with laughter and fell to the ground.

"Oh my God," Ben said, dropping his jaw. "Is *that* my best friend Morgan? The hard-as-nails, take-no-prisoners Ivy League legend?"

"God help us." Candy chuckled softly. "I think they call it *looovvvee!*"

"So she's your younger sister?" Ben asked, following Paige with his eyes and nodding his approval.

"Yep." She nodded and gave him a good-natured punch in the arm. "Oh God. Not you too. I know she's really cute! But I'm getting an inferiority complex."

He turned and fixed Candy with his eyes. "No, Miss Fuller. I'm very happy that you agreed to spend Saturday night with me." He gave her a mock bow. "But I can see why Morgan likes her. She is very pretty and looks like a lot of fun."

"C'mon." Candy nodded and took his arm. "Let's show 'em how to play that game."

He took her arm and they headed for the gate to the back yard. "After you!"

Chapter 20

Cedar Junction, Walpole

Ezra Wilson walked out of the hearing room. After more than fifteen years, he would get the parole he coveted so deeply. Another chance? Maybe. As he walked down the steps from the hearing room, he wondered why they always met on Saturdays. Didn't these people have any better way to spend a fine June weekend than interviewing half a dozen felons? He shook his head. The monthly Parole Board meeting had been easy—almost too easy. Ezra kept expecting to wake up and find himself in his cell realizing the whole thing was a dream.

But this wasn't a dream.

"Gonna miss you, Ezra," the guard escorting him back to cell 124 in D block said with conviction. "These guys—they look up to you." He nodded toward the cellblock.

"Thanks, Wayne." Wayne was all right for a guard. "Can't say the feeling is mutual," Ezra added with a smile.

Wayne grinned and patted him on the back. It was an out-of-character gesture for this hard-nosed disciplinarian and one that would have had him before the shift supervisor if he'd been caught. But that was the kind of reaction Ezra evoked when he set his mind to it. And he had, especially since seeing that story about the kid from Harvard. The boy who could be his son.

Two weeks. Fourteen days until the doors would open and set him free. He'd already found a place to live and had listed Harvard Stadium as his place of employment even though he had no guarantees. Not yet. But Ezra prayed it would work out. Things just had to. Wasn't there karma somewhere in the universe? And if so, wasn't he due just a little good?

But now he was back on the street. Or soon would be. A few old friends were still around, but he doubted they were waiting for his return, and that was fine with him. Friends like them he didn't need. It had taken fifteen long years, but that had all worked out, too. In a way.

After buzzing him through the inner gate at D block, Wayne nodded. "Like I said. I'm gonna miss you. Most of these cons are dumber than shit and have no chance of making it on the outside. But you, you got brains and…charisma I guess they call it." He studied Ezra. "We won't see you back here."

"Thanks for everything, Wayne." Ezra nodded and offered the man his hand. Most guards insisted on being called by their last name preceded by "Mr." But Ezra had a special rapport with more than a few. Wayne was on leave for the next two weeks. So when he got back, Ezra would be a memory. But Ezra always hedged his bets. He had no plans to repeat his mistakes but anything was possible. "I don't plan on making a return appearance." He smiled and nodded "The word 'recidivism' is not in my vocabulary, Wayne."

Wayne shrugged. "I…I got you a little something.

135

Left 'em on your bunk." He looked around warily. "Just don't tell anyone."

Ezra ambled slowly along the elevated walkway. When one of his fellow D block inmates would ask him about the hearing, he just flashed his best smile and gave thumbs-up.

When he got to his cell, Ezra turned and waited while the duty officer in the enclosure opened his cell door. Ezra walked inside and a broad grin worked across his face as he saw the two cartons of Marlboro Lights on his bunk.

No, he thought as he picked up the cigarettes, *I may be dead or I may be somewhere far away, but I sure as hell will do my best to never set foot in this place again.* He crossed to his small desk and slid the picture of the boy back inside his journal, then pulled the small clipping from his pocket and laid them side by side. *I'll be seeing you real soon, son...I hope.*

Chapter 21

"Do you think we can officially call this our tree?" Paige asked as she snuggled into Morgan's chest.

He gave her arm a gentle squeeze.

"I'd say that's fair," he whispered, pulling her closer. "Do you need more bug spray?"

Paige shook her head. "No, I'm fine. Everything is fine," she purred contentedly as she closed her eyes.

But Paige knew one of them had to address the 800-pound gorilla in the room, the unspoken event that could derail their blossoming love. They'd both dodged the subject all night. She refused to bring it up, hoping some miracle might make it disappear. She noticed her dad wasn't his usual self at dinner—full of stories, rhetoric, and sage wisdom. He'd been friendly but quiet, almost withdrawn. She kept trying to forget those strange minutes she'd spent hidden in his office and the call she'd overheard. But they nagged at her.

"Well, looks like Ben and Candy hit it off," Morgan said with a grin.

She returned to the warm pleasure of his arms and joined him in a smile. "Yeah, they hardly came up for air."

The four of them had feasted on the Fullers' sumptuous cookout then sneaked off to get an ice cream and take a long walk on the beach.

"Hmmm." She sighed softly. "Pretty well," Paige

added. "But not as well as some people."

She pushed away so she could turn and find his lips in the moonlight, taking off her glasses and stuffing them in her pocket. The kiss was soft, gentle. Paige remembered the afternoon. She knew the fire, the passion Morgan's touch and lips aroused—knew too well if they kissed the way she wanted they might never stop.

As she backed away slowly, he sighed deeply and broached the forbidden subject.

"What are we going to do, Paige?"

She shrugged. "Wish I knew. We could run away to the South Seas or maybe join the circus," she suggested in an attempt to bring some amusement to the topic that consumed their thoughts.

"Yeah, when I was ten I thought the circus would be the perfect job." He found her eyes in the moonlight. "But seriously, it's gonna be hard enough to leave you on Monday morning, and knowing you'll be gone for a whole year—I don't want to think about that. I can't."

"Please," she begged. "Don't say it like that." She put her hands to his lips angrily to stop the thought. Perhaps if she wished hard enough she could erase the inevitable reality. "I've been thinking. I'm gonna ask Daddy about coming home for Christmas. And I'll be back in May."

Tears filled her eyes as she fell into him, their arms surrounding each other.

"Now I wish I'd never volunteered to be a counselor at that damn summer camp," Morgan said crossly.

"You didn't know. And I have the New England Show Jumping Championships in August."

Morgan pushed her away and fixed her with his piercing blue eyes. "Paige, we'll make it work. Somehow. I swear. We'll find a way to spend every possible minute together."

Watching Morgan, she believed him.

"Sure," she teased. "With all those groupies hanging all over you, you'll forget about me in a day."

"Don't say that! You know better." He ordered, shaking his head. "You're all I want now, all I'll ever want." He found her lips again. Suddenly Paige was in that world again. The private universe of ecstasy she'd found a few hours before. Nothing else existed, no stars, no moon, nothing. Time stopped. Only Morgan's lips, sweet and soft as they pressed into hers. His touch defined her reality.

By the time they stood and reluctantly headed back to the house it was almost midnight. They clung to each other, promising each other continually they'd make the best of a frustrating and painful situation.

Morgan explained he could leave his volunteer job at the camp early, getting away after a month. He'd come home and visit Paige. Maybe bring Ben along if he'd read the signals right between his friend and Candy.

"I know my parents would love to have you come down here—any time you want," Paige promised optimistically.

Originally Morgan had planned to leave on Sunday night. Now he'd wait till Monday morning to squeeze in every last second he could with Paige. They'd still have most of July and early August to be together before his training camp and her departure for Australia.

They'd make it work. Somehow. It had to. Paige stubbornly refused to acknowledge any other outcome. Morgan sounded equally committed. Besides, when Paige put her mind to something it got done, and done well.

When they arrived back at the pool area, several people were talking. Her dad had been drinking. His loud baritone dominated the conversation. The tentative side he'd shown at dinner was lost in too many scotches and his customary adrenaline rush.

"I'm telling you"—he paused for effect, addressing Ben, Candy, and a few of their school friends—"we cannot let our guard down. We have to make every effort to keep our streets safe from the violence running rampant in this country!"

Paige stopped and took Morgan's arm. She looked up at him. An indulgent smile crossed his face. Paige loved her father dearly. Despite being her champion, supporter, mentor, and biggest promoter when he got this way, he was a bear, not someone you enjoyed being around.

Fortunately, as they crossed the pool apron toward the small gathering where her dad held her sister and their friends captive, her mother appeared on the porch.

"All right, Joe. You've convinced everyone," she said as he began another monologue. "Give the young people a rest, dear!" He turned and let his head drop, realizing he'd been holding court.

He held up his hand. "Apologies all around, ladies and gentlemen. Vera's right." The words sounded too precise. He was doing his best to feign sobriety. "To quote Dickens, 'I will retire to bedlam.'" And with a dramatic bow, he turned and went to join her mother on the back porch.

Paige grinned, knowing when her dad began quoting from the classics it was time for bed. She and Morgan sat down joining Ben and Candy.

"Sounds like Daddy was in rare form." Paige watched as her parents disappeared into the house.

Candy nodded. "Yeah. He was more over-the-top than usual. You know how he can get. And he lectured me about proper behavior this afternoon." She chuckled and rolled her eyes. She shot Ben a delicious look. "How 'bout we take another walk, *Benjamin?*" She squeezed every ounce of temptation she could into her words, batting her long lashes. "We could count the fireflies down by the pond?"

He shrugged and nodded with a smile. "Best offer I've heard all night. How could a man resist?"

As he gave Paige a wave and Morgan a high five, he put his arm tightly around Candy and they headed for the secluded spot where the stream emptied into a small pool.

"Hey, you guys sure you don't need a chaperone?" Morgan called after them.

"I think we'll be okay." Ben put his hand behind his back and waved comically.

Paige and Candy's other friends were standing up and heading toward the gate. They all waved and said their good-byes.

Paige's best friend Francie stopped and took Paige's arm, pulling her a few feet away. "Did you have to promise your first born or perform some satanic ritual to get him?" she whispered, nodding at Morgan. "He is one hundred-fifty percent gorgeous!" She faked a swoon and squeezed Paige's hand. "And he seems like a great guy to boot!"

She looked at Morgan and nodded in amazement. "Nope. He just sort of fell into my lap." Paige giggled.

"That's what Candy said. Love at first sight." Francie gave Paige a friendly punch on the arm and showed a mock frown. "Ooooh. I hate you. All that talent and the best-looking guy I've ever seen. I am so jeeeaalous!" she said with a scowl. But Paige knew Francie was a loyal friend—a sweetheart.

"Goodnight, Paige, Morgan," Francie said as she and her date waved and left. They closed the gate and Morgan came up to join Paige.

"What was that all about?" he asked.

"You," she said, grinning without hesitation. "They're jealous I've found the best-looking, kindest, most special guy in the whole world!"

"So," Morgan asked as they sat down in chaise lounges he'd pushed together so they could hold hands. "How 'bout all that fire and brimstone from your dad? Sounded like something out of the Lincoln-Douglas debates."

"My goodness, Mr. Cahill. Amazing! Not only handsome and talented, but an historical scholar." Paige giggled and squeezed his hand as she scanned the pool area. Satisfied they were alone except for a tired bartender well out of earshot, she leaned close. "You have to promise to keep this a secret. Even from your folks."

"Promise," Morgan agreed, crossing his heart.

"Well, the real reason Daddy resigned from the DA's office is because he's going to be the next congressman from our district."

"Really?" Morgan stared curiously. "Ben's the big

guy on law and politics. And I'd read the congressman down here is resigning for health reasons, but don't they need a primary, run-off, or something like that?"

"Yep." She nodded. "But my father made a great name for himself as the DA and the Republicans haven't even got a candidate yet. Everyone says he's a shoo-in."

Had she shared too much? Of course not. Her doubts were foolish. Paige could trust Morgan with anything. She knew that.

****

Paige wrapped her arms around him and pulled him close. She could feel the excitement as they grew close. "Well, Mr. Cahill," she whispered feeling his arousal

"Paige!" Morgan said. He blushed as he backed away.

"My goodness. The idol of every girl in the Ivy League and poster boy for hunky!" She giggled like a schoolgirl. "Don't be shy, Morg," she teased uncharacteristically and took his hand. "Hmmm. I think you need to come up and see my trophy collection?"

He studied her, a smile slowly crossing his face. "Does that mean what I think it does?" he asked, scanning the pool area.

Paige nodded, took his hand, and led him across the massive pool apron into the house.

"Shhh!" she whispered as they tiptoed through the kitchen, the foyer, and up the long circular staircase. Once they heard the sound of a door, but it was inside one of the bedrooms so after a brief halt they finished their climb. She motioned and took off her shoes. He did the same and followed her down the long hallway to her bedroom door.

Once there Paige opened it very quietly. Her face flushed as her heart beat 200 times a minute.

Morgan raised his eyebrows in question, mouthing the words, *Are you sure?*

Paige nodded again. She'd never been so sure of anything in her life, never wanted anyone as much as she wanted Morgan at that moment. Their long luxurious day together had been foreplay, an exquisite tease in anticipation of the moment when they could be completely alone. Paige desperately wanted to give herself to him as she'd dreamt of so often. She took his hand in hers, gently pulled him into her room and closed the door behind them.

"Paige, you're sure this is what you want?" he repeated in a hesitant whisper.

She gave him her most inviting smile and simply nodded. A strange combination of excitement and anticipation enveloped her. Paige held no doubts. Two days ago she never would have dreamed that Morgan would be the one to fulfill her, to make her a woman. Now she could think of nothing and no one else.

"More than anything I've ever wanted," she whispered as she pulled him close.

Morgan smiled softly and found her eyes then her lips. Each of his kisses was like nothing she'd ever known, ever imagined. It was electric, sending a shock through her entire body.

She clutched at his shirt as he pushed into her, hard and firm. She responded and put her hands under the thin cotton of his shirt as he did the same while they explored each other's lips. His tongue played over and around hers, its salty sweetness teasing hers as it begged for more.

They found their way to her bed. Morgan's hands explored inside her sheer blouse, finding the undergarment she'd worn since the accident. A low moan escaped as she lost herself in a fever of passion and desire. "Morgan…Oh, Morgan…"

"Oh—Paige—I—" His words halted abruptly as a soft knock on the door invaded their reverie.

"Paige, you still awake? Can I come in?" Candy asked as she poked her head inside Paige's bedroom. She and Ben had gone for a walk…hadn't they?

Morgan and Paige lay frozen on the bed.

It took her sister a moment to focus in the darkness. But she let out a small cry when she saw Paige and Morgan.

"Oh. Oh my God. I'm so sorry," Candy whispered as she retreated and closed the door quickly.

Paige pulled her blouse around her and turned, lying on the bed, part angry, part embarrassed. "Sorry," she said breathlessly as tears formed in her eyes.

"I think I should leave," Morgan said, as he stood and straightened his clothes.

Paige nodded reluctantly. It was the last thing she wanted, but she knew they had no choice.

"I'm sorry about—" Morgan began.

Paige stood and put her arms around him gently. "No. This was my fault. All my fault." She hung her head and wiped the growing stream of tears as he found a hanky and offered it to her.

"It's all right," she assured him as she touched his cheek and brushed an errant lock of hair from his forehead. "There'll be other nights. Lots of them."

Paige stood on tiptoes and kissed his lips lightly

and followed as he walked to the door. "Lots of other nights," she repeated with a sudden, unexplained sense of foreboding, praying what she said was true.

Chapter 22

Candy stood biting her nails as she stared out the window into the moonlight. Fluffy clouds sped across the perfect blanket of stars dulling their light for a second and moving on. She paid them only token attention. Her shy, innocent sister had vanished like the starlight masked by the passing clouds. What had begun as a casual weekend of fun with her parents' friends had taken an extraordinary detour.

She was thrilled Paige had found someone to care about. Especially someone with as much to offer as Morgan, but their relationship was moving at breakneck speed in a school zone. Candy feared it might burn itself out in one weekend or worse, have consequences that no one wanted or could predict. She had no idea what to think about it or say to Paige. Should she hold her, nurture Paige like a child and counsel her baby sister, or play bad cop and read her the riot act?

But Candy had no time to consider sage sisterly advice since the special double tap on her door signaled Paige's entrance. She tiptoed inside, head hanging as she walked quietly to Candy's bed. Paige exhaled as she sat down heavily.

"It wasn't him," Paige said softly, continuing to stare at the floor.

"I know that."

"Really?" Paige asked with a look of surprise.

"How?"

"Since you were a little girl you've always been the shy one, the one who needed a push, a coax, or a shove." Candy turned and put her arm around Paige's shoulder. "But once you set your mind on something— get the bit in your teeth—whether its show jumping, the piano, or Morgan Cahill there's no reining you in. You're a force to be reckoned with. Even Daddy knows when to get out of your way!"

Paige studied Candy. "I never really thought about it like that. I...I guess I'm sorry."

"I don't expect an apology, Paige. You owe me nothing. That's not my point. The question is what are you gonna do?"

Paige shook her head slowly. "I wish I had the answer. I really don't know. I've never wanted anything or anyone like I want him but—"

"But what, Paige? This isn't a new tone poem on the Steinway or a stunt on Alex. We're talking lives here. Yours and Morgan's. You can't just get up and walk away when you get bored." Candy turned and took both her sister's hands and fixed Paige with her best sisterly stare. "Just remember, you're both very young and unless the world is destroyed by an asteroid, you're both destined for incredible futures—stardom, I'm guessing. I'm probably not the one to counsel you on relationships but please. Don't let your hormones destroy your future or his. You're my baby sister and I love you."

Paige showed a thoughtful frown. "I don't want to, but I don't know if I can be around him, be near him, touch him, and hold myself back. I've never felt like this. You must know I've dreamt about him for years…" She stood, letting her hands fall away from Candy's as she headed for the door. She turned. "If we become a couple—"

"If? If you become a couple?" Candy interrupted with a hollow laugh. "Paige, everyone is talking about you two. You're the biggest thing since Romeo and Juliet. The handsome Harvard jock and the adorable prodigy." She shook her head. "It's a match made by the fucking gods!"

"I'm just so afraid we'll lose control. I can't stay away. But I can't break it off. I'd break both our hearts." She tiptoed to the door and turned, blowing Candy a goodnight kiss. She sighed and said more to herself than to Candy, "Damned if I do, damned if I don't." Her words echoed in the still hallway as the door closed behind her.

Good luck, baby sister. Candy wished she'd given Paige better advice and thankful it wasn't her problem to solve. She'd wanted this to work so much for so many reasons. Now she wasn't sure.

****

Morgan walked through the pool area staring up at the hazy night sky. Was it only last night he'd sat beside her, hoping she'd like him and want to be his friend? Friend? He laughed cynically. Of course he wanted Paige's friendship. She was brilliant, talented, funny, and the most adorable girl he'd ever met, but that was such a small part of what he felt. He wanted so much more. And she felt the same way. There was something so basic between them, a primeval need to be together. Morgan wanted Paige—craved her, had to feel her lips on his, her tongue teasing his, her body sending chills down his spine as it pressed against his, impatient for what they both wanted desperately.

He left the pool by the gate that led the quarter mile to the stable. He walked quietly, thoughtfully, trying to control his feelings, to sublimate the passion that seized him. Despite the insects and the pungent fragrance that hovered as he approached, Morgan already thought of this place as theirs—his and Paige's—the special private place they first met, touched, held each other, kissed. It belonged to them!

As he grew close something caught his attention. A dim light shone in the tack room at the far end of the mammoth equestrian building. He squinted at the luminous dial on his watch. It was after midnight. Why would anyone be out here? He walked inside quietly with the hope Paige may have found her way here after the aborted intimacy in her room. Maybe following his train of thought she came here hoping he'd do the same. They did have an uncanny ability to sense each other's thoughts and feelings.

But as soon as Morgan entered he knew that the soft, melodic voice gently humming an old Sinatra tune was not Paige's. The singer's voice was masculine.

He walked toward the sound. "Sam?"

"Master Morgan?" The question was followed by the clatter of something being dropped.

"Yeah, it's me."

"Jesus, son, you scared the hell out of me." Sam stepped out, his hands full of bridles, reins, and other leather straps Morgan had never seen before.

"Sorry. I was just—"

Sam crossed the few feet after putting his cargo on a work table. "You don't have to apologize or explain, son." He nodded in Morgan's direction and gave a half-chuckle. "I was young once. I was just doing a little maintenance, cleaning and oilin' this tack."

The older man put his arm on Morgan's and led him out back. "Bet you'd like to be standing here with someone else?"

Morgan nodded and smiled ruefully as he studied the night sky.

They sat down on a bench outside, and Sam held up a pack of cigarettes. "You mind?"

Morgan shook his head.

"It's okay. I'll stay downwind so it don't smell bad on you."

"Thanks." Morgan picked up a handful of gravel and began throwing the small pebbles at the giant oak he and Paige had claimed. He turned toward Sam. "Can I ask you something?"

Sam nodded. "Sure, son. 'Bout Miss Paige?"

"Who else?"

"Go ahead and ask. Not much I don't know 'bout these folks. 'Specially her."

"Thanks." Morgan swallowed and took in a deep breath. "This thing with Paige and swimming?"

"Swimmin'?" Sam scratched his head and took a turn looking at the night sky. "Oh." It dawned on him. "You mean why she doesn't like to swim?"

"Yep. Can't figure it out. She's athletic, has a great figure, and—"

Sam held up his hand. "Think it's 'cause of what happened to her brother, Master Robbie."

"Her brother?"

"Sure. I'm guessing she told you 'bout that? He saved her life, then slipped, hit his head, and drowned."

"So it affected her that much," Morgan said, trying

to imagine what it must have been like. What she'd gone through. Relief and joy at being saved from drowning only to have your brother die as a result.

Sam nodded but had a thoughtful look on his face. "Robbie was only a boy, but his parents set quite a stock in him. Everybody did," the older man volunteered. "Seemed like there wasn't anything he couldn't do and do well." Sam shook his head. "He and Paige was especially close. She kind of went into shock for a long time after that. Kep' to herself, wouldn't eat or ride or see anybody. She blamed herself."

Morgan contemplated his words.

Sam continued, "She's had a tough time, son. Like a dark cloud been hanging over her. There was a boy named Eric she set store in. His family moved. He never called her or wrote, then last summer there was the accident at the jumping trials. Miss Paige was lucky she didn't break her neck."

Morgan wasn't sure about the next question but he thought he'd give it a shot. When he'd asked Paige about Monique she'd been vague. He was falling in love with Paige. He knew that something had gone on between them and since Sam was opening up he hoped to find the truth.

"That girl, Monique. It was plain there was some tension, a lot between her, Candy, and Paige. What's the deal?"

Sam sighed softly. "You're takin' advantage of me, son. Things maybe I shouldn't speak about. But if it helps you and Miss Paige, I'll give you my take."

Morgan leaned back against the stable wall. "Thanks."

"Well, Miss Burke—Monique—has been in

competition with Miss Candy and Miss Paige long as I can remember." He stopped and grew thoughtful again. "She does everything they do, but she never done it quite as well—'specially as well as Miss Paige."

"Are you telling me she tried to get even?"

"Not for me to say. There was some talk that she tried to get back by stealing Eric away from Miss Paige." He paused. "And then there was the accident."

"So she flirted with this guy to hurt Paige. Stuff like that happens. But what does she have to do with the accident?"

"Well, the Fullers were off watching another event. When they came back, someone said Miss Monique had been around their trailer. May have even been inside for a few minutes."

"Sorry, Sam. This whole riding thing is new to me. Are you saying that she did something that might have caused the accident?"

Sam put his lips together and looked at the stars. "Well when they checked her saddle after the accident, two of the three billets—straps that hold it in place—were torn. Didn't look like no accident. More like they'd been cut."

"Okay?"

"Mister Morgan. I checked that saddle and all the tack that morning before they left. It was perfect. The saddle was a new Antarès, worth six grand. Mr. Josiah just bought it for Miss Paige."

Morgan swallowed hard. He was beginning to understand the girls' dislike of Monique Burke. "But no one could prove anything?"

"No." Sam shook his head. "And I've known Ms. Monique for most of her life. She's what you'd call headstrong and is a looker, but doing somethin' like that—hard for me to believe. Besides, I know you never been to one of those shows but this was a big one, and there were hundreds of people milling around so…"

"But Paige could have been killed!" Morgan protested.

"Yeah, that's sure true, but like I said there was people all around that trailer and…" Sam stopped. His face wore a hesitant expression. "You gotta remember what Mr. Josiah did for twenty-five years. He was a tough customer. Lots of folks would love to get even. What better way than by hurting his favorite little girl."

"Never would have thought of that." Morgan sat pondering his new friend's words. He hated thinking of Paige as a target of some distorted criminal's plan for revenge but there was a perverse logic in it.

"And Mr. Josiah wouldn't tell the girls that. They'd spend their lives worrying 'bout it."

Morgan could understand that. He'd heard of Paige's dad and his reputation as a no-nonsense, hardcore DA.

"So that was why Monique was at the party the other night?" It made sense if neither Josiah nor Vera really blamed her for putting Paige's life at risk. "And she made a more convenient target than some unnamed thug out for payback."

"Well, I can't say what happened. No one could ever prove anything about the saddle. I never seen Mr. Josiah so crazy, though. 'Tween us I think he thought someone was trying to get back at him by hurting Miss Paige. But after she got better he calmed down. Not much else he could do without no leads. Even had a couple off-duty state police detectives who owed him a favor check it out.

"All I know is that saddle was perfect when we put it in the trailer that morning." Morgan turned toward Sam and opened his mouth to pose a question. Sam shook his head. "Look. I'm just sitting here conjecturing. Probably said a lot more than I should of. Not my place to start blaming anyone for anything."

"But—" Morgan wanted to protest.

Sam held up his hand, repeating, "All we know for sure is that a brand-new world-class saddle that should have been perfect had a problem. Something wasn't right. Can't say nothing else."

Morgan leaned back against the stable wall and exhaled. "Whew."

"Well, what we do know for sure, and I'm guessing she didn't tell you, knowing Miss Paige, is that she not only took a fall but it was bad one. Real bad. Her foot got caught in the stirrup, and she was dragged for a hundred yards. Went over some obstacles, broke six of her ribs, punctured a lung. Internal injuries. She was in the hospital for weeks 'cause she got pneumonia." Sam's voice held anger as he got up, fists clenched. "She was hurt so bad we could have lost her, Mister Morgan."

Morgan watched the kindly man who'd been so warm and welcoming transformed. Sam's affection and anger blended, growing exponentially as he spoke. It occurred to Morgan he'd be a formidable foe in battle.

"Wait a minute. I didn't even think of that. That's another thing 'bout swimmin'. Feeling like she does about you she wouldn't want you to see her scars," Sam said. "Never seen 'em but she's got 'em on the side of her rib cage and her back. She's real self-conscious."

Sam shook his head.

"It wouldn't make any difference to me," Morgan said.

"I know that, but I'm bettin' she doesn't." He shook his head. "Miss Paige is funny. She's driven to be the best, but she's kinda fragile, too."

That agreed with everything Morgan had seen. He extended his hand and turned. Sam's revelations had only deepened his feelings and affection for Paige. "Thanks, Sam. I really appreciate it and all this'll be our secret."

Morgan headed back through the stable to the house, though the kitchen, up the stairs, and tiptoed down the long, thickly carpeted hallway to her room. He gently turned the handle and opened the door, sneaking a look inside.

She stood in a pair of mesh gym shorts and a loose-fitting silky T-shirt. When she heard him enter she turned, her body outlined by the now-bright moonlight shining through the oversize double hung windows. Morgan stopped, aroused.

While he stood letting her initial surprise sink in he watched as her shy smile grew into one that teased, beckoning him. She took off her glasses, walked toward him, arms outstretched, embracing him tightly as they joined. Her body melded into his. They belonged together. Morgan knew it. He pressed against her, thrilled as she responded in kind.

She faced him, fixing her large eyes on his and put her lips to his. Morgan backed away. Paige put her hand to her mouth.

"Sorry," she whispered, wearing an embarrassed expression. "Do I need to brush my teeth?"

Morgan pulled her tightly to him as he kissed her then smiled. "Don't be silly. I just don't want to lose control again."

"Sorry to hear that," she whispered as her face turned crimson in the moonlight. "I can't think of anything I'd like more." She snuggled tightly into his chest.

Paige took his hand and led him to her soft, queen-sized bed. She sat and pulled him next to her. They lay holding each other tightly, trying not to get lost in their desire. Under the loose T-shirt she wore a thin garment that shielded her torso. He remembered Sam's description of her scars. Had she worn it hoping he'd return? The thought excited him.

They held each other and explored each other's lips. It took every ounce of will-power but eventually they separated, holding hands as they fell into a reluctant restless sleep. Despite the excitement of being together, they'd had long, physically draining days. Soon they lay next to each other, their breathing syncopated and rhythmic—young, at peace, and very much in love.

Chapter 23

Paige awoke early as soft sunlight filtered into her room. She'd forgotten to close the sheer curtains on her windows when they sneaked into bed next to each other. As the sun began to climb, it streamed in through the east-facing windows. Reluctantly, she freed herself from his arms. The bedside clock said 5:25 a.m.

"Hey, where are you're going?" he mumbled, tightening his grip.

"You, sir"—she turned and gently pulled free, kissing his lips lightly—"need to make yourself scarce." She touched the tip of his nose, giving it an affectionate squeeze. "I know Daddy thinks the world of you, but I wouldn't want to be within ten miles of here if he found us like this."

Morgan propped himself onto one elbow and brushed away stray strands of hair from her eyes. "But we didn't do anything."

"You and I know that, dear, but—"

"Did you just call me dear?" he asked as a smile spread across his sculptured features.

"I guess I did. Are you upset?" she asked, twisting her face into a frown. "Was I assuming too much?"

"Mad?" A grin appeared. "Are you kidding? I love it…thought it was awesome!" He reached, gently pulling her to him.

"Stop." She stiffened, protesting. "I really do need

to brush my teeth before I kiss you again," she said pulling away.

"You have this thing about brushing your teeth. Too bad. There's no escaping me!" Morgan persisted, sending electricity down her spine. He sneaked around her defenses and hungrily planted a kiss on her lips.

She pulled back and shook her head. "I knew you were going to be trouble, Mr. Cahill."

He sighed and tilted his head. "If it means staying as close to you as humanly possible, you're one hundred percent right. You are in big trouble, Ms. Fuller," he added with a yawn.

She followed suit, yawning and laying lazily on the bed as she caressed his hand.

"But you're right about your dad. He's not a man I'd want to tangle with." A thoughtful look crossed his face. Morgan's chin and cheeks already sprouted a dark forest of whiskers.

He reached up and touched Paige's face gently where he'd lain next to her, then rubbed the stubble on his chin. "I'm really sorry," he whispered.

"You didn't do it on purpose." She shrugged and touched her cheek. "I'm not a makeup magician like Candy, but I can hide it," she assured him.

Morgan took his hand from hers and kissed her palm. "Can you check and make sure the coast is clear?"

"Well, maybe you could stay for *just* a little while?" she suggested, pushing her lips into a pout.

"If it was up to me I'd never leave, but it's not…dear." A shy smile crossed his face as Paige felt a grin cross hers. She loved the sound of it.

She nodded, showing him a look of resignation.

"You're right. But hey, we've got our whole lives ahead of us," she added, squeezing his forearm.

He twisted, putting his feet on the floor and standing as he leaned, groaning as he arched his back. "Oh my God. Riding is a lot more work than it looks."

"Too bad you football types are in such pathetic shape." Paige grinned as she tiptoed to him and kissed his chin, letting her lips work up to his. "My poor baby."

Then she turned, pushed him toward the door, opened it quietly, and put her finger to her lips. "Shhh," she said as she pushed him out quickly and down the hall, blowing him a kiss when he looked back.

"See you at breakfast," he mouthed as he opened his door.

"Get some more sleep," she whispered. "That's an order."

She nodded, closed the door, and ran across the thick carpet throwing herself on the soft quilt as a grin grew on her face. Life was just too damn perfect! How had it changed so much in two days? She looked at her diary but she was too happy and too tired. Paige was sure she could write a novel about what had happened since Friday, but for now it would have to wait.

****

Morgan held the cheerful expression. Why not? He crossed to the window. Outside everything looked so peaceful, so serene. A place for everything and everything, etc. He'd arrived at the Fullers' feeling empty, searching for something. He looked back toward the door and Paige's room. Morgan's search was over. The person he needed slept peacefully fifty feet away.

Tired and sore he lay exhausted on top of the thick

quilted comforter, then slipped off his flip-flops. For just a minute he let his head rest on the overstuffed pillow that invited rest.

He tried to fight the fatigue. All he wanted to do was think about Paige. A smile crossed his face as he yawned. His last vision before drifting off into a deep, dreamless sleep was her face. There'd be no nightmares today.

Chapter 24

Cedar Junction Prison, Walpole, Sunday Morning

"Go ahead, man." The older inmate with the weathered scar nodded at Ezra as he hung up the phone. The Sunday morning line was unusually short. "You making plans for the outside world, you lucky bastard." The man smiled a faded grin that lacked two of his lower teeth. "But be careful."

"Careful?" Ezra asked. "What are you talking about, Zeke?"

"You haven't heard?" The man gave him the I-know-something-you-don't look. "Two of the guys that got released this year are dead. Murdered, the news said."

"What?"

"Yep, Mick Riley and Dub Maron." The man came close and whispered, "Not that it's any loss," as he walked away.

Ezra took the phone. The old man was right. Those two were no loss to humanity. But still. It sent a shiver down his back. He placed his prison number—convicts were charged for calls—and waited while the phone rang three times.

"Is this my main man?" the deep baritone asked sounding amused.

"It's me, Bobby. Two weeks and I'll be at the

gate."

"The job's all set. Has to be before they let you out. Just like you asked. Set it all up. Ground crew at the Stadium?" His friend's voice had a questioning tone. "We got lots of things you can do if…"

Ezra cleared his throat. "But that's what we talked about. What I asked for."

"Right." It was early and Ezra had no doubt Bobby had been living it up all night.

"Gotta be exactly what we talked about… *remember?*"

Anything that varied from the planned job would jeopardize, probably negate Ezra's parole. It was important that he get that job at Harvard Stadium to check out the kid. This was personal. Very personal and very important.

"Sure," his friend agreed. "Just the way we planned. All set."

"Good." Ezra smiled and nodded. "See you at the front gate at nine a.m. in thirteen days." Ezra was about to hang up when he stopped. "Hey, Bobby. You heard anything about some ex-cons getting iced recently?"

His friend was quiet for a few seconds then volunteered, "Think I did hear something about that. But I can't be sure. Why? These guys friends?"

"Hell no." Ezra lowered his voice. "They were bad actors. Just heard about it. No big deal," he said and replaced the handset. He nodded amiably to Wayne, the guard who'd bought him the cigarettes and was going on vacation, then went back to the day room to wait for the call to breakfast. *No big deal!* he repeated silently to himself with a grin. Two less dirt bags in the world. *Good riddance.*

Chapter 25

Paige tried to go back to sleep. But after an hour of tossing and turning, she might as well have tried emptying Buzzards Bay with a teaspoon. Thinking of his arms coiled around her, the subtle fragrance of his after-shave, his rhythmic breathing, and the chiseled face that wore the look of a Greek god was all she could think about. Paige smiled as she touched the mild irritation left from his whiskers. She welcomed it as a symbol of Morgan's affection and love. She wondered if she'd ever confess they'd spent the night together to Candy.

Paige had heard the word "heaven" endlessly—in church, novels, in the movies. Since meeting Morgan again on Friday, she thought this must be the place she'd always dreamed of.

Blowing out a deep breath, she looked lazily at the clock. Somehow she'd managed to daydream her way for almost ninety minutes. It was 6:55. There was no way she could go back to sleep. Paige got up and let the water in the bathroom sink run till it warmed, added some soap, and gave her teeth a brush.

It had been a long evening, full of fun for more than just Morgan and her. Ben and Candy, their friends, parents, and neighbors had all partied till well after midnight. The strange conversation she overheard of her father's flashed by but who had time for that?

Another heavenly day with Morgan had begun.

Paige pulled out a silky T-shirt, her best-fitting jeans, and jodhpur boots. Maybe if Alex was stirring she'd give him a stretch, walk him around the big corral or ride him down to the small pond that served as the source of the stream that flowed 200 yards behind the stables.

Stopping to pull her hair behind her ears, and holding it with a pink ribbon Paige gave herself a casual glance, nodding approvingly as she walked by the mirror. In only two days, Morgan had boosted her flagging ego. And just when she was ready to pack it in. But any girl who could capture the heart of the Ivy League's most desirable heartthrob so completely and quickly had reason to feel good. It occurred to Paige Candy was right again. She liked feeling in control of the situation and had no intention of losing it.

****

Morgan sat bolt upright and turned to find the clock: 7:10. He threw off the quilt, placed his feet on the soft carpeting, and ran to the bathroom. In less than two minutes, he'd washed, run the brush through his close-cropped hair, given his teeth a thorough scrub, and put on an extra splash of after-shave.

He pulled on a pair of Dockers, a long-sleeve Harvard tee and his flip-flops. Without even glancing at himself, he left his room and closed the thick door as quietly as possible running down the back stairs to the kitchen.

"Morning, Morgan," Lizbeth called cheerfully from the back porch. The door was open slightly and he could pick up the fragrance of cigarette smoke from outside.

"Morning, Lizbeth," he said. "Have you seen—?"

"She went through here about twenty minutes ago headed for the stables," the Fullers' portly cook interrupted with a chuckle.

"Great." He nodded as the cook crushed her cigarette in an out-of-the-way flowerpot, came inside, and shut the door against the morning dampness. She walked deliberately to the prep sink against the far wall and gave her hands and face a thorough wash.

Lizbeth smiled as she dried her face. "Yep." The older woman's expression grew into a grin. "And she looked pretty happy to me." She cleared her throat and offered him a plate of freshly baked muffins after drying her hands, adding, "Right out of the oven."

"Thanks. But I think I'll take a walk down to the stables and see if I can find her."

She held the plate with a kitchen towel to insulate her generous hand and insisted, "Go ahead. You'll love 'em. I promise."

Morgan took a cranberry nut muffin and swallowed it in two bites. "Wow!" he exclaimed. "You're right!"

After wiping his hands on a cloth napkin at one of the place settings, he nodded at Lizbeth. "Thanks, again." He headed out the back door and gave the cook a mock salute. "You're the best, Lizbeth."

She nodded with a blush and put the plate back inside the oven's warming tray, then went about mixing up more thick batter with an amazing smell.

"When you find Miss Paige, come back for a special surprise I know you'll love." She called after him, looking up at the kitchen clock and chuckling. "I have a feeling we won't be seeing anyone else for a while this morning."

Morgan stepped out quickly and covered the quarter mile to the stable in two minutes.

As he approached the door, he caught the odor of cigarette smoke again. Sam appeared. After putting out his cigarette and picking up the butt, he approached Morgan. He stuffed the butt into his jeans. Sam saw Morgan watching him and smiled.

"Old habits die hard, Morgan." He shook his head and smiled coyly. "Been doing it since the boss and me was Rangers."

"How are you this morning, Sam?" Morgan asked.

"Hard to be bad on a day like this one." He gestured at the high, cloudless blue sky.

"Thanks for the talk last night, Sam." Morgan offered his hand to Sam. But the groom backed off and shook his head affably.

"Believe me, Morgan, I been here cleaning and rubbing them animals down since six-thirty. You don't want to smell like horses, manure, and stale cigarettes when you meet your pretty little lady." He chuckled. "Matter of fact, I ain't gonna let ya."

Just as he finished Paige came around the long side of the barn from the generous riding ring that bordered it.

Morgan stopped when he saw her. She wore a snug yellow T-shirt, jeans that fit as if they were tailored, and her short hair was held back by an enormous pink ribbon. He stopped to catch his breath, admiring what he saw. "Wow!" he managed as a massive grin crossed his face.

"Well, Sam. At least someone is glad to see me." She gave Sam a haughty expression. For a moment she caught Morgan off-guard. That wasn't the Paige he knew. But her frown broke into a teasing grin as she looked at her old friend.

"Okay, what am I missing?" Morgan asked.

"Well," Paige began but Sam held up his hand and grinned.

"I keep telling her that her daddy pays me so she doesn't have to get her pretty hands all messed up with the horses, chicks, ducks, and the muck."

It was Paige's turn. "And I keep telling my old friend that I like spending time with the animals, especially the newest member of the barnyard crew." She dropped Alex's reins and crossed, putting her arm loosely around Morgan. He blushed, shooting a glance in Sam's direction. Her open affection surprised and excited him.

"Yes," she began taking Morgan's face in her hand and turning it as she looked at Sam. "He is attractive in a basic, roughhewn kind of way!" she exclaimed.

They all laughed, Sam the loudest of all.

Morgan gave Paige a snarky grin, walked over, picked up the beautiful horse's reins, and winked at the groom. "Here you go, Sam. I intend to take this young lady to breakfast!"

Paige opened her mouth to protest but sensed it was fruitless. She was outnumbered and looked happy Morgan was stealing her away.

Joining Paige, Morgan put his arm loosely around her slender waist as he gave Sam an exaggerated bow and whispered in Paige's ear, "After you, dear."

Her face, already pink from their long day in the sun yesterday, flushed crimson at his term of endearment. Paige stole a look back at Sam and seeing he'd become preoccupied with taking care of Alex, gave a big tug on Morgan's waist.

"Nope, after you, dear!" she offered with a giggle, pulling him along toward the kitchen and the surprise Lizbeth said awaited them.

Chapter 26

Ben sat next to Morgan staring at the distant late-morning haze hovering over Buzzards Bay to the west. Without benefit of a breeze, the thick heavy air held a vagrant, listless feel. The clouds hung lifeless and dormant as if suspended in mid-air.

"So, great political guru, what's your take? What's really going on with Paige's dad?" Morgan asked wondering if his friend could figure out the reality of what was happening. Paige had shared that the retirement was a charade, a ruse and to anyone with any political savvy a thinly veiled one at that. But Morgan didn't really care as long as Paige was happy and close to him.

"Well?" Ben shrugged, wearing a thoughtful expression. "Remember, I'm just a tagalong. The surrogate blind date so you and Paige could get up close and personal without attracting attention." He raised his hands and grinned. "But I'm having a great time with Candy. She's the real deal, Morg. Pretty, funny, smart. So, thanks!" He looked at the horizon. "Now in answer to your question. The man's middle-aged, vibrant, and has so much adrenaline he could bottle and sell it, so I'm guessing this is a strategy to do something more… probably far bigger…?" Ben held up his hands and wore a smug expression. "How's that for a guess?"

"Well, let's say you passed the test."

"Come on. *Give!*" Ben demanded.

"Can't. But I think we'll all know soon enough." Morgan said to placate his friend.

"Okay…" Ben shrugged. "But remember my sage words, my friend."

Ben chuckled and shook his head, watching as Candy and Paige emerged. He put his arm lightly on Morgan's shoulder. "And whatever his real master plan, I'll bet he's not exactly bummed that his brilliant and adorable younger daughter has fallen for the scion of one of Boston's best-known families who just happens to be handsome, bright, and the biggest Ivy League sports icon in decades."

As Morgan was about to shoot a snarky comeback, the look on his friend's face changed abruptly. Ben shook his head imperceptibly.

When he turned, Morgan saw why.

"Well, how goes it, mighty men of the Crimson?" asked Josiah Fuller, as he stepped between the two boys and put a hand on each of their shoulders. It occurred to Morgan that Ben was spot-on. Sometimes Josiah Fuller sounded more like a Roman senator than a retired DA. The perfect mixture of testosterone, philosophy, and Dale Carnegie!

"Great, Mr. Fuller," answered Ben with a forced smile. "At least I think so."

"What's the problem, son?" Josiah asked with a look of concern.

"Well, after my buddy's riding adventure yesterday—" Ben nodded in Morgan's direction. "Candy is determined to get me on a horse after lunch."

Josiah's smile grew into a hearty laugh. "Well, I wish you luck! I tell you, Benjamin, when my girls get something into their heads, they're hard to discourage." He continued smiling and stood palms up in a noncommittal manner. He touched his chin. "But knowing Candy, I can almost guarantee you'll come back alive."

He patted Ben on the shoulder and backed away with a smile, heading toward the generous barbecue area where Sam had donned a new role and outfit. He stood proudly and resplendent in a crisp white polo shirt, gaudy apron, and a comically tall, floppy hat, supplied, Morgan had no doubt, by Josiah Fuller. Sam was being capably assisted by a slight but attractive young woman Morgan had seen helping Lizbeth in the kitchen and a wiry middle-aged man who seemed to be everywhere—cleaning up, bringing fresh food, pitching in anywhere he was needed. From the grins, laughter, and robust chatter as they supplied their lunch customers they all seemed to enjoy their assignment. The enjoyment went both ways as the happy recipients left with plates piled high with burgers, sausages, and an assortment of fried treats.

"Yep, I made it back with all my major body parts," Morgan held up his arms, pretending to survey himself. "But I have to tell you," he began, nodding with admiration, "I had a few aches and pains when I got up this morning." Morgan tried to hide his grin as he remembered waking up next to Paige. "There's a lot more to riding than I figured, buddy. Paige is something on horseback and unless I miss my guess, Candy is no slouch either."

As he walked toward the house and the barbecue area, Josiah stopped and turned toward the boys again. "What about you, Morgan? You and Paige have any plans for later?"

The question caught Morgan off-guard. They'd talked about sneaking down to the pretty little pond and lying next to each other. "Aaah…no, sir. Just hanging out and taking it easy." He studied the warm hazy sky emerging as the fog burned off. "When you live on Comm Ave or in Cambridge you don't get a lot of chances to spend time at the beach or with nature. At least not at someplace as spectacular as this."

"I understand. But that town house your folks bought isn't too hard to take, is it? Four floors of hardwood and oak paneling, a few hundred square feet of roof garden, three-car underground garage. I'm not sure Harvard will be offering you financial aid real soon, son." Josiah nodded in respect, still smiling as he looked toward Buzzards Bay.

"Agreed." Morgan smiled at his host. "It sure beats dorm life, even though I have to put my time in at the frat."

"Well. What would you say to a sail after lunch?"

Morgan gave Ben a quick look. "Sure, if that's what Paige wants to do, I'm okay with it. I guess." He nodded, adding, "Did you mean just Paige and me?"

"Well, I thought since Candy and Ben would be off riding, maybe Vera and I and your folks could come along. You know, tag along for the ride." He gave Morgan a shrug. "Unless you mind. We are your godparents, and we never get a chance to spend time with you."

Actually, as much as he wanted to be alone with Paige, he was happy to have company. Like horseback riding, handling a forty-foot Catamaran was not a skill set he'd acquired. His only concern was how his mother would handle a bumpy sail on the Bay. She didn't do well with things she wasn't familiar with but… "Sounds great, sir," Morgan agreed, thinking he'd speak to his dad to make sure everything was okay.

"Good. Of course the girls will want to freshen up. I'll go see how Sam is doing with the barbecue. We can finalize the time later."

Morgan nodded, waiting till Josiah was out of earshot.

"What did I tell you?" Ben asked, adding, "Sailing with the big dog and the missus. What do you bet he shows up at every home game with some press?" he teased Morgan.

Morgan watched as Josiah reached Sam. As he was about to answer, he noticed something. Part of the conversation was friendly, cheerful. Just the way he'd expect between two old Army buddies. But Josiah would snatch a look around between the smiles and pats on the back as the guests passed the grill. He seemed to be whispering to Sam, scanning the surrounding pool area. Sam did the same.

"Catch this," Morgan said to Ben as he gestured toward the barbecue. "What's with that?"

"Got it, bro." His friend had picked up on it. "That is weird, man. But I have no idea what's going on."

Morgan nodded. "If I wasn't looking for it, I'd never have noticed."

"Well, if it makes you feel any better, I think you're right. There's more going on here than we know. Though exactly what I have no idea."

By this time the girls had arrived at the pool.

Candy rushed over and put her hand on Ben's shoulder. Paige joined Morgan. She stretched and gave him a warm kiss on the cheek as she surrounded him with her arms. Morgan looked around, not sure Paige should be so obvious.

She smiled shyly, adding, "Sorry. Every time I see you I smell of horses."

"That's okay," he assured her, watching Josiah again then turning his attention to Paige. "Actually," he whispered as she held him, letting her grip tighten slightly. "I think I could get used to this."

Chapter 27

Paige caught herself in a silly grin as she walked by the ornamental mirror in the foyer. The barbecue had been otherworldly. Of course being anywhere near Morgan would be out of this world to Paige. And Sam was not only an old friend and a great groom, he was the best barbecue chef on the planet. She hummed a few bars from Friday night's Tchaikovsky Overture as she walked past her father's office to go upstairs and change for sailing.

Candy had already washed up, put on a clean polo shirt, and led a hesitant Ben to the stables. Paige had noticed Morgan humorously savoring his friend's reluctance. She remembered how well he'd handled the challenge, sure that Ben would do the same.

As she started up the long staircase, Paige heard her name.

"Paige," her father called from his office. She stopped and turned, walking the ten feet back to the door.

"Hi," he said, turning to face her as he stood hands on hips.

"Hi, Daddy. Did you call me?"

He didn't answer for a minute but sat down, tenting his fingers as he studied her.

"Is everything okay?" Paige asked, thinking about the curious phone call yesterday. His look was so intense her stomach was doing somersaults.

"Of course, dear." He showed a small smile that grew. "Can you come in and sit down for a minute?"

She swallowed deeply. "Well, Daddy, I really should get cleaned up. I've been riding and it's hot outside—" She tried to smile and held her nose.

"Nonsense. Don't be silly." He stood and turned toward the window, gesturing toward the chair in front of his massive desk. "Please, sit down." It had the sound of a plea not an order.

"What is it?" Paige managed in a weak voice. Despite being her most ardent supporter, her father could be intimidating.

"You and Morgan?" He turned. Though she tried to avoid them he found her eyes. Had he found out or have some suspicions about last night?

Oh God! Paige panicked, conjuring up half-hearted defenses when suddenly her father smiled again. "I can't tell you how happy I am about you two." He spoke quietly, deliberately, as he resumed his seat. "I don't know that I've ever seen two young people get so close in such a short time." His words were cheerful, pleasant, but they sounded hollow, almost forced. "And what a couple—two attractive, brilliant, and talented young people, superb athletes—" His words hung in the air as the A/C vent hummed overhead.

A long silence followed.

Paige swallowed deeply again. Part of her thrilled he was happy with what was happening, but her father was complex and driven. Very much so. She wondered if he had a hidden agenda that had yet to appear.

"Daddy, where is this going?" They'd always

spoken openly, but she shifted uncomfortably in the chair.

He studied her again, wetting his lips. "It's too bad you have to leave so soon. I mean after meeting him."

"Yes. But if it was meant to be it'll work out." She nodded, doing her best to offer an optimistic point of view she didn't feel.

"You seem rejuvenated." He studied her. "It's amazing what love can do. Maybe we could revisit the Australia idea? The idea was for you to get away. A change of scenery to help you feel better, wasn't it?"

"Are you serious?" Paige shifted uneasily again, tightening her grip on the chair. "I do feel better and Morgan's wonderful, but we shouldn't label our relationship till we've had time to get to know each other. Of course I'd love to talk more about Australia if you think it would be okay..." Paige loved Morgan so much it hurt, but she had an uneasy feeling about her father's comments.

He turned toward the window again, stopping her in mid-sentence. "Great barbecue, wasn't it?" Australia had suddenly vanished from the conversation.

"Yes it was," Paige agreed. This meaningless banter was getting spooky. If he wanted something, why didn't he just ask her? "Is there something specific you want to tell me or ask me?"

"No. No, of course not." He showed her his best public smile. The rehearsed one she'd seen so many times. *Then why this rambling dialogue,* she wondered?

"Honey, I..." He stopped abruptly. "I just hope you're careful."

Was he talking about being with Morgan? Was this a repeat of Candy's warning from last night? "Careful?"

"Yes. You know in my job I…I had to deal with some very bad people."

Paige swallowed deeply. This wasn't about Morgan. This was something else. She felt perspiration trickle down her back and it wasn't from the heat.

"Are you telling me that we may be in some kind of danger?" Paige whispered.

"No. No, of course not, but I want you to be careful. You're a lovely young woman, and we're a very prominent family. Well!" He stood abruptly, signaling the interview was over. "I think you were right. Why don't you change into one of those fetching outfits your mother is always buying, find Morgan, and meet us at the dock in"—her father glanced at his watch—"about forty-five minutes."

Paige stood and walked across the hardwood floor. Her low boots echoed as she headed for the door. She glanced back and her father nodded.

"See you soon. Looks like a perfect day for sailing," he called after her.

Her stomach was still tied into knots as she left. His words had reinforced his approval of Morgan as a suitor. But there was something more. Was he warning her? This was connected to the strange phone call she'd overheard. She knew it and it sent shivers down her spine. His eyes had that same strange look they had yesterday afternoon. He was normally so focused but his comments sounded like…nonsense. Small talk with a capital *S*. Paige didn't know what to think.

She exhaled, letting her mind drift back to Morgan and lying next to him in the early morning. She smiled, dismissing her misgivings as an overreaction to the exhausting whirlwind the weekend had been. Her dad was retiring from a stressful position. There must be loose ends, issues, and people he had to deal with. Besides, as long as Morgan was with her, everything would be fine. It just had to be…didn't it?

Chapter 28

"Where do you want the extra burger patties and chips, Sam?" Julian stood with a tray of leftover food in his arms. He wore a white baseball cap pulled down low over his forehead and eyes. In the last month, he'd grown a thick black beard that covered much of his face and most of the scar that served as a distinguishing characteristic. That combined with his ordinary appearance served him well as he studied the Fuller estate, making mental notes he would record later in the day and absorb for future use.

"Why don't you go inside and ask Lizbeth, Jed?" Sam smiled warmly and pointed toward the kitchen. He nodded and followed instructions. Jed was one of the many aliases he'd adopted during his righteous crusade. Misdirection, feint, bob, and weave. He'd sat and listened, learning his new craft well from his fellow inmates. They weren't all vicious, mindless thugs like those on his list.

"Extra food, ma'am. Are you Lizbeth?" he asked softly in an excellent southern drawl.

She nodded and fixed him with a stare. "You from below the Mason-Dixon line?" she asked with a wide toothy grin.

"Yes'm. Just up from 'round Mobile. You know, in Alabama?"

"Sure," she offered with another smile. "You can

put the burgers in the walk-in fridge. Anything else that doesn't need to be refrigerated you can just leave here. Molly and I," she said gesturing toward a younger woman, "will put them away."

He did as he was told meekly, so as not to attract attention, always making as little eye contact as possible.

"Thank you, Miss Lizbeth," he said in a quiet voice.

"Seems like a nice man," he overheard her say as he left the massive kitchen, noting the doors, windows and locking mechanism. Next to the door was an elaborate alarm keypad. One he'd never seen in his months of studying security systems. No matter, he'd find a reference.

When he returned to Sam, he asked if there was anything else he could do.

"No, Jed, I think we're all set here." He gestured around the vast grounds. "You did a really good job today. A good service person is like the umpire at a baseball game."

"How so?" Julian asked, raising his eyebrows.

"If he's doing his job no one should notice him."

They both laughed.

"What I'm saying is that if you need some work we could…"

The man held up his hand. "Thanks, Sam. But I have a job." *A sacred quest,* he wanted to say but let it pass.

"Well," Sam patted his shoulder. "If you change your mind. You know where to find us," he said as he handed the man an envelope with ten twenty-dollar bills.

"Thanks, Sam. I'll keep it in mind." He could not wait to get home and tell Sophie what he'd learned. He left the party and found his small pickup, got inside, and headed out the gate. *See you sometime*, he thought with a grim smile as he turned and headed north.

****

Later that evening he lay on the thickly cushioned couch in their living room as Sophie caressed his hand.

"You look pensive, dearest," she whispered putting her moist lips to his hand.

"Yes," he whispered back touching her hair. "I've been thinking more about the idea I mentioned earlier." He sighed deeply. "You know, about using the daughter as a decoy to draw him out."

When she raised the brows over her enormous green eyes, Julian noted how they glittered and changed color when the light struck them.

He smiled, shifting his thoughts to more immediate temptations.

"What's so amusing, darling?"

"Your eyes. They're still the most spectacular I've ever seen."

"So what did you learn on your visit? What are you contemplating?"

"You remember what I said? That if you really want to hurt someone like Fuller the best way to do it is through one of his children."

As she sat up Sophie's eyes narrowed. "Granted, my dear, but I've been thinking about that. And you know I have no sympathy or sentiment for any of these people. But they had nothing to do with his crime."

"True. But is our mission to punish him for what he did?"

She looked into his eyes as a smile crossed her lips. "Yes, my pet."

"The others are useless scum. They deserve to die of course, but this man, the final name on our list was the architect on my misfortune. It occurs to me he deserves a more painful, more personal punishment."

Her smile grew. "I see your point. How would you accomplish it?"

"My research was correct. He has a very special affection for his youngest daughter. Her name is Paige. She really is such a sweet, pretty little thing."

"Be careful. I feel an attack of jealousy coming on." She showed Julian a mock pout then turned thoughtful. "So, when we're ready for him we'll take his daughter?" she continued. "And use Paige—such a charming name—as you suggested. As bait to draw him out?"

"Exactly," he agreed thoughtfully. "But this will have to be well-planned. Fuller is no cheap thug and he's well surrounded. And he's no fool. I suspect he may begin to see a pattern even though he can't prove anything. No. This will have to be masterful."

Sophie purred with satisfaction, running her sleek fingers down his narrow chest. "You'll manage it. I know you will, darling." Her fingers stopped. "And when we're done what about the girl?"

"Sadly, she seems a sweet child, but once we deal with her father she must be sacrificed." He shook his head with something akin to regret. "She's what they call in those cheap, tasteless movie thrillers collateral damage."

"Perhaps," Sophie whispered with a gleam in her green eyes. "We can amuse ourselves with her for a while."

"My goodness. You are becoming quite the little vixen. The thought of toying with such an innocent young thing had crossed my mind."

They studied each other and broke into childlike laughter and stood as they headed for the dining room.

Chapter 29

Sunday night came too quickly at the Fuller estate. Morgan's misgivings about sailing proved wrong. He and Paige glided over and across Buzzards Bay in her parents' sleek forty-foot catamaran. Morgan had been sailing before but never experienced anything like it. The Fullers knew their business, including Paige. Much to Morgan's delight, she spent most of the time subtly flirting, but masking her attempts to tease and excite him as she manned the helm, tutoring him about winds, sheets, tacking, and the sophisticated instrumentation as she guided them over the low swells like they were flying.

"Is there anything you don't do well?" he asked as they hurriedly made their way to the sanctuary of their special oak tree after supper.

"You should talk," Paige said as she sat down next to Morgan and snuggled into him. "But actually," she whispered as she gently trailed her fingertips down his chest, "there are one or two things I haven't had much practice at." She swallowed hard. "I was hoping...maybe you could teach me." She turned her face up, showing a delicious smile. "Or we could learn together."

Morgan lifted her hand from his chest and kissed it. He stood, pulling Paige up with no hesitation and headed for the stables. They tiptoed inside as he looked around warily.

"Sam left after dinner," she said, showing a conspiratorial smile. "I already checked."

He scanned the massive building. "What do you think?"

"The tack room's small and hot, but—" Paige gestured.

Morgan didn't care. He nodded. "I can't wait much longer."

She pulled him to the door and opened it. Inside was dark and warm. It held the musky bouquet of horses. To Morgan it was a suite at the Ritz. Paige was next to him. That was all that mattered.

They found each other's lips before the door closed, kissing so passionately they had to stop, panting to catch their breath. Excitement pooled with nervous energy all at once, fulfilling Morgan's every fantasy.

Paige rummaged around and found several blankets, piling them on the hard floor to give them a cushion. Morgan pulled off his polo shirt.

"I have to tell you something," Paige whispered, eyes on the floor. "When I had my accident last summer it—" She stopped, eyes growing moist. "It left scars."

Morgan pulled her close. "Paige, there's nothing that would change the way I feel."

Paige lifted her damp eyes to his and kissed him softly then slowly pulled off her T-shirt, revealing a thin, lacy bra. On her right side was a thick four-inch scar.

"I'm sorry," she said plaintively, shaking her head.

"Sorry for what? You're the most beautiful and exciting girl I've ever met." Morgan touched her face gently as he lifted her lips to his. "Nothing can ever change what we've found."

As if by a script, they fell to their knees in an embrace so tight neither could breathe, touching each other feverishly in a frenzy of desire.

Morgan's hands caressed and teased her while Paige whimpered.

She placed her hand on him as he moaned in pleasure.

They lay on the old blankets, arms and legs frantically twisting and entwined as if they were one being. Their lips seemed sealed together as he reveled in the sweet temptation of her mouth and tongue.

When they paused to catch their breath Morgan couldn't stop the satisfied smile as he embraced Paige tightly. Their bodies glistened. He reveled in the damp fragrance of her body as it mingled with her perfume and the sharp scent of the stable.

"That was quite a practice session," she murmured in the throaty whisper Morgan loved.

"Paige?"

"Yes." She sighed.

"Remember when I told you about two-a-days?"

She nodded and snuggled closer, immediately grasping his meaning. "Do you want to cool off for a few minutes or—"

He undid his belt and took off his shorts leaving only his underwear. Paige did the same.

"No, I think I'm ready for the next lesson."

"So am I," she said with conviction as they began again.

****

They walked into the damp night air, pausing at

their oak tree, lingering, caressing each other's hands as they embraced tightly to celebrate their night of passion.

"Gotta go tomorrow," Morgan said with resignation.

Paige put her forehead against his. "I know." She shook her head then smiled shyly. "It's not fair. You should just move in. We still need so much more practice."

They'd stopped short of making love, sharing a long and tantalizing feast of kissing, touching, and exploring each other's bodies. "I'm always a willing learner."

"Well, I'll talk to my parents about having you back. How about next weekend?" She raised her eyebrows.

"I think I could swing that."

She hugged him tightly.

"Paige," he began. He had no doubts. Morgan wanted to say the three words he felt so strongly. He took a deep breath. "I want to tell you…"

She put her fingers to his lips. "I know." Paige squeezed his hand, whispering. "We've spent a fairy-tale weekend but those three words signify permanence, a commitment. Your life is so full, so complex. So's mine. Please, just give it a little more time."

He sighed and nodded, surprised at her reticence. "Nothing could change the way I feel, but okay. I'll give it a little more time."

Paige shook her head and touched his face. "I feel the same way, Morg, but I want to make sure that you don't say something you'll regret later on—"

He smiled and took her hand. "You and I are meant

to be together, Paige. I know you think you're giving me some space and time to think about this. But I could never be with another girl, even look at another girl after this weekend."

"I just want you to be sure." She nodded and wiped her eyes as she pushed him gently.

"I am, Paige."

They returned to the house clinging to each other as they tiptoed up the stairway and down the hall to her room. He bent over and kissed her fully on the lips. "Goodnight."

She kissed both his hands and held them for a moment. "You know I'll never sleep tonight?"

"Me neither. But I promise no more secret visits. They're too dangerous."

Showing him a reluctant smile, she nodded. "Goodnight."

He backed away, his eyes fixed on her as he headed down the long hall to his bedroom. Yes, it was going to be a very long night, one filled with vivid, delicious memories he couldn't wait to relive.

Chapter 30

Paige rose before sunrise on Monday morning, knowing Morgan would be leaving. And though her mind was elsewhere, she had to prepare for her classes at the local stables. Part of her was exhausted from the long weekend, another ecstatic having spent it with the most wonderful boy she'd ever met!

She'd spent the night in a swirl of restless dreams and fantasies, reliving their whirlwind weekend, praying to God and every icon she could conjure up that this had been no casual fling for her handsome new beau. Despite all he'd said and done to show Paige he cared, as their time together drew to a close, she fought desperately to erase a nagging sense of doubt.

But watching his adoring eyes throughout breakfast calmed her fears. He sat as close as possible so their legs could touch. When no one was looking he'd sneak his hand into her lap, finding her fingers and tightly weaving them into his. She found herself struggling to stifle the giggle fighting to emerge. No. Candy had called it all along. Right again. She and Morgan were definitely a couple.

"My folks are still gabbing inside. How about a quick trip to our special place?" he whispered as he threw his backpack and overnight bag into his BMW.

Paige needed no prodding. She nodded enthusiastically. They ran breathlessly to the oak tree behind the stable. "It's hard to think we only met on Friday," she said, taking him in her arms and snuggling against his chest.

"I'd never believed in love at first sight. Thought it was something in a movie or a novel," he said as he tightened the embrace. "Till I saw you."

She laughed softly. "Yep, I was really something to look at. Dirty riding clothes, braces, shaggy unkempt hair, covered in sweat, the smell of horses, and in desperate need of a toothbrush. I don't know how you kept from chasing me all over the estate."

He laughed softly as he caressed her back. "Yeah, I've never been sweaty or dirty or needed to brush my teeth." He looked at her and laughed. "Was that why you kept covering your mouth?"

She nodded and grinned. "Candy had just read me the riot act. Told me I needed serious fumigation from top to bottom."

"Not for me you didn't."

His arousal pressed into her belly. She pulled him closer. They needed no words. She just held him, knowing they only had a few minutes.

"I don't care about those things, Paige. People get hung up on the superficial, the cosmetic. I saw a shy, pretty girl, the one I'd been waiting for my whole life. The minute I saw you I wanted to know you better and *voilà*." He released her and threw up his arms.

She punched him in the stomach gently. "You're right. I've heard people talk about chemistry my whole life. When I saw you that afternoon I felt it right away. Like electricity."

"Paige, Morgan!" Josiah called from the back door.

192

"Coming!" Paige answered in a strong voice as she took his hand to begin their reluctant trek to the house.

As they reached the corner of the stable, Morgan pulled her into its shelter and kissed her. Excitement gripped Paige and she clutched his shirt as his lips caressed hers.

After her father repeated his summons, they pushed apart. Paige reveled in the feeling of Morgan's arousal but knew their time was coming to an end.

"Okay," she repeated, waving to her dad as they rounded the corner. She walked slowly as he pulled out his polo shirt to hide the obvious signs of their activities.

As he headed to his sporty convertible he gave her a soft kiss on the lips then thanked her parents for their kindness and hospitality.

"I'll be talking with Paige," Josiah volunteered. "Now you've found us, we hope you won't be a stranger."

"I don't think that should be a problem," Morgan offered politely, sneaking a wink at Paige. "Just tell me when and I'll be back."

And with that he slid into the front seat.

Paige followed him and gave his hand a squeeze.

"And don't forget your friend, either," Vera told him. "He's a delightful young man, and I know Candy thought the world of him."

"I know he liked her a lot, too," Morgan agreed. "Give Candy my best."

He waved to his parents who were in back of him. "See you guys at home."

Then he was gone.

****

If Paige had any lingering doubts, they evaporated when her cell phone rang while she grabbed her lunch break at the stables.

"Hello," she said into the phone not sure who was calling. As soon as she heard his smooth, resonant baritone she giggled and beamed.

"Miss me yet?" Morgan asked.

"Duh! Only for the last three hours and"—she checked her watch—"twenty-two minutes and seven, no make that eight seconds."

He laughed warmly. "Really, Paige. I thought someone with your intellect could be more precise."

"Oh God, I miss you *sooo* much," she whispered into the phone self-consciously. "I am so angry at you for leaving! But there is a slight chance I might forgive you…" she added, looking around self-consciously.

"Well, I might be able to squeeze in another visit this summer," he teased and she loved it.

"I already spoke to my parents and you have an open invitation and so does Ben." She banged the phone against a post for effect. "That means I expect to see you before the sun sets on Friday night."

"Hey," he protested. "Can you not break my eardrums? Is this the sweet, shy girl I met three days ago?"

"She won't be shy or sweet until she sees you again. She is consumed with pent-up frustration and passion," Paige whispered into her phone.

"Okay, look. I've already told everybody I'll be spending every free minute down there. At least till you or your folks get sick of me. So—chill—out—girl!" he whispered loudly into his cell and laughed.

Just as he told her the good news, her afternoon

class of nine- and ten-year-old beginners began to filter in.

"I'm so glad, Morg. I can't believe how much I miss you after only a morning. By the weekend I may explode," she said softly. "Gotta go. Duty calls."

"When do you get home?" he asked.

"Late afternoon—four or five."

"Make sure that phone is charged 'cause you are going to spend some serious talk time with me tonight."

"Can't wait," she told him. "'Bye, Morg. Miss you so much!"

She closed the phone and exhaled deeply as she stood and threw away the remains of her sandwich.

"Hello, girls," she said, greeting her eight students. "This afternoon we are really going to have some fun," she promised them as she thought of Morgan's words and laughed.

Chapter 31

The ground supervisor at Harvard Stadium studied Ezra Wilson's face. Ezra knew playing the macho con and trying to stare this guy down would bring him nothing but grief. He needed this job, and he had no desire to play the tough guy. He was a convicted felon. He'd killed his girlfriend in self-defense, but he was desperate to put that behind him. And this job was special. His application sat on the man's desk.

But this wasn't going the way he'd hoped. Ezra had precious few favors to call in and he had to use every one just getting this interview. The guy behind the desk wasn't making this easy.

"Been away for a while, Ezra," the supervisor said after what seemed like minutes of staring and fidgeting.

"Yes, sir. Almost sixteen years." *A lifetime,* he wanted to add but again thought better of it. It sounded like a complaint. He'd discovered in his short time outside that citizens liked cons to be humble and repentant not the Hollywood version of the hardened inmate.

The quiet returned as the supervisor resumed his study of Ezra's application. "The report says you were a model prisoner."

This evoked a weak smile from Ezra.

"You mind if I smoke?" the man asked after he put the application down again. Either this guy was looking for an excuse not to hire him, or he was having a slow day. Ezra hoped it was the latter.

"No, sir." Ezra shook his head and smiled.

"You want one?" The man, who'd identified himself as Patrick Flynn picked up the crumpled pack and held it toward his guest.

"No, thanks. Try to limit it to a few every day," Ezra shared. "It's a habit you pick up inside. Can't smoke in your cells anymore."

"How'd you get the application for this job, Ezra? We don't usually hire"—Flynn paused as his face flushed—"ex-convicts."

If the comment was intended to provoke or annoy him, Ezra wasn't about to bite. Ezra had an agenda. To find the boy—the phenom he'd read about. He hoped that finding the kid and connecting with him could give his life meaning and maybe bring the closure he sought so desperately. "Friend of mine from the old days owed me a favor," Ezra volunteered. "Mickey Leary. Lives over off Porter Square."

The man nodded. "Oh, yeah. I know Mick. Good guy and tight with the super." The man nodded and flipped the application over, studying it slowly. "You got some good references here," he said thoughtfully. "Had some serious experience before your…time inside." The man stumbled over his words. "And it says here you're a damn genius at landscaping."

And a few other things, Ezra thought sardonically, but offered, "Always tried to stay in touch. Always had a green thumb. And I like to keep busy. We have to learn from our mistakes." He hoped he wasn't pouring on the platitudes too thick.

The supervisor placed the paper on his desk.

"Look, I got nothing against hiring you, Ezra. When I saw your credentials, I talked to my boss. He said he had no problem if you checked out. And you do—so far. You seem like a straight guy."

Ezra nodded. "I 'preciate that."

"But I'm asking you—assuming we hire you, keep your background between us. We get some tough guys on the crew who might take offense. I don't want any trouble."

"It'll be our secret."

The man looked at the application again, then fixed Ezra with a thoughtful look. "Welcome to Harvard."

Ezra stood as the supervisor did, leading the way to the door.

The man held out his hand. "Hope this can be the beginning of a new start."

More like finishing a fifteen-year-old debt. Ezra took the man's hand. But he said nothing. This guy seemed genuine.

"Can I ask you a personal question?"

"Ask away," Ezra agreed, managing a smile. He suspected he knew where the man was going.

The man put out his cigarette as he followed Ezra to the door. "Did you...do what they say you did?"

Ezra stopped in his tracks and turned to face his new supervisor. He stood for a minute, trying to decide how you tell someone you killed a woman, "Yes, sir. I'm afraid I did," he added with a deadpan expression. "Not proud of it, and I can't rationalize it. Taking a life." How do you explain a moment of infinite terror when a coked-out bitch and her lover come at you full speed with a butcher knife and a syringe filled with a lethal overdose while your three-year-old boy is lying on the floor screaming his brains out. You couldn't. So Ezra maintained his neutral expression.

Patrick patted Ezra on the back. "I like that in a man. Honesty. You paid your time. You been honest with me, and I'll return the favor."

So, he thought as he walked into the hazy sunshine, *this guy is all right with me being a murderer.* Ezra looked back as the door closed. He wasn't sure how to interpret that. Maybe this guy was a screaming liberal…a do-gooder. Or maybe he was something else. Until he had a better read on Patrick Flynn, Ezra would make sure he watched his back.

Kevin V. Symmons

PART TWO

Kevin V. Symmons

Chapter 32

Like the fevered minutes of their passionate Sunday evening rendezvous, the summer sped by too quickly. It seemed as if they'd just met when the weeks vanished like the long summer sunsets. Morgan found himself getting anxious as Paige's dreaded departure date loomed closer. Though she was strangely silent, he was sure Paige felt the same way, because they had no secrets. That would have been impossible. From that first magical afternoon under their oak tree they had an otherworldly ability to understand what the other thought or felt.

As they'd promised each other when Morgan left on that first Monday morning, they were seldom parted except when absolutely necessary. But the unforgiving calendar had become their enemy as Morgan counted the dwindling days till Paige boarded the 747 that would spirit his love away and leave them both empty and alone.

As July dashed into August, the partings grew more difficult, more painful. Their Monday mornings, once filled with laughter and anticipation, knowing they'd be together again soon, became gloomy. Their anguish over their dwindling days together grew palpable.

So it was strange when Paige called Morgan to make sure he was coming to watch the hunter-jumper

competition that Saturday in Andover. Where else
would he be but as close to her as possible. It was now
August second. In two weeks he'd begin two-a-days,
sequestered at the small New Hampshire college where
they were held. And to add to his misery, the team's
training site had been changed to a location on Lake
Winnipesaukee. Another year he would have been
oblivious to the change. Now it meant losing ninety
precious minutes getting to Paige.

Knowing that time was closing in around them,
Morgan had determined to make this weekend a special
one. The competition was at the Andover Hunt Club. It
was a major event, and Paige took no prisoners when
she got the bit between her teeth and Alex's. Morgan
had never been there, but Paige emoted about Andover
Hunt, saying it was a first-class equestrian facility
located in an elegant community of the same name
twenty miles north of Boston.

The strangest thing about the conversation was her
tone. As the weeks fled and her departure approached,
she'd grown even more quiet and withdrawn than
Morgan. But when she called him that Thursday, she
was ebullient, teasing him, and kissing the phone like
she had in the weeks after they met.

Either she was doing her best to keep the world's
stiffest upper lip or the unthinkable—Paige had found
something new to draw her attention. While that might
have seemed impossible Paige had that strong-willed
competitive side Candy had warned Morgan about. But
since they'd been a couple it had been on hold. Was this
the first crack in the walls of their apparently timeless
relationship?

****

"You should have told him on the phone," Candy scolded her sister as they waited for Morgan and Ben at the farm. "You owe that to him. He is so bummed out. Last weekend when I'd catch him looking at you, I thought my heart would break. And you've known about this for two weeks. Do you have a hidden sadistic streak?"

"C'mon, Candy! You think I want to torment him? You know there were some last-minute complications with the high school. Daddy had to pull some serious strings." Paige made a silly face at her sister. "But I have to admit, I just can't wait to see his face when I tell him."

Paige continued her goofiness and pushed past Candy in the hallway, stumbling clumsily down the long circular staircase at the sound of the doorbell.

"Paige, please be careful," Vera said from the gleaming marble hallway. "Morgan and Ben are here, and you have a competition this weekend. Try not to break your leg." She shook her head but wore an amused smile.

Candy took note of her mother's newfound willingness to accept Paige's manic behavior—flighty, clumsy, almost distracted one minute, driven the next. From the upstairs railing the antique grandfather clock struck two thirty. It was never more than ten seconds off so she felt no need to check the time.

The early afternoon had slipped away. She'd helped get everything ready for tomorrow. Her father was equally committed to indulging Paige's every whim, though that was nothing new. But lately he hovered over both of them with a newfound attention, like a sheep dog guarding his flock.

Paige had laid out her new custom-tailored breeches and gleaming field boots. Candy smiled. Her baby sister had certainly grown up over this surreal summer. She suddenly filled her clothes and riding attire like a woman. Candy knew Morgan adored everything about Paige but the way her figure had matured was something to behold. And suddenly as if a spell had been cast over her, Paige seemed happy wearing the designer outfits Vera now purchased with enthusiasm. It wasn't that she begrudged Paige any of the newfound attention or happiness. Especially because Morgan had brought Benjamin into her life. No, she was happy over the metamorphosis. Because Candy held a dark, terrible secret stored deep in her memory. One that no one else knew or could have suspected. One that would haunt her for the rest of her days. It had held her captive for ten years. And Candy also knew her parents too well. She couldn't shake the feeling there might be more to their doting than Paige or anyone else suspected.

And there was the change in Sam. The happy-go-lucky groom and handyman had been transformed. His affable smile and casual demeanor had been replaced with the wary face of the watchman. He now stayed on the estate with Lizbeth and the other servants and had acquired a staff of several "helpers" who were young and strong. Something was going on, but her dad kept his own council, refusing to say anything other than the standard line about adding a few bodies to give Sam some help because of his advancing age and arthritis.

Candy put her musings on hold, bit her lip, and double-timed it to her bathroom to brush her teeth. She'd learned how to compartmentalize. She put her doubts and her guilt in their proper place and stole a glance toward the circular drive to stare at the gorgeous hunk of man waiting impatiently for her. A long gargle with Listerine to make double-sure her breath was pristine and sweet and Candy moved toward the stairs, pulsing with excitement, imagining Ben's arms around her. Yummy!

****

Paige was determined to tease Morgan till the evening barbecue when her revelation would knock him over. She sauntered out to the circular driveway, doing her best to look casual. As the tiny stones reflected the late summer sun, Paige pulled her designer shirt away from her damp skin and waved her hand in front of her face. "Hot huh?"

Morgan sighed and forced a smile. "Yep." He looked around and took a deep breath. "God I love it down here. It's my oasis—" He shook his head and closed the five feet separating them, taking her into his strong, gentle arms. "Paige, I've missed you so much."

Paige backed away and gave him a practiced smile, opening her mouth widely to put it on display.

"Well, look at that," Morgan whispered. "No more braces."

"Nope, just this tiny retainer. Don't look too close and maybe you'll miss it. And no more glasses," she added batting her eyes.

"Funny, but if you hadn't mentioned it I might not have—"

She swatted his arm playfully. "Here I am so proud that the metal is gone—well almost gone—and I got new contacts and you don't even care." Her face twisted into a pout.

"Paige," he whispered. "You just don't get it."

"What don't I get?" She pushed her mouth into a peevish frown.

"That I care for you because of who you are not how you look."

"Oh…so now you don't like the way I look?" she asked, showing him a wounded expression.

"Paige," he growled. "I love the way you look!"

She broke into a giggle and punched him in the stomach. "I'm sorry. I know what you mean. I can never resist teasing you."

He made a faux scowl, but her amusement was infectious. Morgan joined her laughter.

"Want to see the new saddle I got for the competition?" She winked and gestured toward their spot.

"You know, Ms. Fuller, seeing that new saddle is all I've been thinking about all the way down. How 'bout you, Ben?"

Ben had his arm around Candy and nodded vigorously. "He's right. It's all we talked about, seeing the new stuff in the barn. Don't know about you, buddy, but I don't think I can wait." He hid a laugh as Candy pinched him.

They all grinned broadly and headed off toward the barn, splitting up. Paige and Morgan made straight for their oak tree as Candy and Ben headed for their private spot by the small pond near the river.

"Oh and Paige," Morgan studied her intently as they found their tree. "I kinda liked the glasses. I think they gave you that shy sexy look," he teased.

She stuck out her tongue and laughed.

****

Paige pushed Morgan's lips away. "We have to stop. Someone may see us," she managed between halting breaths.

"C'mon Paige. We only have a few weeks left. We need to make the most of every second," Morgan protested.

She looked into his pleading eyes and gave in, sighing as she snuggled into his waiting arms.

"I know," she said standing up and taking his hand. Paige pulled him behind their oak tree so they were out of sight and gave him a nudge till he backed against the thick trunk. "You have training camp in two weeks and then I have the Hampton Classic on Long Island on Labor Day Weekend."

She'd wanted to tell him so often since her parents had agreed to call off her exile but was determined to wait till the barbecue that evening to see his reaction in front of everyone. But after seeing his sad, forlorn look Paige couldn't wait one minute more.

"Yeah, training camp with only a quick visit that middle weekend and I'm still not sure about that," he began. "I have to ask the coach. I am a captain so he may—" He stopped abruptly. His face showed a mixture of surprise and suspicion. "You mean that show on Long Island you told me about? But you're leaving the weekend before Labor Day."

Her excitement bubbled over, forcing her to spill her news. She couldn't keep her delirious announcement any longer. "What if I told you, that I will be here for Labor Day and Halloween and Thanksgiving and Christmas?"

His eyes widened as he straightened up and put his hands on her shoulders. "Paige, don't tease me. I might get suicidal." A smile spread across his face.

She nodded fiercely. Tears of joy and relief overflowed. "Yep. My parents and I talked and we agreed there was no reason for me to go anymore! Someone I met miraculously brought me out of my depression!" Paige announced, putting her hand to her mouth as she laughed hysterically.

Morgan hugged her so tightly she lost her breath. Paige dug her fingers into his back and sighed again as she whispered, "I love you," into his chest.

He caressed her back gently. She sneaked a look up at him. His eyes were closed, perhaps lost in her heavenly surprise and the fact that she'd finally given in and confessed her true feelings. Morgan kissed her hair, whispering, "I love you, too. Paige. I have ever since the moment I saw you that June afternoon."

Chapter 33

"Jeez, babe. This is quite a place," the crude man at the wheel shook his head as he studied the grounds of Julian's sumptuous family estate.

"Yes," Sophie answered quietly. "My parents were very fortunate. I'm so glad you're impressed." She showed the lout her warmest, most endearing smile. Despite her overpowering love for Julian, entering the sad bar where this creature spent his time had been humiliating, especially having to suffer the leering and overt sexual comments she'd endured as they watched her.

"So," he said showing her his chipped, yellowed teeth and the gaps between them. "You're sure you'll be okay? I mean, this is a big place and you said your folks were away."

"I…I'm not sure." She bit her lip and frowned to look wary and tentative. "You've been so kind, giving me a ride home and all. Would you…would you mind walking me to the door?"

"Well sure, honey. If it'll make you feel safer."

"Yes. Yes it would and that's so kind." She nodded meekly, amazed that this piece of filth would think she was so naïve or so desperate she would have any interest in him. But then using their egos against these men had been the most rewarding part of this exercise in ultimate payback.

They covered the quarter mile to the house in silence. When he parked in front of the double front doors, the driver slid out of his seat and raced around the front of the car to her door. He opened it in a pathetic pretense at being a gentleman.

"Thank you." She grinned inwardly as they headed toward the door. Even from four feet away the man's sour breath stunk of stale cigarettes and cheap whiskey.

"My pleasure, sweetheart." He beamed, taking the key she offered him.

He twisted the oversized key and threw the door open gesturing for her to enter.

For a minute she froze as he stopped at the threshold. She breathed a sigh of relief as he entered and closed the door, putting the key on the table in the entry hall.

"You've been so kind," she whispered flashing him her most delicious smile. "Can I get you a drink?"

"Why, sure, missy. I'd love—"

Julian stood behind the door, clearing his throat, a cattle prod in his hand.

The man stopped. "Jesus! You. What the hell?"

The three-foot-long device wiped the smirk from the man's face.

"Didn't you hear? Several of your friends have been killed in the last several months," Julian commented casually.

The man looked like a caged animal. He watched the cattle prod then spotted the silver-plated Smith & Wesson .40 caliber revolver Sophie now brandished in her hand.

He held fast then seemed to realize the desperation of his situation. He glanced back then took a tentative step followed by a lunge at the revolver.

She sidestepped as he fell, hitting the hard marble floor heavily with a groan. Julian took three steps and thrust the cattle prod into the large man's rib cage, pulling the trigger as the man shook and screamed in agony. His eyes rolled back in his head as he passed out.

"Any problem, my dear?" Julian asked as he stepped over the man's body.

"None." She shook her head. "It went just the way we planned."

"Good. Now let's get him to the basement and see how he likes being the victim."

She nodded as they pulled his limp frame toward a wheeled cart they would put on the elevator that serviced the basement.

She lifted the oaf's large meaty arms onto the spotless stainless steel vehicle. "I can't wait."

Chapter 34

The Andover Hunt Club was the image Morgan would have conjured up had he closed his eyes and let his imagination run wild. A rambling low white house sat nestled between rows of stables and outbuildings sprinkled across neatly groomed green lawns. An eighteen-hole golf course beckoned in the distance. A plaque at the main house and pro shop touted the course's challenge, boasting it had been the site of the highest four-day score in U.S. Open history. Despite his upbringing as a child of privilege, as he followed Paige to her riding events, Morgan found himself falling under the spell of the romance and elegance surrounding Paige's equestrian contests.

After life in contact sports where sweat and grime were commonplace and the grunting of athletes the rule, he found the rhythmic beating of hooves, the fluid movements, unity of purpose and precision between the riders and their mounts like nothing he had ever seen. Watching Paige bent over Alex's braided mane as they glided over the course and fences flawlessly was intoxicating. Morgan swelled with pride when they entered the ring to claim another first-place ribbon. Having found a kindred spirit to match him award for award and triumph for triumph brought a heady sensation. He treasured every minute of it.

In the few months he and Paige had been together,

Morgan had taken advantage of the beauty and challenge riding offered. Had anyone suggested in the spring that he'd be cantering over the lush Mattapoisett countryside on horseback Morgan would have snickered…probably outright laughed.

By August Morgan had even grown accustomed to the pungent fragrance of the stables, looked forward to it in a perverse and provocative way because he associated it with Paige and their precious, intimate interludes. But most of all, riding gave him the chance to be alone in picture-postcard settings with the girl he loved. Paige wasn't simply a girlfriend or lover; she was his soul mate, a part of him. The connection begun on their first afternoon made Morgan wonder how everything he did or said related to Paige. Yet to their credit and frustration they had yet to consummate the overpowering passion drawing them together. Having come deliriously close several times one or the other would manage to pull themselves from the fever that resulted whenever they touched.

When the Fullers parked their trailer in the generous staging area it occurred to Morgan as it had more than once when in the stables at their Mattapoisett farm that their family's horses had quarters that half the population of America would be happy to occupy.

Despite the fact that the competition was a major one for Paige, she was already the undisputed number one rider in her class again, so the whole family was in attendance as were Ben, Sam, and two of the new employees at Cedar Acres. Both seemed to accompany them regularly. They were pleasant, charming, and appeared to do what they were charged with—helping Sam run the stables and maintain the Fullers' estate.

But Morgan didn't believe that for a minute. They seemed to pay special attention to the girls. Nothing out of line and certainly no attempt at being flirtatious. Quite the contrary. Just politely there whenever Candy or Paige were. No, something told Morgan these men were no grooms, but then, Morgan had never believed that Sam was the simple servant he appeared. He'd tried to bring it up with Paige, but she only shrugged and stared at him blankly. Morgan let it go.

Candy had to leave for Columbia in two weeks so she'd opted out of competing, choosing to spend her day clinging tightly to Ben. Morgan was sure she was falling in love with him. And to no one's surprise, Ben was just as consumed with Candy. Though not as obvious in their displays of affection as he and Paige, Ben and Candy were as well matched as designer bookends—funny in their own special way. They'd often get into deep, sometimes heated intellectual debates about government, politics, and social issues. But whatever their cerebral differences, when the lights went out their affection and caring for one another was obvious.

Having learned the basics from Sam at Paige's earlier events Morgan pitched in. He enjoyed the physical work and helping Sam do all the small things required before Paige began the competition. It kept him busy and helped to calm his nerves, because Morgan's stomach flipped before Paige took to the ring. Her events were more nerve-wracking than taking the field for football. Part of it was the nagging thought that despite every precaution and safeguard she could still fall and hurt herself—seriously. But it was more an extension of the bond that forged them into a single consciousness.

It was another steamy day, so after helping Sam with the tack and giving Paige's new riding clothes two thumbs way up, Morgan headed to the refreshment stand while Paige added her own final touches in their trailer. Morgan grinned as he watched, wondering if he should feel jealous. She and Morgan were not the only perfectly matched pair. Paige and Alex had an uncanny connection. and he knew Paige would spend several minutes patting him while talking to him in whispers as she smoothed his lustrous mane in its elegant plaits.

After last season's tragic mishap, Sam refused to leave the trailer despite Paige's presence. His new helpers sat in their spanking pickup as if on stakeout. Needed or not Sam kept vigil, only leaving his post when Paige or Candy were in the ring and then nodding at his new assistants to stand guard. Morgan had grown very fond of the old soldier. Despite the more serious attitude he now showed, his engaging often sentimental anecdotes gave Morgan more insights into the Fuller family and Paige, for whom Sam seemed to have an almost fatherly affection.

Ben agreed to tag along and help get drinks. "Wow, Paige looks amazing," he said looking back toward the trailer.

Morgan nodded. "Twelve on a scale of one to ten. But you better keep your eyes to yourself, my friend," Morgan teased as he gave his friend a push.

Ben surveyed the area and took Morgan's arm, pulling him aside. His face grew a bright shade of crimson. "I'm thinking about making a serious move with Candy," Ben confessed.

"Serious move? Look, I don't know. I mean if you

guys are about to…"

"Shit no!" Ben said, looking around as he held up his hands. "That's not what I'm talking about!" he added with a frown. "She told me she loved me last weekend and I know this is crazy, but I was gonna ask what you thought about my asking her to…" His friend swallowed deeply. "To marry me."

"What?" Morgan faced his oldest friend. "Marriage? She's only eighteen, and you're just a sophomore at Harvard!"

"I know it's a crazy idea 'cause we have so much ahead of us. But when I'm with her it's like I'll never need anyone or anything else again." Ben shook his head. "She's going off to Columbia and the big city. It's a glamorous place with a lot of temptation. I guess I'm afraid of losing her."

"So you'd make a prisoner of her with a ring—assuming she says yes." Morgan shook his head slowly. "I'm still learning, buddy, but that's not how it works. If it's gonna be, you can't put her under lock and key."

Ben exhaled. "I know, but I care so much about her."

"Well, what do I know? Maybe it's not so crazy," Morgan said thoughtfully as he shrugged. He didn't tell his friend but he'd been thinking the same thing about Paige. She'd turn eighteen just after Labor Day.

Ben nodded. "Look, if you've got any sage advice I'm all ears."

"When I come up with some, you'll be the first to know." Morgan patted Ben on the back as they resumed their walk and got in the endless line at the refreshment stand. As they waited patiently for drinks Morgan straightened at a light touch on his shoulder. Before he turned he had a sinking feeling. The light breeze blew her fragrance toward him. The strong luxurious scent he remembered from his first night at the Fullers' that June.

Chapter 35

Candy fidgeted, pushing her lips into a pout as she helped Paige. She fumbled with the bridle, bent over to check the saddle, and gave the stirrups a pull.

"What's with you?" Paige asked as she walked over and took her sister's hand.

Candy was always the wise one. Calm and cool. The sister with the worldly advice. But since last weekend she'd been acting like one of Paige's ten-year-old students afraid to mount a horse for the first time.

"Noth…nothing," Candy stuttered, forcing a smile.

"C'mon, Candy. You been acting goofy since Ben left last weekend. What's going on?"

Candy continued nervously, biting her lip, finally twisting her mouth into a frown as Paige studied her.

"Hey, remember me? Your baby sister. Got a competition in twenty minutes, and now I'll be worried about you. I'll probably knock down a gate at the first fence."

Candy stopped the oral gymnastics and closed the distance between them, taking Paige's hands in hers. "Oh, Paige. I'm so sorry. Please don't…"

Paige held up her hand as a smile crossed her lips. "Come on, Candy. It's okay, honest. I was just kidding. I shouldn't have said that."

"I told Ben *I loved him!*" Candy blurted out as her face flushed. "And he didn't say it back so I'm afraid…" Her words died as Sam re-appeared in the trailer door.

"Time, Ms. Paige. They're ready for you."

Paige gave him a nod. "Be right there."

She took Candy's hand and squeezed it tightly. "I know he feels the same way."

"Really? You think so?" Candy whispered.

"Give it this weekend and I'll bet he tells you." Paige gave her sister the most reassuring smile she could muster. "And yes. I'm positive."

****

"Ili." Morgan turned at the sound of Monique Burke's voice. He noticed that she wore a casual outfit. He assumed she wasn't competing. Probably because Paige had kicked her shapely butt at every jumping competition in eastern New England this summer.

She turned her siren's stare on his friend.

When Morgan stood mute, she held out her hand to Ben. "Hi. I'm Monique Burke."

He took her hand. "Hi, Monique. Ben Littlefield."

Monique showed Ben her dazzling smile. Morgan wished he'd worn his sunglasses. "Would you mind awfully if I stole your friend for just a moment, Ben?"

Ben shrugged curiously. "Guess not. We're a long ways from the counter." He gestured toward the snack bar window.

Morgan looked at Monique and then scanned the area. The last thing he wanted was to have one of the Fullers find him talking to Monique. "I don't think that's a good idea."

"Afraid your new love will object?" she asked, sounding amused.

"You can tell me what you want right here."

She studied him thoughtfully. "You really *are* afraid she'll see you talking to me, aren't you?" Monique shook her head, making no attempt to hide a frown. "All right." She gave in. "Look, I know you and Paige are together, but you seem like a decent guy so I...I just wanted to tell you not to believe everything you hear. Okay?"

Morgan stood watching her silently as the line moved slowly forward. "Don't know what you're talking about." He was in no position to start making judgments about what may have caused Paige's accident. Sam had even said he thought there might be a more sinister motive. It had occurred to Morgan on more than one occasion that might be the reason for Sam's new helpers. But Morgan didn't want to frighten Paige, and he didn't feel comfortable enough with her parents to bring it up.

"Well, in case they do I just wanted to tell you. It's not true," Monique began. Morgan studied her emerald eyes. He thought he saw a sheen of moisture. "We've always competed, but I'd never do anything to hurt her." If Monique was acting, she deserved an Academy Award. "We liked the same boy a couple of summers ago and...I won that one. But I swear I didn't do anything to hurt Paige. When he moved away, we both lost out. I think you're a decent guy, so be careful. Paige may be what she seems—sweet and innocent but..." She grew close and took his arm. "She's the best of them..." She shrugged, shook her head, and backed away. "Nice to meet you, Ben. Take care of your friend," Monique threw back as she turned and headed back to the staging area, adding, "He may need it!"

"Wow! What was that about and who was she?"

Ben asked as he followed Monique's graceful departure.

Morgan stood mute, thinking about Monique's warning. The frightening thing was what she said had the ring of truth to it. Morgan thought of Sam's words again. They sounded eerily similar to Monique's.

"Come on, buddy, share. What's the deal?" Ben asked as they approached the counter.

"Paige had a serious riding accident at a competition last summer, and some people think Monique may have been involved." His eyes followed her as she disappeared in the crowd. "Because Paige was always kicking her butt in competition."

"Sounds like serious shit." Ben shrugged, pausing. "Look. I'm no shrink, but I didn't catch that vibe from her."

"I know." Morgan nodded. "There's no proof. And Monique came across like the evil queen from *Snow White* the night we met. I guess I assumed it was true, but I'm not sure I believe it now."

They turned their attention to the refreshment stand, now only three customers away. But Morgan's stomach did gymnastics as he wondered exactly what Monique meant. Could it be true? Morgan loved Paige so much it hurt, and he knew she loved him right back. But while Ben was placing the drink order, Morgan thought about some things he'd never understood: Sam and the way he doted on her. How did he really fit into the Fuller picture? Morgan was sure his role was much more than the simple role he played, and now he had two muscular back-ups that looked like weightlifters. And that trip to Australia. Was that overkill? The Fullers were a wealthy and influential family. But it was more and more obvious Josiah Fuller was on an adrenaline high fueled by his ambition. And Vera seemed to be the power broker, feeding it behind the scenes. Were they exiling a troubled and depressed daughter to the outback for her sake, selfish reasons, or was there something more? And if so why the sudden turn-around?

"Got a five?" Ben asked, bringing Morgan back.

"Ah…sure," he answered pulling out his wallet and handing his friend the money. As he let his mind return to the questions, another surfaced. Over the course of the summer, he'd seen a change in the Fullers. When he'd arrived on that warm June afternoon, Candy was the queen. Paige more a concern. Or so it seemed. Now *both* were pampered and fawned over her like starlets.

Morgan put his wallet away as Ben handed him a cardboard holder with four drink cans in it, carrying two iced coffees himself.

"Everything okay, Morg? You look kinda funny."

"Yeah," he said. "Everything's one hundred percent." He hoped he spoke the truth.

Chapter 36

Early September 2001

The Harvard team finished its daily workout at the Stadium. Their Ivy League schedule would begin in ten days on Saturday, September fifteenth. Ezra sat high on the cement bench seats of the famous stadium doing his best to look invisible. When he'd first heard and read about Morgan Cahill it seemed simple. Sort of. But Ezra now realized that his task—that of reuniting with the son he'd been forced to abandon fifteen years ago— would be monumental if not impossible.

His idea had seemed sound: seek the boy out and find a way to become a part of his life. But Ezra had been unable to investigate any of the details of Morgan's life over the fifteen years since they'd been separated. In the short time he'd been working at Harvard, it was obvious the boy had everything he could ever need or want. From what little he'd been able to glean and his observations of Morgan, the kid was not only handsome, brilliant, and a superb athlete, but he'd been adopted by one of Boston's finest families. He even had a pretty girl whom Ezra had seen on more than one occasion. Watching the interaction between the two it was obvious what they had was very real. So why would Morgan need Ezra? Good question. Not an answer in sight.

"You thinking about applying for a coaching job?"
It was Patrick Flynn, Ezra's boss—the man who'd hired
him.

Ezra swallowed and shrugged. "No, Pat. May be
hard to believe, but I used to play myself. And this
Cahill kid. I love just watching him. Even heard about
him at Cedar Junction. Never seen anything like what
he can do with the football."

"Yep—he is something all right."

The man sat down next to Ezra. Since they'd been
working together, Ezra had noticed that Pat was a fair
man but never mixed much with his workers or the
others on the staff. Ezra wondered at his presence. He
still remembered the man's pointed question about his
guilt. But whatever he thought, Pat sat next to him
watching in silence as the boys went through their final
drills and headed into the locker room.

Ezra stole a look at Pat's eyes. They held no malice
or contempt. "Just that I've noticed you hanging around
after work watching the team," his boss offered quietly.

"Yeah, well I can't drive, drink, and any family I
had has long since deserted me. Not that I blame them.
My parents were straight-laced and having a drug
addict and a murderer for a son wasn't one of their
long-range family goals. And I haven't heard from my
sister since the day I was arrested. Anyway, so it's not
like I got a lot to take up my time." Ezra laughed self-
consciously. "If it wasn't for the library and the books
at the Harvard Coop, I'd be going crazy."

Pat stood up. "Tell you what. Three years ago my
wife left with the guy who sold us our new living room
set. Get that. Sounds like the punch line from a bad
joke, but it's true." He motioned toward the stairs.

"Come on. How does Chinese take-out sound?"

Ezra had developed a special sense in prison for knowing the good guys from the bad. Maybe it had gone sour on him, but he hoped Pat was legit. Whatever the case, it sounded okay to Ezra. He'd spent enough nights alone regretting his mistakes.

Ezra stood and gave one last look at the players as they headed into the locker room.

"Sounds good to me, Pat." He held out his hand. "Thanks."

****

Early September found Paige on Long Island at the Hampton Classic. Attended by many of the best riders in the US and Western Europe, Paige finished fourth in one event and fifth in another.

"Are you bummed?" Candy asked on her cell phone when they spoke late in the afternoon.

"Not as much as I thought I'd be," Paige admitted. "After all, Gwen took the Europeans last summer and that guy Erwin from Gloucestershire was the talk of the indoor circuit last fall." Paige paused and looked around about to share a highly guarded secret. She whispered, "And since I've been with Morgan, it isn't as important as it used to be."

Candy whistled into the phone. "Whew. Now that is an admission coming from my driven baby sister."

Paige smiled to herself. "I used riding and the piano as surrogates. Something to take my mind off living 'cause I was afraid of being hurt again. By someone like Eric and really being hurt…like in the accident last summer."

"Well, Paige, you were right about Ben," Candy said. Paige could imagine her sister glowing, lying in her dorm room just thinking about his admission of love. She'd been floating on a cloud ever since he'd confessed his feelings. "Have you ever thought of becoming a psychologist?"

"Nope. Still want to take care of animals and one hunky Harvard jock!" They both laughed. But as she turned, she saw a young man staring at her. He'd been hanging around all day. "Gotta go," she told Candy as she saw Francie gesturing her to come over. Her friend had her eyes on the same man that Paige had spotted several times during her rides.

Paige watched the man but headed toward her friend. As she arrived in front of Francie, the man approached her father and handed him a business card. He smiled and they shook hands as he nodded in Paige's direction.

"Oh my God! Do you know who that is?" Francie said in a loud whisper as Paige watched him talking to her father.

"He does look kind of familiar, but..." Paige shrugged.

"Derek Talbot," she interrupted Paige.

Of course. Francie had pointed him out more than once this summer when she'd come to Paige's events. He was a legend. Two-time national show-jumping champion and bronze medalist at the '96 Olympics in Atlanta.

"What's he doing here, talking to my dad?"

"Duh—jeez. World to Paige." Francie hit Paige lightly on her riding helmet. "He coaches the Brown University Equestrian Team. One of the best in the country!" She turned toward Paige. "And since he's talking to your dad, he may want to talk to *you*!"

"You think?" Paige asked, watching as he turned. He shook hands with her father again and headed toward them. "Wow! And I didn't even get a ribbon."

"Paige, I swear. Sometimes you're so naïve I think it's an act." Francie giggled into her hand as he stopped in front of them.

"Paige." He nodded politely. "My name is Derek Talbot, and I just spoke with your dad," he said in a mellow baritone, fixing her with soft brown eyes. "I was wondering if could buy you a soda or cup of coffee and talk?"

"Ah, sure," Paige said. "Oh, this is my friend Francine Winthrop."

Derek Talbot turned his gaze to Francie who took his offered hand and blushed. Paige didn't blame her. He was very good-looking and exuded a quiet confidence when he spoke.

"Will you excuse us?" Paige asked Francie.

"Sure," Francie agreed, raising her eyebrows and beaming, pointing and making a silly face when she got behind Derek.

He gestured to one of the small tables under the refreshment tent and Paige took his cue.

"Can I get you something?"

"Ah, how about a Pepsi…or Coke. Either is fine."

He disappeared into the busy line at the counter and returned in five minutes with two soft drinks. Paige's stomach fluttered with nerves. "Pepsi it is."

"Thanks," Paige said as she sat, hands balled tightly in her lap. "My favorite."

"Mine, too."

Derek explained that he coached the Brown University Varsity Equestrian Team.

"I know. And you medaled in the Atlanta Olympics."

"Only bronze," Derek said modestly, his face flushing. He pulled several brochures out of the backpack he carried. He told Paige he couldn't offer her a scholarship since riding brought in little revenue, adding that his family summered on the Cape and he'd followed her riding career for a couple of years.

"But Coach Talbot, I…"

"Please call me Derek, Paige." He showed an engaging smile and had great dimples. "I don't stand on formalities and neither does the team. Which you may have guessed is why I'm here."

"All right—Derek. But I was terrible today," Paige said shaking her head.

"Paige, I've seen you mature as a rider over the last two summers. You were up against some of the best in the world today. You just missed medaling in two events."

"Really?"

"Paige," he said quietly as he looked around and drew close. "We have some fine talent on the team. But you're better than any of them right now."

Paige couldn't hide her smile. "I don't know what to say." Paige felt the blood rush to her face. "Thanks, Derek."

He explained their training routine, the time Paige would have to commit, and gave her several handouts to review.

"I'd be proud to have you on the team." He smiled and stood, holding out his hand. "I'd like you to think about it. The names of this year's captains are on that list. Call them and ask any questions you want answered. Trust me, we really are a team, Paige. No hazing, no pettiness, no jealousies. I promise. And…" he began quietly as he glanced around. "I know you teach and can see you being a captain in no time."

"Thanks. I will." She met his gaze. "I saw you talking to my father."

Derek nodded. "Well, I know your mother attended Brown. You'd be a legacy. Not that you need it with your grades and talent."

"How do you know that?" Paige asked, feeling a little uncomfortable.

"I have my secrets." He put on a funny face and looked around pretending they were being watched. "Actually, I called your mother and asked if she'd be okay with my talking to your school. But I asked her to keep it between us till I had the chance to talk to you in person. I hope you're all right with that?" He looked concerned. "Once or twice I've had some ugly experiences, so I wait till I talk to the candidate. If they show no interest, I drop it."

"Oh," Paige answered, nodding. "I understand. And I can see it might be kind of sticky."

Derek nodded. They shook again. He headed out of the tent and turned, giving her a wave.

Paige was so flattered that as soon as she spotted Francie she went to tell her what he'd said. Taking the folder, she headed back to their trailer to help pack up so they could head home.

****

At a table several removed from where Paige and Derek Talbot had sat, a fit, slender figure glancing occasionally at the pretty teenager and her companion. Yes, Paige, that was her name. Something about it suited her.

Julian found something quite fetching about her. Had since the day he'd acted as a helper at the Fullers' celebratory weekend. There was a sensual innocence to Paige that attracted Julian in ways nothing had in some time. His thoughts about how they would use her had changed into something that would not please his lover and accomplice.

Of course, he was still with Sophie, but as he watched Paige, her sweet, youthful face, and studied her fluid movements it stirred something in him. This was something he had never expected. He thought of the soft, fragrant days when Sophie was a child—a child he loved and wanted deeply. Days when they'd taken their own mounts on long lazy rides over the lush North Shore countryside. And the more he watched Paige, saw her laugh, smile, tilt her head in a pleasing way the more he wanted her the same way he'd wanted Sophie in her delicious early years. Before the accusations about their forbidden relationship.

Of course he would keep his desire to himself, knowing Sophie's immediate reaction would be to do something cruel and violent to the girl. Sophie had no idea he followed Paige, watched her, and had even taken pictures of her.

But, he rationalized, they had planned their escape knowing they could never stay after they lured Fuller into their trap. But Paige need never know she had been the cause of her own father's undoing. Once Fuller was dead, Julian toyed with the idea of taking Paige on his escape and leaving Sophie behind to keep the district attorney company. Or even leaving the DA, now running for congress, alive. Paige might even forgive and bond with him as long as he promised no harm would come to her father and that would solve two problems. Torment Fuller at the loss of his favorite child and give him this shy delightful girl he had grown to want so desperately.

It would take work of course, Julian thought, admiring her lithe form as Paige left the tent. He had every confidence he could orchestrate the plan as he had everything else since his release. And Sophie… Well, what had he said about Paige? Collateral damage? A sad ending?

But Julian had a life to rebuild and what better way to begin than with the very daughter of the architect of his undoing. Wasn't there a certain subtle justice in it all?

****

The next day Paige showed the information to her father and mother and explained the conversation with Derek. They both thought it was a great idea and agreed to meet him.

"But, honey, you're top of your class and have so much talent," her dad offered at dinner. "You're sure you don't want to check out other places? What about Julliard or the Conservatory. Your teacher says she thinks you'd stand a good chance at—"

"No." Paige held her hand up. Interrupting her father wasn't something she did often, but she had no doubt that being at an Ivy League College forty-five minutes from Cambridge and Morgan was as close to heaven as she could imagine. "You know what I want. What I've wanted since I was ten years old."

Chapter 37

"I think that's great and certainly no surprise. But didn't we talk about you looking at schools up here?" Morgan asked her when she told him about her meeting with Derek. He paused. "What's this guy look like anyway?"

"A little taller than you. Kinda hunky with big brown eyes—oh, and did I tell you he won bronze in the '96 Olympics?"

"Come on! Tell me he's forty-five and dumpy. Please?" Morgan asked.

"Nope," she answered. "He really is cute. I thought Francie was gonna faint." Paige tried to stifle her giggle.

"Paige!"

"Stop it!" she scolded him. "You know you have nothing to worry about. And we talked about what would happen if I went to Boston. If you and I were three miles apart how much work would we get done? Less than zero!"

"Okay," Morgan said grudgingly. "But I want to meet him."

"Yes, dear. Whatever you say," she agreed, envisioning a macho hand-shaking contest. "Gotta do some work. Love you!" she whispering in her most sultry voice adding a deep sigh.

"Oh, Paige," he whispered back. "Love you, too."

****

Morgan had taken a rare weekend off from visiting the Fullers' because his father was going to New York for the week. Paige had driven up to spend the weekend at the Cahills' even though Morgan had to spend most of Saturday at the Stadium. His dad's new position as Managing Director of the Boston office of Cantor Fitzgerald meant a week-long series of kick-off meetings for the fall.

"You are so lucky, Dad!"

"Yeah, I get to sit a thousand feet in the air and listen to endless rhetoric about our exciting plans for two thousand-two."

"Remember what you promised?"

His father nodded. "Yep. Your coach has given you the day off so you, Paige, and your mother can fly down on Thursday and I'll take you to Windows on the World. Already have the reservation for seven o'clock."

On Sunday evening they all said their good-byes, and Paige got back into her red VW Beetle and headed back to Mattapoisett.

Morgan turned in early since he had an eight a.m. class. As he drifted off to another peaceful night's sleep, he mused on how the bad dreams he'd experienced had miraculously disappeared since Paige had been in his life. She'd been like a life buoy for him and he for her. Each had fulfilled something in the other that had made them complete.

His last thoughts that night were of her and the rush he'd get showing Paige the view from 100-plus stories above New York.

****

It happened just as second period began on

Tuesday morning. Paige checked her watch: 8:50 a.m. Miss Wilkins was late. That wasn't like her. When she entered the room she wore a serious expression. No, more than serious. Somber. Her tanned face had gone pale.

"I'm sorry to be late. But—there's been an accident. A bad one involving the World Trade Center."

Paige swallowed deeply. Any casual disregard vanished. She raised her hand not sure she wanted to hear the answer. "What happened, Miss Wilkins?"

"Aaah…it appears that a small plane accidentally flew into the North Tower about ten minutes ago. The principal's wife called. No one's sure yet as to the details."

The North Tower? Paige pursed her lips and concentrated. Was that where Morgan's dad was and even if he was, if it was a small plane maybe there wasn't much damage. Paige had been eleven when some terrorists had set off a bomb in 1993 that killed half a dozen people.

She checked her watch: nine a.m. Paige raised her hand.

"Yes, Paige."

"Miss Wilkins, my boyfriend's dad was at the World Trade Center this morning. Could I…?"

"Of course," her teacher agreed and offered her best smile. "Francie, you go with her."

The two girls grabbed their books and headed toward the door. As she passed several of the other girls took Paige's hand and gave it a quick squeeze. But everything would be fine. When she and Morgan were together nothing bad could happen.

They headed down the corridor and had almost

reached the large double doors at the front entrance when a booming voice called them to a halt.

"Good morning. It is my sad duty to inform you that both towers of New York's World Trade Center have been struck by large aircraft. At this time we will be evacuating the building in an orderly manner. Those students with vehicles please proceed to your homes. Buses will be available within fifteen minutes to take those students home who need them." The principal's bass voice boomed over the intercom.

"This is not a drill, and there is the strong possibility that these were the planned acts of terrorists. We ask that you proceed in an orderly manner, return to your homes, and stay there.

Thank you."

Paige ran out to her car, pulled open the door, and pulled out her phone.

"Let me drive, Paige," Francie said calmly as she took the keys.

Paige nodded, tears covering her face as she dialed Morgan's number.

He picked up on the first ring. "Have you heard about…?"

"Yes," she whispered. "I'll be there in an hour. I'm in my car now with Francie."

"No…no. Let me call you when I talk to my mother. She doesn't even know. She's gone to her book club." He whispered, repeating, "She doesn't even know."

Then his phone went dead.

Chapter 38

Paige called his phone again immediately. He must
have hung up or dropped the phone—right? But then
why didn't he answer or call her back? *Oh my God!*
Suddenly her thoughts turned to Candy. Paige knew
very little about New York City. Was it possible she
was somewhere near where the attacks took place? Was
she all right?

****

The rest of that week passed like Paige was in a
dream. Not a dream, a nightmare, but one she couldn't
escape. Sadly, this was not the romantic fantasy that
had consumed June, July, and August. No, something
had happened she could not explain or understand.
Morgan Cahill, the boy she had shared so many
passionate nights with and all her most private and
guarded secrets, had gone dark. He was there
somewhere but hidden so deep within himself she
couldn't reach him.

He didn't answer his phone, and the two emails he
sent her were brief—a few barely polite words in
response to her impassioned pleas. When she told him
on Wednesday that she was coming to Boston to see
him and his mother his response hurt and terrified her:
Please do not do that. Very difficult here.

She talked to Candy, who was okay. Columbia had
dismissed classes after the Trade Center attacks, and

she and her roommate had been holed up in their dorm room.

An atmosphere of tension, fear, and anger pervaded everywhere. When Paige went to the Emerald Square Mall in search of something for Mr. Cahill's memorial service it was deserted. The few patrons spoke little, never looked each other in the eyes, and scurried out the door surveying their surroundings suspiciously.

Declared or not, the country was at war. Word from the news media, her friends, and their boyfriends was that some were going to enlist and fight the "terrorists," whoever that might be. Foreign names—names like the Taliban, Al Qaida, and Osama Bin Laden were bandied about on the TV and in the media, but Paige cared little about that. She had one concern: Morgan. What had happened to him? And to them?

All Paige wanted was to see him, dry his tears, and hold him to help assuage the terrible pain and anguish he must be feeling. But as the week passed by in confusing slow motion it became obvious that was not going to happen.

She talked to Candy about it.

"What's happened? He's completely shut me out," she whispered, choking back a sob.

"I don't know, honey. All I do know is that Ben is giving me the same info." Paige could hear her sister breathing on the other end. Candy sounded like she was fighting back emotions of her own.

"Candy? Are…are you okay?" Paige asked hesitantly.

Candy started but stopped before the first word was out, finally managing. "I guess so," adding, "You're not the only one who cares about Morgan and the Cahills."

Her answer was soft but filled with feeling.

"I know, Candy." Paige stopped and caught herself. It suddenly occurred to her that since the attack her entire focus had been on how it had played out for *her*. Her mother had told her that Mrs. Cahill was devastated. Morgan not only had to deal with his own grief but must be caring for his mother. "I guess maybe I'd lost track of that."

"I'm sorry, Paige. Maybe I'm the selfish one." Her sister sighed deeply. "But I gotta tell you. You're not the shy, withdrawn little girl who met Morgan on that June afternoon."

"Thanks. That's nice, but what's your point?" she asked not sure whether to be flattered or angry.

"You're stronger than this. Remember how much you love Morgan. Give him some time and space if he needs it. Ben's trying to do that."

Paige was quiet for a long moment. Her older sister had hit the target again. "You're right. I...I guess I've been playing the poor spoiled little girl." She brushed the dampness from her cheeks.

"No, Paige. You've just found someone that means so much to you that you expect every feeling, emotion, and secret of his belongs to you." Paige could hear Candy swallow on the other end. "That's not how it works. Sometimes the people we love need some distance."

"Thanks," Paige said, swallowing a sudden wave of emotion. "I wonder what it would be like to have a sister who wasn't so great."

"You'll never get the chance to know," Candy said softly. "'Bye..." They both laughed self-consciously and hung up.

****

Morgan walked the doctor down the winding mahogany staircase in the Cahill townhouse on Boston's fashionable Commonwealth Avenue.

"She needs to get some rest, Morg." The tall, silver-haired man shook his head. "I don't think that I've ever known a couple as close as your parents. They were completely devoted to each other," he said softly, adding, "and to you of course."

Morgan tugged at his chin. "You think the medication will help?"

"Hard to tell. Under normal circumstances she'd sleep for a week but stress and grief can be a pretty frightening antidote to sleep medications." The doctor put his hand on Morgan's shoulder. "Keep your eye on her and call me if she gets agitated or if this doesn't work. It's important she gets some quality rest and it looks like you could use some, too. Here." he reached in his bag and handed Morgan a small vial. "These are less potent, but they should help you. Do something to try and get away from this for a while."

"Thanks," Morgan said offering his hand.

The doctor headed for the door, stopped, and turned. "Your dad told me you had a wonderful girl. Someone you really cared about. Let her help you." He nodded and opened the door. "Good luck. Keep me in the loop. And I'll see you at the service this weekend."

Let Paige help him? Morgan stood, eyes fixed on the second floor where his mother lay in bed. All Morgan had wanted since he heard the terrible news on Tuesday was to get in his BMW, fly to Mattapoisett, get lost in her arms, and never leave that embrace. But he couldn't. His mother was in a desperate state. He worried she might fall into a depression she might not recover from. Few knew she'd been deeply troubled by that curse for years. He loved her so much. She was a great deceiver, hiding her frailty and weakness, while depending on his father for so much.

He trudged up the stairs closing his eyes when he reached the top. He turned sharp left and headed into his room, flipping on his desktop. He opened his email account and found her email from yesterday.

Morgan,

I can never tell you how sad I am. Your dad was one of the finest men I've ever known. Please, please, please, my darling, let me come to see you on Wednesday, hold you...help you through this nightmare so we can move on together.

All my love, always. XXXXX,

Paige

He thought he heard a cry and got up, tiptoeing across the hall, leaning into his mother's room to watch her. She seemed restless but asleep, so Morgan crept out and returned to his room. Exhaustion dragged at him. But his sleepless nights weren't filled with the strange frightening dreams of past years. No, since Tuesday morning the frightening visions that filled his days and night were all too real. Morgan closed his eyes again and sighed then headed into his room and sat down at his desk. He'd take the doctor's advice and let the girl he adored help him through this.

He began typing his reply telling Paige he looked forward to seeing her and how much he needed her with him. His finger was poised over the keyboard and he was about to press Send when he heard a chilling cry from across the hall. He jumped up, sprinted across the twenty feet in seconds, and stopped as he saw his mother sitting up screaming, holding her head and calling, "*Malcolm!*"

Morgan rushed to her side and took her hand, gently pulling it from her hair. He whispered "It's all right, Mom. Everything's all right. You just had a bad dream."

She seemed to understand him and slumped as he helped her lie down. He did his best to quiet her as she closed her eyes and seemed to be drifting off. Morgan found the overstuffed chair in the corner and pulled it over to her bedside. He took her hand and did his best to hum a lullaby he recalled from childhood.

When she seemed to be resting quietly again he stood and walked into his bedroom. Picking up the phone he called the doctor.

"She's still having trouble, Doc."

"Morgan, I think it's time we called in some reinforcements." The man put his hand over the receiver and Morgan heard muffled conversation. "If you need me to come over I can be there in half an hour, but we need to get you some help beyond the housekeeper."

Morgan exhaled deeply. "I called my aunt in Springfield. She just got word about Dad, but she's in England, and they don't even know if they can get back here for a while with the flying ban. But I agree," he said wearily. "I love Mom so much but I need some help, at least till the service is over."

"Do you think you can make it through the night?"

"Sure. I'll be okay."

"As soon as I hang up, I'll make some calls. I can think of a couple of private nurses that would fill the bill, but I have to see if they're available."

They worked out the details, then Morgan called his coach to explain what was happening.

"Morg, you know that Saturday's game against Holy Cross has been called off. You'll have to let me know about next week against Brown. Whatever you decide is okay, just let me know so we can plan around it."

"Okay, Coach. I'll let you know."

"That's fine, son. Do whatever you need to and the whole team will be there for you at the service."

"Thanks, Coach," Morgan said quietly and hung up. He rose and dragged into his mother's room to check her. She was resting comfortably or so it seemed. He backed out very quietly and returned to his room, sitting down at his desktop again.

As he sat trying to get his mind around the surreal events of Tuesday morning he spotted the delicate embroidery his mother had made him on his tenth birthday—the same day she'd first read Frost's simple sixteen-line allegory. His gaze shifted to the last four lines:

The woods are lovely, dark and deep
But I have promises to keep
And miles to go before I sleep
And miles to go before I sleep...

Morgan hit the mouse to bring the screen to life. *Miles to go before I sleep?* The words rolled around in his weary mind. They said everything.

The message telling Paige to come to Boston stared back at him. He loved his mother so much and she needed him desperately now, but Paige was a part of him, not another person. She was an extension of his being, his soul. But he'd spent the whole summer with her. The first emotion that came to mind when he heard about the attacks was guilt. Guilt because Morgan realized that he'd deserted his parents to spend every possible moment in Mattapoisett. He had never wanted anything as much as he wanted to see Paige, but he shook his head knowing what he had to do.

He highlighted the intimate message he'd framed a few minutes before and hit delete. It disappeared. Morgan replaced it with a terse refusal of her offer:

Paige,

Please do not do that. Very difficult here.

Morgan

Morgan could only balance so many balls in the air and until he knew more about his mother's care and the memorial service was over, he would keep his own council. Paige loved him so much she would understand. When he saw her at the service he'd steal a private moment and explain what was happening. He knew Paige. If he told her, she'd insist on flying to his side to help. Much as he wanted that, it wasn't fair to her. He'd been selfish in spending the entire summer in her arms. Now he had to man up and help his mother deal with their loss. Paige would understand…he just knew she would.

Chapter 39

Ezra sat in the living room of his apartment in Cambridge. He stared absently at the endless news coverage of the attacks as he considered how strange and fickle life could be. For months he'd been hiding in the shadows, watching his son's life like a spectator.

He'd muted the volume but now turned it up again as the news replayed some of the heated debate in congress over what to do about the terrorists who had launched the attacks. As he watched the anchor team discussing what actions the President was proposing, he wrestled with his feelings about it.

Ezra had been a soldier himself, a marine right out of high school. Even risen to the rank of staff sergeant before his life had taken a tragic and misguided detour the disastrous night he met Jo Ann Murphy. He remembered his commanding officer telling him what a good marine he was—had a real future in the corps, were his words. Ezra smiled ironically, wondering what Captain Mason would think of him now. But of course that would never happen since he died in the Gulf War ten years ago.

Ezra stood and walked to the window that fronted on Massachusetts Avenue. He thought about Morgan, asking himself if this somehow changed the anonymous role he'd adopted since his parole. Would the kid be any happier to know who his real father was now that his adoptive one was dead? Perhaps, if he was an astronaut, a diplomat, a sports icon, or something else that garnered respect but not if the man was a convicted murderer. That offered nothing to assuage the pain and loneliness Morgan must be feeling. Quite the contrary. No, when a fine man like Malcolm Cahill was killed in a senseless and brutal way, shaking hands with the devil would bring his boy no solace, no joy.

Ezra put on his windbreaker and headed out to meet Pat at a local coffee shop. He'd done the straight and narrow since his release, but tonight he might ask his new friend if he could pick up a fifth of Absolut vodka and sneak it back to Pat's place. All Ezra wanted was the pleasant numbing effect of the alcohol to help him forget what a shit place the world had become.

Chapter 40

"Paige…you want to talk about it?" Her father stood at the door of the great room. She fiddled absently at the Steinway with one hand. Strange how she'd always heard a girl and her mother could be best friends. Because at the Fullers' it was always her father she ran to when she needed consolation, a warm shoulder to cry on, or arm around her.

"Not much to say," she offered, working to manage a smile. "Morgan's gone silent on me."

He nodded slowly and came inside, sitting down next to her. "I think he may have his hands full right now."

"I'm not sure I understand, Daddy. I know he must be going through hell, but all I want to do is help him," she whispered choking back a sob. "I know I need to give him space, but I want to be there to help share his grief."

He reached across and put his hand on her shoulder, pulling her close. "You're really hurting, aren't you?"

"Yes," she managed, remembering Candy's advice on the phone.

He sighed and stood, crossing the room and looking out the double-doors onto the streaks of sunlight as it descended over the Bay. He put his hands behind his neck and bent his head. Letting his hands fall to his side he turned to face her, his face a mask she was unable to read.

"You know that Malcolm and I go back a long way? Right. Decades?" he asked, his words deliberate.

"Yes, Daddy," Paige answered, recalling an earlier apparently pointless monologue on that June weekend when she'd met Morgan, wondering where this one was going.

"Well at one time he and I were like brothers. Very close."

Paige continued to stare. He averted his eyes.

"Do you remember anything about their visit in June?"

She shook her head. "Not really. What do you mean?"

"Maybe you didn't notice because you were so consumed with Morgan. But Mary Jane, Mrs. Cahill, wasn't around a lot."

Paige stopped and tried to focus, to think about what he was saying. "I guess you're right. I saw her at all the meals, and she went sailing with us. I mean, she seemed very nice. What am I missing?"

"Did you ever wonder why despite always referring to Malcolm as my best friend we never saw them except that time seven years ago?"

She shook her head again. "I guess I never did. But I'm beginning to see that maybe I spend too much time worrying about myself so…" She paused not sure she wanted to hear the rest of this revelation.

"I guess there's no way to sugar coat this. Mary Jane, Morgan's mother, has serious mental health issues."

"Mental health issues. Sounds like sugar coating.

What does that mean, exactly?" Paige found his eyes. They looked downcast, almost sad.

He made his way to one of the large couches and sat down, patting the place next to him.

Paige followed his lead and sat down next to him, pulling her legs up under her.

"When Mary Jane was young she was attacked...sexually assaulted." Her father swallowed and took a deep breath.

"Oh my God." Paige inhaled quickly as she touched his hand.

"She was pregnant at the time," he continued. "The attack was not only brutal, it took her baby and any chance she had of conceiving again."

"Oh my God," Paige repeated. "That's terrible. I had no idea."

"How could you?" He shrugged. "She was hospitalized for a long time. When she was released, she was never the same woman. I can see Malcolm's face when we met for a drink and he told me about it. I think I was as devastated as he was." He reached out and took Paige's hand.

"I'd heard a different story, but I can understand why they wouldn't be telling everyone about that."

"The story they told their friends was that Mary Jane had a miscarriage. I was working for the Suffolk County DA's office at the time. We never found out who did it, but it was one of the reasons that I pledged to do everything I could to get scum like that off the streets even if the one we wanted the most had eluded us."

Paige had seen her father give animated speeches, whipping his audience into a frenzy. She respected and loved him but never so much as she did at that moment. Until this instant Paige had always thought him a great showman. Suddenly she'd discovered that this man she loved so desperately was more than a rousing and eloquent speaker. He *was* the dedicated public servant he appeared to be. And she was proud. She squeezed his hand.

"So she was traumatized by what happened?"

Her dad nodded. "More than you can imagine."

He went on to deliver a litany of how the terrifying event had transformed Morgan's mother from a sensitive and beautiful young woman into someone sad and detached.

"So what you're telling me is that Morgan is dealing with far more than the loss of his father." Paige stared out at the distant sunset, just disappearing below the western horizon.

"Yes, Paige." He nodded. "I know he loves you very much, but he has so much on his plate right now."

She opened her mouth to protest.

He held up his hand. "I see the way he looks at you. Like someone worshipping at an altar, Paige. No one can steal or destroy that. Please. Give him some time."

Paige fell into him and hugged him tightly. "Thank you, Daddy," she whispered and closed her eyes.

Chapter 41

On Saturday morning, September fifteenth, close to 800 people assembled in the largest of the function rooms at the main location of the Harvard Club. The club was the epitome of Boston elegance. But all that was lost on Morgan.

After a hellish week managing his mother's care and trying to deal with the aftermath of his father's death, he was operating on adrenaline, nerve, and instinct. He knew he would see Paige today and try and make amends for excluding her from his life since the attacks on Tuesday.

He wore his best black suit, the one he and his dad had picked out for the funeral of a teammate's grandfather, never imagining he'd be wearing it again so soon and for something so personal. Morgan helped his mother into the limo that would transport them to the club. "Are you okay, Mom?"

She sighed deeply. "Yes, thank you. Much better. Thank you for being so thoughtful and taking care of me," she whispered, taking his hand tightly in hers. "Just like your father did for so many years."

"It'll be over in a couple of hours."

She nodded and did her best to show him a courageous smile. "You've been wonderful, Morg," she repeated as she brushed aside a tear.

He returned the squeeze and for just a moment

rested his head on the plush seat as they headed cross town on their twenty-minute journey.

****

Paige had come up from Mattapoisett in her own car. Insisting on it despite her parents protestations. She wanted to have a car if Morgan asked her to stay or help him. Her mother told her it was foolish and her father reminded her of their talk earlier in the week.

"He still has so much to take care of, honey," he whispered.

"I know," she whispered back and nodded. "But I just have a feeling. He may need me."

In the end as often happened they gave in and indulged Paige. Candy had driven home from Columbia for this solemn service since the airlines were still in a state of chaos. A frightening pall hovered over every flight. Despite assurances from the government and the airlines, the fear was palpable. Many worried that the terror attacks would come in waves and were reluctant to jump on a plane again, even a short commuter flight.

Candy joined Paige for moral support. She had given her sister the condensed version of her father's revelations about Mrs. Cahill's condition. And Candy, after sharing a good cry with her baby sister, had given her the patent older sister, I-told-you-so look.

The trip up on that morning took almost two hours. At first the two girls struggled, making clumsy small talk. But as they drew closer to Boston, Paige let the traffic serve as an excuse to go quiet as she silently prayed that Morgan wouldn't keep her out of his life.

****

Ezra sat in the back of the huge hall. He'd never been inside anything like this. The room resembled places he'd only seen in movies or read about in books. A massive vaulted ceiling was flanked by walls shrouded in black bunting out of respect for the somber event they were here to observe. He'd worn his only suit—navy blue with a striped tie—and sat as far back as he could, having taken the subway and a bus to get here from his Cambridge home. Members of the football team were here as well as other's he'd seen around the Stadium, but he wasn't sure who they were.

He did his best to look inconspicuous, shrinking in his seat and moving to the far right as people filtered in to fill the hundreds of seats in the hall. But people did seem to notice him. Especially women.

It had taken him a while to understand, because in prison everyone is a number, nothing more. At first he felt strange and exposed. Did they know who he was and what he'd done? Why would anyone give him a second look? It had taken his new friend Patrick who laughed and put him straight.

"Ez, I'm not into guys. Promise you I never have been but you're six-one, have a full, thick head of hair, big baby blues, and look like George Clooney." Pat grinned.

Ezra pulled on his chin, confused.

Pat's grin grew into a soft laugh as he looked around the neighborhood restaurant where they'd been hanging out, lowering his voice. "He's a movie star. All the ladies think he's the hottest thing going." His friend shrugged. "And you, buddy, could be his twin brother."

Two older women slid in next to him, nodding with the hint of a smile.

"Terrible tragedy," one offered.

"Yes, terrible," Ezra agreed, nodding in

affirmation. He began to say more but thought better of it.

As he was about to move again a tall, slender redhead spied the empty seat next to him and worked her way along the aisle, sitting down. She nodded.

Ezra returned the nod.

The woman looked about forty. Her short red hair hung casually over sculptured ears. Fierce, translucent eyes that changed color as they reflected the lights stared straight ahead as Morgan ushered a middle-aged woman by the arm to the front. They were followed by several people who could have been family or close friends. Ezra thought he recognized the girl he'd seen with Morgan at The Stadium.

As he strained to see the procession make its way to the front, he felt the stare of the woman next to him—the woman with the red hair. He glanced her way and caught her studying him. She nodded with the hint of a smile and turned back to join those watching Morgan and his companions take their seats.

Despite Pat's ego building assurances of a few weeks ago Ezra still felt uncomfortable when someone watched him, especially an attractive woman. It gave him the jitters. Would she jump up and point at him, yelling, "Here's Ezra Wilson, convicted murderer." But of course it didn't happen, and Ezra exhaled under his breath as the large crowd settled in for the service.

****

Her VW was taken by one of the small army of valets as Paige and Candy got out and headed toward the massive front door of the Harvard Club. She'd heard the word austere. As she studied the entrance and peered into the lobby of this edifice, she knew in the future this would be her prototype when she heard the word again.

As soon as they stepped inside on the polished hardwood, someone took her arm. She closed her eyes and exhaled. Paige knew by the scent of his after-shave who it was and despite the tragic circumstances for her visit her heart beat faster.

She turned, finding the wide steel-blue eyes she saw in her dreams. He worked at a smile though it held little enthusiasm.

"Hi," he said in a whisper.

"Hi back," she said taking his hand.

Their fingers intertwined immediately as if they had a mind of their own. Paige breathed a sigh of relief.

He looked at her in the dimly lit entry hall, asking, "Are you okay?"

Paige tried to hold her composure but could do nothing to stem the tears. Tears of joy knowing that nothing had changed between them—that Morgan still loved her and wanted her to be close mingled with tears of sadness at the senseless thing that had taken his father away.

"I am now," she said, nodding. "But what about you?"

Morgan's eyes looked hollow, dark, and exhausted. Circles ringed them.

"Same here." He shook his head. "I still can't get my head around…this." His voice cracked and he swallowed. His eyes filled with tears, but he managed to brush them away.

"Mom, here's Paige, Mr. and Mrs. Fuller, and Candy."

Mrs. Cahill smiled wanly and patted Paige's

shoulder, then touched her father and mother on their forearms. She nodded at Candy who stood on the other side of her parents.

"We don't have anyone left except my aunt and she couldn't get a flight back from London so will you sit with us at the front?" Morgan asked her dad. "I asked Ben to sit with us, too. He's like the brother I never had."

"Of course," her dad agreed and squeezed his arm lightly.

As Malcolm Cahill's oldest friend, Paige's father had been asked to say some words at the service. Morgan explained that his family had attended the Arlington Street Church for generations but had no strong religious inclination. Arlington Street was a Unitarian Universalist church that took a less formal attitude toward Christianity so the minister's words would be more secular than theological.

Morgan's dad had been a well-respected, popular figure in the Boston community. In addition to his strong business ties and leadership on a variety of boards and committees he was legendary in his charitable activities. Paige, Morgan, and the others walked slowly down the center aisle formed by the hundreds of chairs the staff had deployed for the overflow crowd.

As Paige surveyed the solemn crowd it was evident he had many friends. Paige had attended her share of funerals. Often, despite the loss of the departed smiles and conversation were evident among the attendees. She saw no evidence of anything other than genuine grief and a sense of disbelief on the faces of those they passed on the way to their seats in the first row.

Adding to the somber atmosphere of tragedy and loss pervading the event was the musical selection echoing throughout the medieval hall. She recognized the melancholy largo movement from Dvorak's Ninth Symphony known as the "New World Symphony."

Malcolm had been a Harvard alum, and with his son now enrolled there, this zenith of academic excellence and tradition left nothing undone. Their award-winning brass ensemble played the selection to perfection.

Paige squeezed Morgan's hand tightly as she felt her eyes fill and overflow again. She stole a glance at Morgan standing straight, strong, and erect as the ensemble completed their flawless rendition. She had never been more in love with him than she was at that moment. She gently pushed away her tears and moved as close to him as she could, wishing she could somehow erase the last week, have the world stop and spin backward as she'd seen in a science fiction movie once so everything would be as it was before 8:45 on Tuesday morning. But that was never going to happen.

They stood as the minister said a prayer after which the large group took their seats. Paige had never been in such a large group that was so quiet. When someone in the midst of the throng of attendees coughed, it echoed around the large hall. Paige looked at the vaulted ceiling. The room wore the appearance of feudal halls she'd only seen in books.

Her father gave an uncharacteristically brief but touching tribute to his dearest friend's life and legacy, pointing to Morgan as his example.

"Some leave this world better for having lived but none has ever left a more fitting legacy and tribute in the person of his son than did my dear friend Malcolm."

He left the lectern to respectful nods at his well-chosen words, stopping to bend and hug Mrs. Cahill and shake Morgan's hand as he sat down. All three had tears streaking their faces. The minister made a few polite remarks but none with the powerful and poignant insights of Paige's father.

And then it was over.

****

Ezra swallowed deeply and felt traces of tears on his cheeks. He self-consciously put his hand to his face and brushed them away quickly. The redhead next to him had turned and caught him.

"Were you close to Mr. Cahill?" she asked swallowing a sob of her own.

"No," Ezra answered. "I didn't really know him."

"Oh. I see." She nodded and touched his forearm, showing a smile that held warmth and understanding. "Me either really. I worked for him when he got transferred here. He was an amazing man."

The rear of the large crowd seemed to be a collection of people like Ezra. Some alone like him and his neighbor or a group of two or three comprised the rear guard of this tragic observance. They all turned and watched the small group of seven people who seemed to be close exit the hall before moving.

He waited behind the woman next to him while the crowd of hundreds filed out. Finally, after almost twenty minutes they worked their way across and turned left at the end heading for the exit.

A small crowd had gathered outside but there was little talk or laughter. Ezra took two steps down and stopped, pulling out his pack of Marlboro Lights. He pulled out his disposable lighter and was about to light his cigarette when he felt a touch on his shoulder.

"Would you mind?" asked the redhead who'd sat next to him, waving her unlit cigarette.

He nodded and gave her a light.

She inhaled deeply and looked around. "Don't want to bother anyone," she said raising her eyebrows, adding, "I think we're in the minority."

Ezra looked at her casually and nodded. "I think so."

She started down the steps and stopped, turning to face Ezra. "Are you okay?"

"Sure. What do you mean?" he asked defensively.

"Not my business and I don't usually talk to strangers at funerals, but you look pretty shaken up for someone who didn't know Mr. Cahill very well."

Ezra took a drag on his cigarette and blew it out. "I knew someone very close to him. But thanks."

"Okay," she said and started to turn.

On an impulse, Ezra touched her arm. "I don't usually talk to people at funerals either. My name's Ezra Wilson." He offered his hand.

She put her lips together and tilted her head for a moment, watching him.

She stuck out her hand. Ezra noted she had no wedding ring on.

"Hi, Ezra. I'm Karen O'Malley."

She continued to stand looking at him. This was virgin territory. It had been decades since he'd made small talk with a good-looking woman and Karen fit that description.

"Karen, you probably got a job, a house full of kids, or something to get back to but…"

She held up her hand. "Got nothing pressing today. Took it off not knowing how long this might take. Would you like to buy me a cup of coffee, Ezra?"

"I'd like that. A lot."

Both put out their cigarettes and he bent over and picked up the butts throwing them in a trash container as they passed it.

As they headed from the Harvard Club, Ezra froze.

"What's the matter?" she asked. "You look like you've seen a ghost." She raised her eyebrows.

"Not a ghost but an old…" Ezra threw over his shoulder as he broke into a trot and followed a slender figure he knew. Or thought he did. But he let the thought die. He'd been going to say friend but that was never true. No one at Walpole had ever been his friend. Not like in the real world. This was a man he'd sheltered in prison. Someone who'd been accused of pedophilia and tormented endlessly by some of the crueler inmates. They used his crime and his frailty as an excuse to torment and use him. Ezra and his cell mates had done their best to help the poor kid and he was glad when he read Julian had recently been exonerated.

"Hey…*Julian,*" he called toward the retreating figure who pulled his hat down over his narrow face as if hiding as he slipped into a cab and sped away. Why would he be here, at this funeral?

Karen caught up with him and shrugged. "Something I did wrong? My mouthwash?" she asked with a look that mixed amusement and confusion.

"No," he stopped short as the cab disappeared. "Nothing like that. Just someone I…" Ezra still had no good way to finish the thought so he just shook his head. "Sorry."

"So, you lived in Boston a long time?" she asked as they turned and headed for the trolley.

"Been away for a long time," he volunteered.

"Really, that sounds interesting." She smiled at him. "I'd love to hear about it."

"I'd rather hear about you, Karen," he said. "My story is really pretty dull."

Chapter 42

Two-dozen people stood on the second floor of the
Harvard Club. The service had taken less time than the
staff had anticipated, so they were still setting up in one
of the small function rooms.

There was some muffled conversation, but for the
most part everyone just stood looking at each other and
smiling weakly or staring in some neutral direction
avoiding the eyes of Morgan and his mother. The
tragedy was still so raw and so surreal no one knew
how to deal with it or what to say.

For her part Paige stood as close to him as she
could without clinging. His mother, who held his other
hand, moved toward her and offered a kind smile.

"Thank you so much for being here with Morgan.
He tells me you're heading to Brown next fall, Paige."
She took Paige's free hand and nodded. "That's
wonderful. I've read they have quite a riding program,
dear. You must be thrilled."

"Yes, I am. But it's not a *fait accompli* yet." Paige
went on to explain that despite assurances and her
legacy status she still had quite a few things to do
before she was accepted.

"Anyone would be crazy not to want you," Morgan
said, squeezing her hand and smiling at her. "My
lovely, talented genius."

Paige turned crimson at his enthusiastic

263

endorsement.

They continued to make small talk. Several of the small crowd drifted over to tell her father how moving his words were. As the doors to the small function room were opened, Candy stole away from her hold on Ben and maneuvered next to Paige.

"Can I steal my younger sister for a minute?" she asked Morgan.

"I'll time it. One minute starting now." He smiled and held up his wrist with the watch.

"Well, looks like you two have kissed and made up," she whispered as she held Paige back.

"So far there's been no kissing involved," she said, hiding a smile, hoping no one noticed. "But I hope we can rectify that soon." She held up crossed fingers.

"If I know you guys, I have no concerns on that score." Candy gave Paige a quick squeeze and went back to find Ben.

****

"So you're going to play next Saturday?" Paige asked him as they left the Harvard Club.

His mother was being escorted to a limo by her parents.

"Yes." He nodded. She looked curious and concerned.

"Morgan," she whispered looking around self-consciously. "You've been through…*hell*." She paused. "And you look exhausted. I'm sure the team and coach would understand. I heard him tell you to take some time off."

"Paige, when you compete, it's just you and Alex, right?"

She nodded.

"When I compete it's with fifty other people. And I'm one of the keys." He held up his hand. "Sorry. I don't mean it like that. Like they can't live without me, Paige but—"

She touched his lips with her fingers. "I've never known anyone with so much talent who was so modest. No need to explain, and if you say you can play, all I can say is I'll be in the stands cheering you on."

"No. No, you won't," he said turning her to face him.

She frowned, showing concern again. "But…"

It was his turn to put his fingers to her lips. He'd shut her out since the attacks. But seeing her today, being with her, holding her close, inhaling the intoxicating musky scent that clung to her, Morgan knew no matter what the problem he could never be away from her again. Not ever. Even for a moment.

He pulled her close. "You'll see the game from our sideline. I already okayed it with the coach."

"If you say so," Paige whispered, sighing as she surrendered to him. "I never want to be away from you again."

"And you never will be," he promised. "For as long as I live."

Chapter 43

As promised Paige sat on the sideline that first game on the following Saturday against what she hoped would be her future alma mater, Brown University. Despite two difficult weeks and the responsibilities of caring for his mother, Morgan performed in the way his teammates and the thousands in the Stadium had come to expect. He ran for 212 yards, caught five of Ben's passes for seventy more, and scored one rushing and two receiving touchdowns as the Crimson forged a hard-fought twenty-seven to twenty victory.

After the terrible fear of losing him, Paige was in heaven after the way he'd shown her so much affection and attention since their reunion at the service. Paige had helped Morgan with his mother that day and spoken to him every day since—sometimes two or three times.

She'd been invited to stay in one of the Cahills' generous guest rooms on the weekend of the opening game. She felt uncomfortable knowing what Morgan's mother had gone through. But Mrs. Fuller seemed like the kind, thoughtful lady they'd seen on her rare visits to their home.

She joined them for dinner both nights and even stayed long after the meal was over seeming in unexpectedly good spirits as she offered a story about how she and her husband had met while they attended college—she at Radcliffe and he at Harvard.

When she left the table and the housekeeper cleared away the dishes after coffee and dessert, Paige led Morgan into the large walnut-paneled den to watch a movie, or that was their cover story.

Despite the warm September afternoon, the evening held the crisp feel of fall and Paige shivered. It could have been the cool air or it could have been a chill as she saw the host of family photographs that lined each of the dozen or so bookshelves that flanked either side of a large screen TV in the wall.

"You cold?" Morgan asked as he put his arm around Paige.

"Never, when I'm with you," she purred, nestling into his muscled chest. She loved the warmth, the feeling of safety and contentment she knew whenever he held her like this.

He released her and walked to the fireplace. Flipping a switch he pointed at it. "Magic!" he decreed as the gas fire came to life.

Paige joined him and laughed then moved closer to Morgan till they were only a few inches apart.

"This looks familiar," he whispered as they slid down onto the couch. "I think we've done this before." He offered a smile that tempted and teased.

"I believe we have, sir," she agreed closing the short distance to find his lips. She kissed him softly at first, finding his cheek, his neck, nibbling on his ears.

"Oh, Paige," he said closing his eyes as he found her lips, opening his as he explored her mouth and tongue. "I'm so sorry about…everything. I have to explain."

"No you don't," she said breathlessly as she moved

away from his lips and found his ear again. "I can't imagine what you've been through. I forbid you to punish yourself, understand?"

"Yes, ma'am!" he agreed in a whisper.

They held each other, kissing with a newfound passion, as if going through this tragedy together had forged an even stronger bond. Paige broke the embrace and touched his cheek letting her hand drift down over his chin.

"You know, you missed my birthday last Thursday."

Morgan closed his eyes tightly. "Oh my God, Paige." He shook his head taking her hand. "I'm so sorry. Can you forgive me?"

"There's nothing to forgive, dear." Paige gave him her warmest smile. "I just wanted to remind you that I am eighteen now…"

He sat up and looked at her. "Are you saying what I think you are, Paige?"

She took his hand, asking, "Can we go upstairs?" When she thought about seeing him again, Paige had dreamt of this moment. In their long passion-filled summer they'd come so close so often. The events of the week had given Paige a strange sense of foreboding as she realized how fragile life could be. She was ready.

Paige pulled him up and put her arm around his waist, standing on tiptoes to find his cheek.

They made their way up the stairs. Arms around each other they padded silently along the thick mauve carpeting to his bedroom. When she looked up at him he showed her a soft smile. He was about to speak when Paige put her fingertips to his lips.

"Yes," she said, nodding. "I've never been more

sure of anything."

Morgan turned to face her as he closed the door quietly. He bent, finding her lips and kissing them softly, adding, "Me, too."

Paige reached behind her and turned off the lights. As if on cue, they both shed their clothing. When Paige had removed her top and Morgan his sport shirt, he approached and took her in his arms. They found each other's lips, kissing with the passion they had a few minutes before. Morgan played over and around her neck and shoulders as she turned and gently kissed his chest.

Paige backed toward the bed and he followed her choreography flawlessly. They fell breathlessly onto the soft quilt and kissed again. Paige closed her eyes and let his touch and her desire take control. This would be the most wonderful night of her life.

Chapter 44

The man hung in the basement of the remote estate on Greater Boston's North Shore. Sophie held Julian tightly as they studied the thick figure suspended from the sturdy ring in the eight-foot ceiling.

Julian moved from her toward the inert man. He had stopped gasping and kicking several minutes before.

"No," she said taking his arm. "Leave him there till after dinner."

He froze and turned toward her. "You are cruel, aren't you?" he asked with a frown.

"Not cruel, just practical." She moved toward the man and pushed his body, watching as it swung and twisted in a slow arc. "I've studied this, and it's possible he may not be dead. Sometimes it can take fifteen minutes for them to die from hanging."

"All right," he agreed, watching the man continue to spin slowly.

She took his hand and pulled him toward the stairs. "That makes four."

"That's right. We're almost done."

"Ah, yes. But these oafs were just a rehearsal. The next two will be the frosting on the cake…especially the girl. She's the key to getting her father."

"Yes, I have something special planned for her. Something that will draw her father out from behind his tight web of security and into our hands." A smile of satisfaction crossed his lips, never revealing his desire for Paige. "I want to keep it a secret but it's something I saw and read about. Something he will never be able to resist."

"I can't wait." She linked her arm into his as they mounted the stairs. "But that man. The paroled convict who saw you at the funeral." She turned to face him, when they reached the kitchen. "What was his name?

"Wilson, Ezra Wilson?"

"Does he concern you? He concerns me," she whispered, finding his ear with her lips. "We haven't made it this far by leaving loose ends, darling."

"I don't see how he could be any trouble. Besides, he and his friends were decent to me. I'd hate to repay his kindness by killing him." He pushed back and found her eyes. "So far we've managed to stay below the radar. No one has put together any connection. Just three scumbags, now a fourth, who got what they deserved."

She put her lips together and looked at him thoughtfully. "All right. I always defer to your wisdom, darling. But he was there for some reason, and circumstance has a way of getting in the way, finding people and events."

He nodded. "If it's necessary to deal with Mr. Wilson, we will, my dear. I promise. We will."

Chapter 45

November 2001

Since that miraculous night in September, their lives seemed destined toward an even more heavenly course than Paige could have dared imagine. Romeo and Juliet minus the tragedy—or most of it. She lay in bed at the Cahill townhouse, smiling after having returned to it only minutes before after spending another long, passionate night with Morgan.

Of course nothing could erase or mitigate the senseless and tragic loss of Morgan's father and the 2,995 others who perished on nine-eleven. Nor was there any way to return his mother to a complete state of reality. Or at least one Morgan was willing to act on. Mrs. Cahill acted normally around casual acquaintances, but when the door was shut and the lights turned off, one of two things happened: she sank into a state of gloomy despair, or she retreated to some netherworld that was happier and more welcoming than the cruelty this one offered. Both showed the extent of her departure from reality and need for treatment but Morgan, realist though he was with everything else, turned a blind eye to his mother's condition.

Paige talked to him about getting her more substantive care, perhaps even sending her someplace for a time where she could get the in-depth attention she really needed. Between his studies, football, and having to suddenly assume the duties as head of an affluent, influential, and well-connected Brahmin family, Morgan's schedule overflowed. Not to mention the time he stole from everything else for Paige. He'd promised after that terrible week he would never take her for granted or fail to show her how much he loved her, cared for her, and needed her. And to date, he'd been as good as his word. Better, much to Paige's delight.

Paige loved him so deeply and cared so much for him. Wanting to help and be a partner in his life, Paige read tirelessly about depression, bringing Morgan articles and texts on the subject. While he thanked her politely and smiled warmly at her concern, he refused to discuss the idea. That, Paige had discovered sadly from her extensive research, was one of the major roadblocks to defeating this insidious disease: well-meaning family and friends pretended it did not exist or that their particular family member was not afflicted badly enough to need long-term or ongoing care. Like too many forms of debilitating psychological afflictions the most difficult problem in helping to find a cure was not the availability of treatment, it was unwillingness on the part of loved ones to admit a family member was in need. So in the end she did all she could, supporting Morgan and spending as much time as her schedule would allow at the Cahills', helping to minister to Mary Jane.

As she lay, eyes closed, Paige did her best to put that out of her mind, choosing instead to luxuriate in delicious recollections of another night of passion at Morgan's side. She thought back to that first weekend in Mattapoisett. Their first weekend together, remembering with amusement the warning Candy had issued when she and Morgan had spent the night in her bedroom. *"Unless the world explodes you two are headed for stardom. Please, don't let your hormones ruin your lives,"* she'd begged. Well after a summer on the edge of passion they'd given in to those hormones and to date no penalty had been forthcoming.

Six o'clock. The anniversary clock on the mantel above the small fireplace in the elegant guest room rang cheerily. Paige recalled her fear about her scars—a constant reminder of that terrifying August afternoon she worried would turn him away. How could she have sold him so short? She no longer wore the undergarment to conceal it any longer. Paige turned onto her side and smiled broadly looking at her glasses on the night table, recalling his comment when she'd proudly shown him her new contacts. She now wore the glasses again knowing he really did like them. She curled into the fetal position and pulled the pillow down and around her head as she closed her eyes and let sleep overtake her. Morgan's mother seldom rose before eleven and it was Sunday so there were no other pressing matters that needed attention. She'd try again to make some headway with Morgan about his mother.

Paige stifled a yawn as she coiled tighter under the welcoming warmth of the thick down comforter. She sneaked one eye open and saw the gray of another cold November day in New England. Sighing contentedly she closed her eyes again and fell into a deep sleep filled with visions of high blue skies, endless swells on Buzzards Bay and of course, Morgan cantering along beside her.

****

On Monday Paige was back in Mattapoisett. Getting out of her VW Beetle in the school parking lot, a giant smile crossed her face. Making love to Morgan was the most exquisite experience she could ever recall. The first time had been more difficult than she'd imagined, even a little painful. But in spite of that, she'd been in a state of uncontrolled euphoria afterward. They'd done it several times now, each one better than the last as they learned how to tease, tempt, and satisfy each other in ways she'd never imagined. To her delight, despite Morgan's rock star status, Paige discovered he was as new to intimacy as she was.

She waved to a few of her classmates, marveling at how Morgan had not only fulfilled her romantically but given her the confidence she'd lost after a long, miserable year. Francie said it best: "It's like you're a whole new person, Paige. We've been best friends since grammar school but you're so…different!" And she was.

The new Paige took the time to put on makeup, spending long minutes in front of the mirror tending to things like hair, nails, and eyebrows. She not only wore the new outfits her mother bought for her, but found herself disappointed if Vera came home from the mall empty handed. Now that Candy was away, they even went shopping together, something that would have been unheard of in the spring. Friends told her their secrets, invited her to parties, and called to ask her advice on everything from homework to their love lives. When your man was a local legend, the toast of America's oldest and most revered college, you got respect and then some. You had to have something really special going for you to attract a guy like Morgan

Cahill. When Paige opened her locker with his picture on the inside of the narrow wooden door, the underclass girls would gather round and swoon. And Paige had to admit she loved every minute of this newfound respect and adulation.

****

She lay in her bed on Sunday night, the eighteenth, falling asleep after coming home from the last Harvard home game. Morgan, the love of her life and best friend, had contributed three touchdowns in a 35-23 trouncing of Yale. That capped off a perfect 9-0 season for the Crimson. Paige drifted off thinking about the butterfly she and Morgan had seen emerge from its cocoon on their very first riding date. Paige wasn't a believer in omens, metaphors, or foreshadowing, but she knew how that beautiful yellow-winged creature felt. She had finally broken free, shed the fears and misgivings that had preoccupied her since losing her first boyfriend and the accident eighteen months ago. *Paige Fuller*, she thought, brimming with love and a newfound enthusiasm for life, *you have arrived!*

Chapter 46

"Wow! That was—I don't know exactly what but it was great," Karen O'Malley said breathlessly as she lay next to Ezra in his compact Cambridge apartment while the faint street noise drifted up from Massachusetts Avenue.

"Yep!" He turned over, finding her full lips, touching them lightly with his fingers. "We were great."

She nodded and took his hand. "Were you ever frightened? I mean you know, when you were in prison?"

"Sure, lots of times." He sighed. "There were nights when I first got there I was afraid to close my eyes." He shook his head. "I was lucky. Got in with some guys who were tough but decent. I know that may sound crazy considering we were at the state prison for major felonies, but we looked out for each other."

She played over and around his fingers, caressing them lightly as they talked.

He'd told her he'd been in prison. In the world of 2001, there was no way to hide the fact. Anyone with modest computer skills could find out that information if they wanted. So he'd taken the proactive route and told Karen. But he'd danced around the truth, telling her he'd been the driver in a robbery where a woman was shot and hoping she'd accept that and not search

277

any further.

At first she looked shocked. It took a few cups of coffee before she agreed to go out with him. But he had to explain why he couldn't drive, drink alcohol, or leave the state. Better some distorted version of the truth than a complete fabrication. They started with a movie, then a few lunches before she gave in and agreed to have dinner with him.

Strange, Ezra thought as he smiled, studying her face. He'd changed his attitude and outlook at Cedar Junction to get out so he could find his son. And he had. But in doing so, he'd found a new life. One far removed from the violent addictive behavior that almost swallowed him.

Karen was somewhere between pretty and cute…Ezra wasn't sure which as she lay next to him. Round freckled face with a great smile, a hint of dimples, and waves of thick red hair that swirled provocatively whenever she moved her head. She had the most unusual and striking eyes he'd ever seen. Depending on the light they could be green, amber, brown, or all the above. They sparkled mischievously when she laughed and Ezra loved it.

And Karen wasn't the only bright spot. After only four months on the job, his friend Pat had promoted him. Ezra's knowledge of landscaping and yard maintenance had won Pat's respect and that of most of his co-workers, many of whom were immigrants.

But the real frosting on the cake was that over the course of the fall, he'd actually spent time with Morgan. Briefly at first when they'd see each other as Morgan came and went from practice. But much to Ezra's delight and surprise they bonded. Ezra took the initiative and would ask about a particular play or series of plays. He'd been a fine high school running back himself, so he spoke from a position of knowledge. Now, Morgan thought nothing of stopping and talking about the upcoming game, the weather, or on rare occasions even a comment about his life. Ezra had met Paige, the sweet, pretty girl who looked at Morgan adoringly. They were such a special couple. Despite the tragic loss of his adoptive father, Morgan was living the life Ezra would have wished for his son.

Ezra laughed to himself when Paige studied him and commented that he looked very familiar. Ezra wondered if someday it would dawn on her or Morgan that he was a worn down, world-weary version of his son, not sure whether that would be a good thing or bad.

Yes, all that was good. Far better than he had any right to expect. But Ezra had learned long ago that the good usually kept company with his old friend the bad. In Ezra's case the downright miserable. So when the buzzer rang as he lay watching football on a Sunday afternoon in November, he had a premonition that this was going to be the cloud in the silver lining he'd just been reflecting on.

Karen had gone shopping, so he was sure it wasn't her. Pat was busy visiting his ex and their kids, and no one else knew where he lived unless the Jehovah's Witnesses were canvasing the neighborhood. Ezra's stomach churned as he got up and pressed the talk button on his intercom.

"Hello," he said, keeping his tone even. "Who is it?"

"Is this Ezra Wilson?" a mellow bass voice asked.

"Allen Koval gave me this address."

Allen Koval was Ezra's parole officer. So this was no social call. Ezra pushed the release and heard the door open in the lobby two floors below. Thirty seconds later an authoritative knock signaled that his visitor was outside.

Visitors as it turned out. Ezra looked in the peephole and saw two men whose appearance cried out "cop." He opened the door and the lead man showed him a gold badge and a card. It said he was a detective sergeant with the state police.

"Paul Winston," the man said as he held out his hand.

"Should I be worried?" Ezra asked.

Winston looked at his partner who also handed Ezra a card. "Not by our visit, Mr. Wilson."

Ezra stuck out his hand and shook Winston's hand then his partner's.

"What can I do for you?" Ezra asked gesturing for the men to come in. He led them to the small kitchen table and they all sat down.

Paul Winston fixed Ezra with a pleasant expression. "I'm sure you've heard about the recent killings of ex-convicts, Ezra? May I call you Ezra?"

"Yes and sure." Ezra nodded with a shrug. He was both curious and concerned but had learned to keep his mouth shut. To volunteer nothing.

"Well, you served time with all four men. Right?"

Ezra studied Winston. Was the detective trying to trick him? "Four?" he said tentatively. "I'd heard about three of 'em. When did the fourth one happen?"

"On Friday night we think. Found his body in the Fenway like the others." He looked at his partner. "It's

Sunday afternoon. Figured you might have seen it."

"No." Ezra shook his head. "Who was it?"

"Small-time muscle guy. Jeremy O'Toole."

Ezra couldn't help letting a smile cross his face.

"Something funny about that. Ezra?" the other detective asked raising his bushy eyebrows. His voice was tinny. Almost shrill compared to Winston's.

"Sorry. No. Nothing funny at all about murder. You'd have to know these guys."

"So the warden at Walpole told us." Paul Winston shook his head as he looked at his partner.

"A who's who of low-life scumbags was the way he put it," the second man offered. "But please don't repeat that."

"Well. Let's say that my best guess is if you put together the attendance for all their funerals you'd be lucky to get a crowd big enough for a poker game. And no. The warden was always straight with me so I'd never say anything to embarrass him." Ezra immediately regretted his words. He'd violated his own rule and told them something when he should have kept silent. But as he watched both nodded passively.

"That's what we hear."

"So, why is it you're here?"

The men exchanged glances. "Well," Paul Winston began. "The warden also said some things about you. Good things."

They both nodded again. "Said everyone respected you and your friends." He paused, looking at his partner for support.

Ezra held up his hand. "I understand what you're getting at, Detective." Ezra said. "You think I may know something that may help you?"

"Look, Ezra," the second detective said. "In any social group, there are things that go on no one outside the group knows. The warden said you were a leader up there. People looked up to you. And he thought you might know something. Maybe what these characters had in common that would cause someone to want to kill them all."

Ezra shrugged, pondering the Psych 101 comment and thinking about it. "Maybe there's a vigilante out there. I have no idea. I've thought about it." And he had. Since the day of the funeral. The day he thought he'd seen Julian.

"You and your friends had a few run-ins with these guys we were told."

Ezra stood slowly. "Look, Detectives, these guys were the kind that you couldn't avoid having a run-in with…unless you were dead."

Paul Winston stood and held up his hands. "Okay, Ezra. We really came here looking for help. No one's accusing you of anything."

The buzzer rang three times. Karen's signal she was coming up.

Winston looked at Ezra.

"My girlfriend's back. She was out shopping and look—she knows I was at Walpole but…"

"No sweat. We're not here to hassle you or mess up your life. Koval tells us you're doing great. So…"

Before he'd finished, Karen had unlocked the door and came in with a couple of bundles in hand. She looked at the two men and stopped short.

"Is everything okay, Ez?" she asked hesitantly.

"Everything's fine, miss," Winston said. He turned back to Ezra. "One more thing before we leave, Ezra."

"Sure. What's up?"

The second man pulled a picture from his inside coat pocket, handing it to Ezra. "You recognize this man?"

Ezra studied the photo and felt a tingle run down his spine. "Sure. You know I do. Is this a test?" He shook his head. "That's Julian. Julian Warren."

"Sorry, wasn't trying to trick you. Yeah, Julian Warren."

"Is there a reason you ask?" Ezra knew exactly why they asked but was back to playing mute again. These bad guys had made this kid's life a living hell, but as he handed the picture back to the detective, he wondered. Julian had always seemed so quiet. Meek. Downright mousy.

"Well, we won't play games with you if you don't play any with us. It's no secret the guys we found on the Fenway used him as their personal plaything until you and some of your buddies stepped in."

Ezra looked at Karen. "You could say that about ten other guys. They were a nasty bunch that enjoyed violence." He forced a smile. "Are we about done here?"

"Sure." They turned and headed for the door, nodding at Karen.

"You have our cards. If you think of anything that might be helpful. Give us a call," Paul Winston said as he closed the door.

"Is everything okay, Ez?" Karen repeated, adding, "Who were those guys?"

"State cops. They're working on that series of murders. You know, the ex-convicts that someone's killing and dumping in the Fenway?"

Kevin V. Symmons

"They don't think…"

He closed the distance and surrounded her with his arms. "No. Guess the warden at the prison thought I might be able to help them."

"But you couldn't?"

"No. I have no idea what's going on, but those guys were bad news, so it's not hard to imagine that someone had a grudge against them."

"Wait a minute," she said pulling away from him. "That name. Julian. Isn't that the name you called at the funeral the day we met?"

He nodded. "You got a good memory, and yeah it is, but he's not the type to go around murdering people."

"You're sure?" she said holding herself as she shivered.

He pulled her close again and kissed her fragrant red hair.

"Positive. And even if he was. I'd be the last guy he'd come looking for. 'Cause if it wasn't for me, he'd most likely be dead now."

Chapter 47

Thanksgiving weekend arrived bringing a taste of things to come. A blanket of powdery snow descended on the Greater Boston Area on Wednesday night. Morgan and his mother had been invited to spend the holiday weekend at the Fullers' ski house at Sunday River, the massive ski resort near Bethel, Maine. He'd asked Paige if they could ride up together. Saturday would be the breakup dinner and awards night for the football team and he and Ben, who was also invited, would have to go back on Saturday morning since it could be a four to five hour drive depending on traffic and weather. But everyone had been so busy he looked forward to two glorious days and three nights with Paige, despite the probability of having to forego any intimacy.

Morgan thought his mother had made a remarkable turnaround after his father's tragic and senseless death. Paige felt differently but he was confident that given time she'd recover from her bouts with depression. She still took medications, but after a couple of very difficult weeks, she seemed to rally. Much to Morgan's delight and hers, she had found something new and meaningful to focus her attention and energy on. She was doing volunteer work for the New England Home for Little Wanderers, a 200-year-old charitable operation whose mission was to help disadvantaged children and families achieve independence and success. His mother was helping to plan the annual Christmas toy collection and fund-raising campaign which would swing into high gear after the long Thanksgiving weekend.

As they left the Maine Turnpike and headed straight north, the three of them were glad to see a few fluffy snowflakes tease as they proceeded along winding Route 26, the one-lane access road that would cover the final forty-five minutes and get them to Sunday River.

His mother beamed and oohed like a teenager as the snow began to thicken. "I can't wait," she enthused. "I haven't been on skis for a long time." She stopped, knitting her brows as she concentrated. "Must be ten years."

"Next to riding, and the piano of course, I think skiing is the greatest thing going," Paige volunteered from the back seat. She and Mary Jane had shared the co-pilot seat next to Morgan on the long drive.

"Well, I really haven't done it much since I was ten or twelve but from what I remember it is quite a rush… flying down the hill and stopping on a dime!" Morgan played the enthusiastic partner and son but was so tired from prepping for finals and football he was exhausted and looking forward to some serious time on the couch snuggling next to Paige.

But she could see right through him. "Yeah, I can tell," she teased as she leaned over his seat and squeezed his shoulder. "That's why you've been yawning since we hit New Hampshire."

"Well, you'll find out next year what it's like going to an Ivy League school," he said giving her a smug expression. "I confess I wouldn't mind lying around and doing nothing for a couple of days, but I know you love to ski and I wouldn't want to disappoint you, *my precious*!" he said, raising his eyebrows as she smiled at him in the mirror.

The car skidded slightly on the snow-covered secondary road. Morgan snapped to attention and corrected the skid. "Paige," he said with concern. "It's getting a little slippery. Will you lean back and put on your seat belt?"

She stuck her tongue out at him. "Hey, you just keep those baby blues on the road, huh?" Paige commanded with a grin.

His mother shook her head and laughed. "I agree with Paige, Morg. We don't want to end up in a ditch."

They drove in silence for a few minutes, listening to country western on the radio. It was the only thing on the radio in central Maine. Morgan hummed along with the simple repetitive song as the snow grew thicker. Visibility had dwindled to a hundred yards. Morgan yawned again. He was more tired than he wanted to admit.

"Maybe we should stop for coffee at the next roadside café?" Paige asked. *How did she always know how he felt?*

"Naw, we've only got about twenty more miles," he told her as his stubborn streak kicked in. "I just want to get there."

"Okay, but the next couple of miles are tough. I know it pretty well so if you want me to drive…"

"No. I'm fine," Morgan insisted as he smiled at her in the mirror.

Paige closed her eyes, but Morgan watched her. It

was difficult not to. She was everything he'd ever wanted. The father he'd worshipped had died. He could never understand or make sense of that but it seemed as if his life was...

"Morgan!" his mother screamed as he turned his attention to the narrow snow-covered road. A large tractor trailer spun out of control around the blind corner ahead. Morgan turned their large SUV to elude the mammoth vehicle, but there was no escaping it.

As he watched, the truck twisted in slow motion and skidded into the Tahoe he drove. His vehicle had skidded and turned so the passenger side faced the oncoming truck. He heard the cries from his mother and Paige as the cab's headlights bore down on them. He reached across the seat in a futile attempt to shield his mother, but there was nothing he could do. The last thing he remembered was Paige screaming his name and reaching for him as he hoped his father would be there to welcome them into heaven...

Chrysalis

PART THREE

Chrysalis

Chapter 48

Candy stood next to Ben. It was the Saturday of Thanksgiving weekend. They should have been happy, stuffed, sleeping off the tryptophan from the leftover turkey and in a couple of hours Ben and Morgan should have been standing on the podium getting their awards as the Crimson football's co-MVPs for the 2001 season. Instead Ben held Candy tightly, doing his best to offer her consolation as her sister and best friend remained immobilized and in jeopardy.

Her parents had taken a brief respite from their three-day vigil since the accident, retreating to the hospital's cafeteria while Candy and Ben stood watch. Ben tightened his grip on her hand as they stared at Paige's unconscious form at Boston's New England Medical Center. This was her first day since being moved out of intensive care.

"You may not believe this, but it sounds like she was lucky," the attending doctor said as he studied Paige and scanned the numerous monitors. "She should recover completely. Paige will have a few bruises and a nasty scar on her face. But she's a lovely young woman so a good plastic surgeon will fix that so you hardly see any evidence," he offered as he turned to look at them.

"Did you say lucky?" Candy asked with skepticism despite his reassurances as her eyes filled and overflowed. The electronics beat a steady rhythm as she stared, eyes transfixed on Paige. As always, when Paige was hurt, sad, or in danger, pangs of guilt rose up into Candy's throat like sour bile that choked her. They had ever since that afternoon ten years earlier on the riverbank when…

"I think she looks better today. Don't you?" Ben asked as he continued squeezing her hand for reassurance. Sometimes Candy thought she didn't deserve Ben. He was so special and he loved her so much.

Her sister's head was covered in thick bandages. For the second time in less than two years, the sister she adored lay in a hospital bed. Paige had awakened several times asking for Morgan, her father, and Candy, returning to her drug-induced slumber after a few confused moments. She moved tentatively to Paige's side, taking her hand and squeezing it so hard her sister let out a weak groan. Reluctantly Candy replaced Paige's hand delicately on the bed clothes and bit her lip as she backed away.

"The police report says that she wasn't wearing a seat belt. She was thrown around violently on impact," the doctor explained his "lucky" comment. "Her injuries could have been much worse."

Candy wiped the tears away and looked at Ben as the doctor nodded and excused himself.

"How's Morgan?"

"Still in critical condition," Ben whispered as he turned and put his arm around her again. "They said it'll be touch and go for a while."

She sighed deeply as she continued to study Paige's inert form, hot tears rolling off her cheeks.

"Who's going to tell him about his mother?"

Candy asked thoughtfully. "And who's going to tell Paige about him?"

****

"What's the matter?" Karen asked as they sat and watched the Saturday evening news.

"Shhh," Ezra whispered as he sat transfixed in front of the TV in her Back Bay apartment. "Jeez, the kid's still in a coma."

"What's your interest in this story, Ez?" She touched his shoulder. "I know you work at Harvard and knew the Cahill kid. We met at his dad's funeral, remember? But you've been fixated on this accident like these people were family."

The newscaster had gone on to something else so Ezra muted the TV and turned his attention toward Karen. "Sorry," he acknowledged. "I just feel sorry for him. The kid lost his father on nine-eleven and his mother when that tractor trailer hit them."

She shrugged. "I know you got to know him and said he's a great kid. But you really do seem almost obsessed with this."

Should he tell her? No, that would mean revealing the truth about his crime and imprisonment. His involvement with Karen had begun as a diversion, something to take his mind off the situation with Morgan and what he could do to connect with his son, but somewhere in the midst of it all, he'd grown to care for her. Very much. So much so that he'd abandon the holy quest he'd spent years dreaming about? No. Not that much. At least not yet. But perhaps fate or circumstance had taken a hand. At least now he had something, someone else to care for, to worry about and give some meaning to his life again.

"Yeah, you're right." He gave her his best smile. "Sorry," he repeated. "Let's go get something to eat."

****

It was a bleak Tuesday afternoon in mid-December at the intensive care ward at Boston's New England Medical Center. Paige stood and stretched, yawning. She was still weak and prone to moments of disorientation. But she would not leave his side. Heading to the window, Paige looked at her watch. It was almost three p.m. She hadn't eaten anything since breakfast, but she had no appetite. The doctors were optimistic assuring her that he'd awaken soon. Part of her was thrilled at the idea of seeing him, his smile, his laugh, the dimple that cleft his chin when he spoke or concentrated. Another part was terrified.

The tractor trailer that hit them had hit the passenger side of the large SUV. Morgan's mother had been directly in the giant vehicle's path as it skidded and bore down on them. Twelve tons of metal gone wildly out of control on a narrow back-country road it had no business being on.

Mrs. Cahill never had a chance. Paige's father, the former district attorney and newly-elected congressman had taken up the challenge, vowing to see the driver charged with everything but the Kennedy assassination.

Paige took a more restrained view of the tragedy. The man had come to visit them in the hospital with tears in his eyes. Apparently, the use of Route 26, though prohibited, was common and had the unexpected snow squall never materialized no one would have been the wiser. The man had four children and worked two jobs to make ends meet—at least that's what her father had told her. Accidents were just that.

That was why they're called accidents. Paige had grown up, emerging from the shelter of the cocoon she had dwelled in, pandered and protected by her parents and Candy. Since Morgan had come into her life she'd even managed to gain some perspective on the accident at the jumping trials. She wanted no retribution to be extracted from the driver.

She sighed, trying to think of how to tell him that two months after he'd lost his father the mother he'd doted on and protected like a guardian angel was dead. Other than his aunt in Springfield, Morgan was all alone. Paige promised herself she would be everything that he'd ever…

"Aaah…" he groaned. When she turned, Morgan fumbled with the call button. When he saw Paige, a smile spread across his face. "Hi," he managed in a hoarse whisper.

"Hi back at ya," she stammered. Her stomach did somersaults while she tried to decide what to do—how to deliver the news.

A nurse appeared at the door looking confused. "Excuse me, Ms. Fuller, but we have a problem downstairs."

Paige smiled at Morgan and squeezed his hand then walked to the door.

"A problem? What kind of problem?"

"There's a man at information who said he wants to see Morgan…Mr. Cahill, but we only allow family while someone is in intensive care, or in your case when we have written permission."

"All right. Well Morgan's father died on nine-eleven and he has no male relatives," Paige explained politely as the nurse peered around her. "So I don't see how that could be true."

"Well, this man said that Mr. Cahill was adopted and…"

"That's true but so what?" Paige interrupted impatiently.

"He says he's Mr. Cahill's real father."

Paige stood, mouth open. She shook her head as she glanced back at Morgan who'd already fallen back into a deep sleep after a brief moment of awareness.

"All right. Let me go down and see him." Paige had no idea who the man was or what his game was. Perhaps part of her father's cynicism had rubbed off, but she could immediately see half a dozen possibilities. Morgan was alone. The surviving scion of a wealthy Boston family. While she didn't take her dad's jaundiced cynical view of humanity she was no fool. As soon as word got out about the accident and his mother's death, Paige could imagine people coming out of the dark to claim some relationship for the potential gain it might engender.

"Can I get you a wheelchair?" the nurse asked.

"No." Paige shook her head. She'd learned from her father, too. That would put her at a disadvantage, and she wanted to confront this imposter face to face. She hobbled down the hall to the elevator concerned Morgan would be alone if he awoke again. But Paige had appointed herself his unofficial guardian, and she was determined to put this imposter, whoever he was, in his place.

Chapter 49

Paige pushed her way through the crowd when the elevator stopped. She was on a mission. The nurse who'd ridden down with her directed her to a man sitting with his back to them on one of the sterile utilitarian sofas that populated the generous waiting area. She managed her way clumsily using a cane. By the time she reached the man the nurse had pointed to, Paige's anger had grown into focused fury.

But as she came around the sofa and saw the man she stopped suddenly.

"You," she said quietly when she saw his face. "I know you. I've seen you around The Stadium. Morgan introduced us."

He fidgeted, touching his face and looking nervous and out of place. "Yes. I remember. You're Paige." He worked at a smile and held out his hand. "Ezra Wilson," he managed after wetting his lips. If he was a con man, he was doing a poor job.

Paige studied his face. She was no great judge of character, but she saw no false bravado or pretense in his nervous gestures.

She held out her hand and took his, shaking it. "Hi, Ezra." She nodded. "Ah, I know you and Morgan spent some time together, but there's a misunderstanding." She gestured toward the information desk and forced a smile. "They said you claimed to be Morgan's real father?"

He put his hand to his mouth, studied the floor and then directed his gaze at her. "I'm…I'm sorry, Paige. I'm not sure what's best for Morgan, but there's no misunderstanding." He paused and swallowed deeply. It was cool in the massive lobby but a telltale sign of perspiration showed at the man's hairline. "For better or worse it's true."

And as she watched him, studied him, his expressions, his features, she knew. This man was no gold digger, no opportunist. She could see Morgan in everything about him from his solid build to the cleft chin and blue-gray eyes that held hers.

She sat down next to him and smiled softly, instinctively taking his hand. Paige had no idea where this would lead or how it would play out but something, somewhere in the recesses of her mind told her she needed to listen.

"I love Morgan very much, Ezra." She brushed aside the tears that had begun to overflow. "And if you're willing. I'd like to hear your story…."

****

Paige stood at his bedside, holding his hand as he faded in and out of consciousness. Her parents, Candy, and Ben surrounded him.

"I told you. I believed him, Daddy." She'd been having a running debate with her father about her thirty minute encounter with Ezra Wilson.

"I'm sure he was very convincing and when Morgan is up to it in a few weeks, it'll be up to him to decide what to do. But until that time, it's our duty as the only people who are close to protect him."

"I had the same misgivings, but he showed me no

evidence he was driven by greed or anything other than his need to reconnect with his son now that his adoptive parents are dead," she said firmly. If Ezra was putting on an act, he was doing a good job. "He said he wants nothing but to be there if Morgan needs him."

He looked at the others. All showed skeptical faces. "I'll call in some favors and do a background check on him."

Paige bit her tongue, knowing that what he'd confessed would alienate him from her father and the rest of her family. Fifteen years at the state maximum security prison would be a shaky foundation to build a relationship on. She had no idea what his crime was, but it wasn't shoplifting if he'd spent a decade and a half at Walpole.

"What if you don't like what you find out?"

"Paige, be reasonable, dear. This man appears out of nowhere, conveniently after Morgan becomes the heir to a substantial fortune," her mother chimed in.

"All right," Paige agreed, holding up her hands in surrender still unable to shake the feeling that what Ezra Wilson said about his reasons for wanting to see Morgan were genuine. "But no matter what his background or where he came from, he seemed sincere. I would never want to stop Morgan from meeting his real father."

Candy came around the bed and put her arm around Paige's shoulder. "I think for now we need to worry about how he'll react when he finds out about his mother."

Everyone nodded in solemn agreement.

But Paige stood wondering if that blow might be softened if Morgan knew that he wasn't without a family. That someone who cared and seemed to love him might still be in his life?

Chapter 50

Ezra sat glued once again to the six o'clock news. He patiently awaited another meeting with Paige Fuller. Morgan had great taste. She was not only the cutest thing on two legs, Paige was one of the most genuine and thoughtful people he'd ever met. She could have blown him out of the water easily. Her family name was iconic, and her father was a big deal. A famous DA for twenty-five years and now a congressman who'd wasted no time in getting his name in the press. She had no reason to listen to or even meet with Ezra, but she did. But tonight the headlines drew him away from his personal problems.

"Earth to Ezra!" Karen bent over and kissed his ear. A delicious combination of tomato sauce, onions, and her perfume did their best to pull his attention away. He sat frozen.

She came around the couch and plopped down next to him with a thud.

"Ten weeks and I'm already old news?" she teased, taking his hand.

He shifted his gaze and found her lips. They were soft, sweet, and very spicy tonight.

"No, I promise. You're the best thing that's happened to me in decades," he assured her. "But have you heard the latest?"

"Latest?"

"About the ex-cons?"

"Ezra, what are you talking about?"

It had been on his mind for two weeks. Ever since the visit from the state police detectives and the discovery of the fourth mutilated body of a Walpole parolee near the Fenway in the Back Bay.

"Look, remember you asked me about this once? Kidded if I was nervous 'cause three ex-cons had gone missing?"

She sat up wearing a thoughtful expression. "Yeah. I do."

"Well last week they found another guy. That's what those cops were here about. No specifics but it sounds like he didn't go easily. Ritualistic was the word they used on the news. Like someone was sending a message and he had a number four carved into his chest. They're telling us now that the earlier guys had numbers, too."

Karen put her hand to her mouth. "God, that sounds awful. Do they have any ideas as to who or why someone would want to do that? What did the state police say?"

"No leads at all, or so they say."

"Ez, are you worried?"

"No. Not about me." He shook his head, taking her hand. "But here's the thing. I knew these guys. They were thugs, bullies. Could make your life a living hell."

"And so…? I hate to be callous but maybe the world is better off without…"

He nodded vigorously. "No argument but last night they found someone else. And this person wasn't a con or a bad dude. At least not that I know of."

"So what's that have to do with a bunch of ex-con

career criminals?"

"She was a big-time lawyer. A defense attorney."

"Okay, so she didn't get the local head of the Mafia acquitted or double-crossed some big-time hood." Karen shrugged. "Not saying it isn't a tragedy but…"

Ezra held up his hand. There was something eerily familiar about these four convicts and the lawyer. Something they had in common. But it remained in the darkness…just beyond his reach and that was what was so troubling. He was tempted to call Paul Winston but had nothing specific to offer. But somehow, he had a terrifying feeling these deaths were not only related but he was getting a sick, sinking feeling he knew the architect of the massacre. "She was tortured, too. Like the others."

"All right, maybe it's a coincidence."

"I don't think so. She had the number five carved in her chest," he said as he pictured Julian Warren running away and hiding after Malcolm Cahill's funeral. He had to think more about it, but he was terrified he knew why the fragile inmate he'd helped save was there…

Chapter 51

Morgan sat in the visiting area on the sixth floor, staring out the window still trying to come to grips with all that had happened in the last three months. He'd lost both his parents and the injuries he'd suffered meant that his promising intercollegiate athletic career might be at an end.

He wasn't angry or depressed, though those emotions would have been the logical reactions for someone who'd held the world within his grasp only to have it vanish like smoke. No, those feelings would have been a relief of sorts. Instead numbness, an almost disembodied sensation consumed him.

But then, of course, he had Paige, the beacon that kept him from surrendering into a state of misery, depression, and oblivion. She had been there throughout the weeks of his slow rehabilitation and return to life. Others—teammates, classmates, the Fullers, would drop by frequently offering him encouragement and pledges of undying loyalty but it was Paige, only Paige, who kept him from screaming at the gods and cursing them for teasing him, offering him so much, only to snatch it from his grasp.

A gentle knock brought him back to the present, the reality of what his life would be from now on.

"Hi," she whispered. "Remember me?"

He turned in his wheelchair and took in the face

that kept him getting up each morning, going to therapy, sweating and straining to return to a semblance of what he once was…what he could have been.

"You're late," he said with a smile.

"Traffic getting up here was a bear." She shook her head and showed him the picture-book smile that he waited for every afternoon. "And some of us don't have a life of leisure."

He snorted. "I'll be back to fighting form in no time."

She crossed the few feet and bent, finding his lips. The kiss began in a friendly way, a gesture of welcome and affection. But as had always been the case when they were anywhere close, it grew passionate and intense in a matter of seconds.

She backed away, her face flushed as she caught her breath. "Now, let's not get carried away," she whispered self-consciously. "You still need time to get better."

He nodded and took her hand. "I just want it to be like it was between us, Paige." He searched her eyes. "Promise this won't change anything."

She found a chair and pushed it next to him. "There's nothing short of death that would ever change what we have," she reassured him. "What we are together."

He put his hand to her face and touched the scar from the accident. "I'm so sorry about that."

"I've told you, if you apologize one more time I'll get up and leave. Right now! Damn it, Morg. It was not your fault." She put on a frown but he could see right through it and he laughed softly. "Besides they tell me with some plastic surgery I'll be good as new. I've thought of running for Miss America. Whaddaya think?"

"You'd win hands down," he said managing a quiet laugh. They sat for minutes, knees touching, fingers locked together tightly, Paige gently caressing his hand. "I'm here to tell you Mom and Daddy insist you recuperate at the farm. I know you missed Christmas, but we'll have a lifetime of Christmases. My dad's in Washington a lot and Candy's away at Columbia, so I'm just plain lonely."

"Only if you promise to dress up in a sexy nurse's outfit and answer my *every* need, no matter how strange or demanding."

"Darling, you know I will never be more than a few feet away from you for as long as we live." She touched his forearm. The electricity worked up to his shoulder as she did. "Do you remember that first weekend?"

"I spend my downtime fantasizing about it…" It was Morgan's turn to blush.

"Well you told me when we both thought I was going to Australia that someday you might have to leave me, too."

He nodded and squeezed her hand.

"I have to tell you that you were gone for almost a month and I—don't—like—it!" She gave him the signature giggle he'd fallen in love with on that long sultry weekend in June. "So, don't ever do it again!"

Morgan swallowed deeply after listening to her. He'd been wanting to ask her that special question since the summer. Morgan had no idea when there would ever be a good time so he blurted it out. "Paige, I have never in my entire life met anyone who fulfilled me the way you do. Someone who was a part of me the way you've become so…"

He was sure she knew what was coming. "Yes…?"

"And I know we have so much ahead of us that no one can foresee but…"

Tears filled her eyes and she moved as close as possible taking both his hands in hers. "Oh, Morgan. Of course I'll marry you." She stood and bent over, hugging him tightly.

"Oh," he teased. "I was only going to ask you for a soda."

She swatted his arm and they laughed out loud. "Yes…yes…yes! But when you're back on your feet I expect a formal proposal. On your knees with a ring!"

Maybe there was a silver lining to the cloud that had hung over him since September.

****

Sophie closed the door on the tiny closet in their basement. "Your little friend is going to enjoy the nice space we've set up for her."

Julian studied her, then the small cell. It looked medieval. Manacles, straw on the floor, a thick noose suspended in the center. A strange gleam shone in her amber eyes. He'd seen it before. He was exacting revenge. She was enjoying their unholy crusade. He recalled how she'd left their fourth victim hanging for an hour. Long after he was dead, face bluish and swollen, while she studied the man. Julian hated their victims. Sophie reveled in this quest, and he knew she had some deranged scheme in mind for Paige.

"Paige is to be the lure, the incentive to draw Fuller here."

"You call her by name all the time." She stopped.

Julian felt her stare. "You do recall Alexander, don't you?" she asked pointedly with a patronizing smile while she positioned the video camera they intended to use to take video footage of the poor girl to force her father to come, to sacrifice himself to save Paige's life. But Julian knew that unless he intervened, Sophie would not only kill Fuller but his daughter as well. And by the cruel look in her eyes, Paige would not be dispatched any too quickly.

Her reference to Alexander, the name of Julian's favorite pet, a tiny cocker spaniel that had an unfortunate *accident* recalled bitter memories. Julian had never been certain about the poor little fellow's demise, but Sophie's reference to him erased any lingering doubt. Sophie's jealousy had been the cause of his death. And what she was telling him of course was that should he indulge or show any kindness or mercy to their young hostage—the bait to attract their final victim, she too would befall a cruel, perhaps even more sadistic fate.

"Yes, of course I do, my dear." He found her eyes and fixed them with a purpose. "I would suggest that Paige not befall the same tragic end." He took her slender arm and twisted it painfully till she winced.

Sophie refused to give him the satisfaction of registering any pain but looked away having read the message in his eyes. "I understand, *dear*."

Chapter 52

Paige turned her red VW Beetle into the long driveway that lead to her family's estate. She let go of Morgan's hand since there were several sharp turns in the first quarter mile and both of them had learned a cruel lesson about concentrating on their driving on that slick night of Thanksgiving weekend.

"The doctor says you should be back in the gym by late February," she said confidently in her ongoing attempt to buoy his sagging spirits.

Morgan was silent then nodded stoically. "So he tells me."

She stole a glance in his direction thinking how strange and cruel fate, the gods, or whomever arranged the chaos of the universe could be. Six months ago he'd arrived at this same place…driven down this very road holding the world and his future in his hands. And though neither of them could have suspected it, Paige's, too. Now, the athletic career he'd coveted and perhaps even his dream of one day studying distant worlds from space had all but vanished. Sometimes, it seemed to Paige that Morgan was letting that happen. She refused to let it. Morgan had taken her from the depths of despair and pulled her into a world of love and beauty and confidence. Everything her life had lacked. Paige loved him so much she owed it to him to return the favor.

"Morg," she began, knowing what she had planned for this weekend was taking a massive gamble. Her parents, Candy, and her best friend Francie thought Paige had lost her mind. But Morgan needed something. A jolt to reawaken the *joie de vie* that had filled him till the fall's events had robbed him of it. "There's someone I want you to meet this weekend. Someone special that I think may be able to help you."

He cast a forlorn sideways glance her way, shaking his head slowly. "Please, Paige. No more shrinks, psychs, or other well-intentioned do-gooders."

She stopped the car at the spot where they'd first met. "Do you remember that first day? You kept trying to get my attention and I ran off, escaping to the stables."

"Yep." He looked around at the light cover of snow resting on the icy surface that now covered the stalks of grass on the open fields. "Thinking about you and how we met is all that keeps me going some days."

He leaned over to give her a kiss but she backed away. "The person I want you to meet isn't a doctor or shrink, Morg. You already know him. Just not in the way that you..." Paige stopped. Hesitant as she tried to describe what she had in mind. "You should."

He leaned back against the passenger door, a curious, almost suspicious look on his face. "What's going on, Paige?" He shook his head. "I've had enough counseling and well-intentioned pats on the back to last me a lifetime." A tired, strained look crossed his face. "This isn't one of those gurus, you know, the Wayne Dyer types who are going to bring me back to life by meditation or—"

"Not one of those either. I promise," Paige

interrupted angrily, putting her car in gear as she headed toward the main house half a mile ahead. "Jesus, Morgan. When I met you in June you were bigger than life. A legend. Now you're acting like some spoiled kid who didn't get dessert!" She put her lips together then continued. "I know you've been through hell! But I love you for Christ's sake. I've never loved anyone else and I never will. Now what the *fuck!* You helped me escape that chrysalis I was imprisoned in. I want to do the same for you."

"I'm telling you, Paige. I'm tired and sore and so confused my head is spinning so please no more *pleasant surprises*," he responded with equal and unexpected anger.

"Deal," she promised him as they pulled up in front of the large granite pediment that lead to the massive double doors.

As she put the Beetle into park and turned it off, the entry doors opened. Morgan turned toward the entrance and spotted a man heading toward him.

"What the hell?" He looked back at Paige, a mixture of curiosity and apprehension showing on his face. "Isn't that Ezra? The guy from the Stadium ground crew?"

"Yes," Paige acknowledged. "It's Ezra. Ezra Wilson."

"Okay. Has he gone into the counseling business on the side?" Morgan asked with a snide tone as he looked back at the man approaching. "Come in. Game's over. What's he doing here?"

"He came to spend the weekend with his family. He only has one surviving relative. And I thought— hoped maybe talking with him could help you," Paige said quietly, waving at Ezra as he stood next to the small vehicle shivering in the cold wind blowing in from Buzzards Bay.

"I'm totally confused." Morgan shot a look at Paige then back at Ezra. "Do we know his family?"

"Yes, very well, Morg." She took his hand and squeezed it as Ezra forced a smile and opened the door. "He's your father. Your real father, Morgan. And his only living relative is you."

****

Ninety minutes after the revelation at the Fullers' front door, a non-descript black panel van took the turn into their long gravel driveway. Sophie sat behind the wheel. Both she and Julian had on dark clothing and ski masks sat in their respective laps to be used when they arrived at the Fuller house.

"So just your little sweetheart and the kid are at the house?" Sophie asked quietly.

"How many times do I have to tell you? Yes." Julian was growing impatient with her. He had made up his mind a few days before. He would take Paige but do her no harm. Something in her innocence and beauty had consumed him. Sophie would be the one who'd become expendable.

"The congressman and his wife are in Washington, the sister is still at Columbia, and this is the staff's night off. They will be alone." He repeated the location of the cast of characters for the fifth time. "The boy is recovering from a serious auto accident for Christ's sake. I will disarm the alarm circuit, we'll be inside, give him a strong sedative if we need to, and then take the girl. We'll wait till the middle of the night when they're completely asleep."

"Why not just kill the kid?"

"I have told you that a dozen times, too!" Julian did his best to stay calm and keep Sophie from engaging in more of the sadistic blood rage she had grown so fond of over the course of their vendetta. "There is no need for that. He can do us no harm. He'll never know we were there. Why take the chance? In and out! The more people we kill, the more angry and frustrated the cops and the world gets. Why anger them any more?"

"Because you're leaving someone alive who'll get stronger and hound you till he finds us. You don't think taking the love of his young life may arouse some anger?"

"Not if we're ten thousand miles away and he has no idea who, where, or what we are."

"But…" she began.

"Shut up, Sophie. Just drive the damn van! I'll repeat: we'll wait till the middle of the night when they're both asleep and out of it. With any luck we may not even have to sedate the boy. We'll be in and out before he knows what happened."

She gave him a scowl and hit the accelerator. "Just remember I warned you. Loose ends like this will come back to haunt you. Haunt us."

Julian would hear no more of her complaints and incessant groaning. She was jealous of the mental attachment Julian had formed for the girl. But taking Fuller's only daughter, his favorite by all accounts and everything Julian had read and seen, would be punishment enough. Paige would be made to understand. She was giving herself to him as a payment for her father's life. In time she would grow to understand. Julian could see to that. He had his ways.

Sadly his lover would have to suffer the consequences of her unwillingness to recognize the new dynamic in their situation. Julian pictured Paige in his mind's eye and smiled broadly. Had he planned this it could have turned out no better.

Chapter 53

They sat in her father's study. Morgan Cahill, all-Ivy tailback; Paige Fuller, award-winning show jumper and concert pianist; and Ezra Wilson, convicted murderer. A fire blazed warmly but he could find no joy in his heart. Ezra sat quietly, staring back and forth between his son and Paige. In the weeks between hearing his shocking pronouncement and the subsequent talks in the Cambridge coffee shop that served as their rendezvous, Ezra had opened up to Paige, telling her things he'd never shared with anyone. She seemed to encourage frank and open dialogue. He told her things about his life, thoughts, and secrets he had never imagined sharing. At their first impromptu meeting Ezra immediately saw what his son had seen in this sweet, pretty young woman. She was the least judgmental and most compassionate person Ezra had ever met.

She had been the one who'd decided on this clandestine reunion at her home in Mattapoisett. At some point, despite her parents' strenuous objections, Paige had come to the conclusion that Ezra and Morgan had to meet. Ezra was sure that her parents must have raised holy hell when she suggested this sit down. He had no idea what else to call it. But she had held her ground or perhaps simply gone ahead and made the arrangements without their permission.

After getting weak-kneed when hearing who and what Ezra was, Morgan had made a modest recovery. Now he sat staring into the embers of the small fire that imparted an eerily cheery feeling to the austere wood-paneled den and the chill that pervaded this surreal confrontation.

Morgan turned to face Ezra. "I'm assuming there's some long, soul-searching explanation as to why I've never heard of you and why you and my mother gave me up for adoption."

Ezra looked at Paige. When she shrugged he saw no reason to sugar coat the truth. "Neither long-winded nor soul-searching, Morgan." He fixed his son's eyes with his. "It's really quite simple. Your mother and I were drugged-up petty criminals. She and her latest boyfriend came at me one night with a butcher knife and a meat cleaver."

Morgan's eyes grew wide as he sat up and swallowed. "Really. And…so?"

"I defended myself. I'd been a marine instructor in self-defense and as fate would have it on that particular Saturday night I wasn't stoned or coked out of my mind. They were so…" He hesitated. "It wasn't much of a struggle. I went to prison for it…."

Morgan closed his eyes. When he opened them, he wore a look of recognition and resignation.

"Those terrible dreams you've had for years, Morg?" Paige said in a voice barely above a whisper. "When I heard Ezra…your dad, explain what happened I knew right away. They were repressed memories of that terrible night."

"Well." Morgan stood and approached the fireplace, leaning against it and facing away from Paige

317

and Ezra. "At least that answers one of the big questions in my life. So you're a murderer and spent time in jail and yet somehow Paige thought this would what? Give me hope for the future?"

He turned and shook his head. Anger and disbelief showed in equal parts on his face. "So you two set up this…this intimate meet-and-greet thinking that I'd walk over, hug you, and say, 'Hi Dad, you may have killed my mother and spent years in prison, but it's really great to meet you?'"

Morgan looked back at the fire as he picked up the poker and moved a few of the embers.

"Look, son…Morgan, if my calling you 'son' makes you uncomfortable. Paige thought it might help you to know you still had a living relative." Ezra paused. "Even if it's an ex-con like me."

"I guess it's gonna take some time to sink in."

Morgan turned and studied Ezra's face. "How would you feel? In three months I lost two of the most loving and devoted parents a person could ever have. And now…"

Ezra stood and held up his hands in surrender. "I really appreciate what you tried to do for Morgan and me, Paige." He shook his head. "But he's right. Morgan's been through hell since nine-eleven. And we've just delivered a major kick to the head. You're replacing two perfect parents with the man who spent fifteen years in Walpole for killing his mother."

****

Paige watched Morgan hobble up the stairs, walk down the long hallway, and slam the door of the bedroom they'd come to think of as his. Tears ran down her cheeks, and she brushed them aside, looking at

Ezra, doing her best to muster a smile.

"I really thought he was a bigger person than that, Ezra." She swallowed deeply and shook her head. "That it would be good for him to…"

Ezra held up his hand and came to stand next to her, putting his arm gently around her. "Don't sell him down the river yet." He squeezed her shoulder. "He needs time to process what we've thrown at him."

"Was I wrong?" she asked, looking into Ezra's eyes. "Should I have just let him go on feeling sorry for himself?"

"No," he whispered, offering her a confident smile. "He's better than that. And you, Paige. You're the best thing that ever happened to him."

"I wish I could believe that." She shook her head. "I thought I knew him, but since the accident?"

"Shhh," Ezra reassured her. "When the chips are down, Morgan'll come around."

"I know you're right. He's the most—the most amazing man I've ever known." She gave him a smile. "Now," she said taking his hand. "Do you mind staying down here in the servants' wing? I feel guilty about it."

"Paige. Please. I'm not the kind of house guest your folks are used to having." He let go of her hand, managing a smile. "My stuff is down the hall. I'll be fine."

"Okay. Just call me if you need anything."

****

Ezra lay on the bed, lights off, wishing he felt confident about what he'd told Paige. The clock said one thirty, and he felt stressed and exhausted, but sleep refused to come. He turned onto his side, reliving that terrifying night that had changed so much in so many lives. Jo Ann had gone out and he'd stayed home with Elias, the three-year-old son he adored. The boy who'd be turning four soon, and Ezra had promised himself he'd give the kid the best birthday party ever.

He'd made up his mind to leave Jo Ann. He knew she was seeing some other guy, and she was useless around the house. Something—maybe his affection for his young son—had given Ezra the strength to spend less time doing drugs. He'd found a decent job with a local landscaper and even seemed to have a flair for it. Jo Ann continued to spend most of her time coked up, drinking, or high on something else.

Ezra fell asleep on the couch watching the Red Sox about ten thirty, only to be wakened sometime later by the clatter as Jo Ann stumbled in the front door. She was loud and had brought home the guy she was hanging around with. They were both drunk and stoned out of their minds.

He remembered the screaming, the mumbled threats as he looked at them. Her new friend was a big guy, but Ezra knew from his years as an instructor in the corps that the man was no threat so he got up, ignoring Jo Ann's rants as he went to shut Elias's bedroom door.

As he turned around, Jo Ann was coming at him yelling something as she brandished a kitchen knife while her new friend held something like a cleaver...

Suddenly a strange sound brought Ezra back. After the four years in the Marines as an NCO and fifteen at Walpole you had an instinct. A sixth sense and this sound didn't register as one he expected at the Fullers' home.

The sound was muffled, but it had the overtone of a

struggle. Not what he should be hearing in this opulent estate with only three people in it. Ezra moved stealthily off his bed and made his way to the door, opening it with no noise.

Yes…there it was again. A muffled cry and despite the muted tone he thought it was Paige's voice trying to be heard. He tiptoed down the long hallway of the servants' wing, and there standing at the base of the circular staircase was Paige.

Two individuals stood on either side of her both dressed in black and hooded, but she'd been tied and gagged. The smaller of the two kidnappers hissed, "Shut up, you spoiled little bitch!" and gave a tug on a collar or rope they had placed around Paige's neck. She coughed but tried to pull away. Despite the terrifying situation, Ezra had to admire her courage. Paige was no compliant victim, struggling and crying out violently despite her bindings and the gag.

Ezra assessed the situation at light-speed. She was the daughter of a very wealthy, influential man. He had no idea why these people were kidnapping her, but he saw no positive outcome. Instinct told him she would be leverage for some plan these devils had in mind but he couldn't imagine what. The same sixth sense told him that her father was the intended target—Paige was simply a pawn, but that did little to assuage his fear for her. In the few weeks he'd known her, Ezra had developed a strong, almost paternalistic affection for Paige. He had no intention of letting someone take her whatever their intentions.

Certain the kidnappers were well armed, Ezra stood in the shadows of the hallway and calculated where he could find a weapon—anything he could use.

As they pulled Paige toward the entry hall, Ezra heard a familiar voice. Suddenly his mind connected so many events that had seemed unrelated. He understood who these people were and why Paige was being kidnapped. Despite the cool air, Ezra felt beads of sweat run down his back. His stomach lurched knowing she'd meet a terrible fate if he failed to act quickly.

He sneaked back into the kitchen and spotted a long knife in a rack on the counter, grabbed it, then rushed back to the hallway to confront them. He was sure that his opponents had firearms, but Ezra would never let them take Paige. Not without a fight.

****

Paige did her best to halt the intruders who had burst into her room and bound her. She struggled against the rope the smaller one had placed around her neck. But when she did the collar tightened, strangling her.

She was terrified—had almost lost control of herself but after a minute of confusion and fear, Paige knew her best chance, perhaps her only chance, was to stay in control. Like on the jumping course when they raised the fences or moved the obstacles. You had to be ready to assess each new situation and react. Hot tears flowed onto her flushed cheeks but she bit down on the gag determined to stay…in…control.

She tried to think—to comprehend what they wanted and who they were. The few words spoken between them had given her no clue. One voice was female and harsh. The other was soft and male. The man had promised her everything would be all right. She had no intention of believing him and was determined to do everything she could to make noise and resist, hoping Morgan or Ezra might hear and call the police.

"She's being a pain in the ass! Use the sedative on her and let's get going." It was the woman who spoke. There was a cruel, menacing tone to her voice. Paige had no idea why.

"Look, Paige," the man said in a soothing, almost friendly voice. "We don't want to hurt you. Just go with us. I promise everything will be all right."

He knew her name and seemed gentler than his female companion. A thousand things flashed through Paige's mind, but that one drew her attention because she realized it might be useful. He almost sounded as if he knew her and was sympathetic to her plight despite causing it.

She did her best to mumble "Yes" through the gag, stopped struggling, and nodded when she spotted something on the far side of the large entry foyer. A reflection! It had to be Ezra. That was where he'd be coming from. Maybe all hope wasn't lost.

****

Morgan had awakened abruptly. It took a moment to remember where he was. But something had gained his attention despite his fitful sleep. It was the sound of a struggle and the muted cries were definitely female.

Paige! Something or someone was hurting her. Or was his imagination running wild? Could it be that like him she was troubled by the strange circumstances that had brought them together at her parents' home?

Before he had the chance to guess, he heard someone—it sounded like several people—going by his door. He arose and tiptoed to the door. His first thought was that Ezra was involved. That his whole appearance had been an act. A ruse to gain Paige's trust for some more sinister purpose, but when he sneaked open the door he caught sight of three figures heading down the stairs in the moonlight that shone through the skylights. And one was Paige. She was tied and from the sound of it had been gagged. The other two were clothed and covered in black, wearing ski masks.

When they had disappeared down the staircase, Morgan made his way down the hallway, hugging the inner wall so that no one could see him from below. As he approached the landing, muffled voices and the sound of a struggle reached him. Paige wasn't giving in without a fight. Neither would he. He saw a large metal sculpture that sat on a small table. He crept over to retrieve it. As long as Morgan drew breath, no one would take her.

****

Julian had done his best to convince Paige that she had nothing to fear. She didn't. At least not from him. But Sophie was enjoying Paige's captivity far too much. He intended to put a stop to it.

"Let go of that rope!" he commanded as he yanked at it in Sophie's hand. "She's not a dog to be pulled on a leash."

Sophie held tightly to the rope that was fastened like a noose around Paige's neck then gave it a yank, causing Paige to stumble and choke.

"Give me the damn rope!" Julian ordered a second time and slowly brought his 9 MM automatic up and pointed it in Sophie's general direction.

"You stupid little fool! I knew it. You've got a crush on her," she hissed, holding tightly to the rope, pulling it higher so Paige was choking. "Yes, you're sweet on this stupid spoiled little thing, aren't you?"

Just as he was about to answer, the air was cleft by the sound of an object flying by. It smashed violently into the elaborate crystal chandelier over their heads. Bits of broken glass and light bulbs rained down on them.

"Let her go!" A voice demanded from the upstairs hallway. "I have my cell phone and have already called nine-one-one. The game is over."

"It's the damn kid, Julian!" Sophie exclaimed in anger. "I warned you. You stupid fool! You should have taken care of him when we were upstairs!"

"It would have done no good, Julian," another voice echoed from the rear of the entry hall as a figure emerged from the shadows. "Because he's not alone and I've called the state police, too."

"Ezra?" Julian managed as he stared in disbelief. "What…what are you doing here?"

"That girl you're trying to kidnap is going to be my daughter-in-law."

"Your daughter-in-law?" Julian asked in confusion.

"I don't believe any of you!" Sophie screamed. "We're going to take her, and you'll never find her!" She put a gun to Paige's head and yanked on the rope again as Paige staggered and coughed weakly.

"No, I don't think you are," a soft voice said from behind.

When they turned a tall, lanky man in his sixties stood, flanked by another, younger man. Both held large automatic weapons pointed directly at Sophie.

"Now, release that rope and let Paige come to me before we have to do something we regret."

Julian stood frozen, but his angry accomplice

screamed, "Damn you all!" and lifted her smaller automatic. As she did both men at the door fired. She fell, clutching her chest as blood pooled at her lips and onto the ornate terrazzo floor.

Ezra ran at Julian, hitting him in the kidneys and grabbed his weapon as he fell, crying like a baby and mumbling, "Sophie..." as he lay on the floor, crawling and sobbing like a child as he hung over his lover's lifeless corpse.

It was over.

Chapter 54

Morgan held Paige so tightly she thought she might suffocate. She purred contentedly in his arms, loving every minute. She dug her nails into the back of his Harvard T-shirt sobbing, partly from relief, partly a delayed reaction to the events of the last hour.

A state police detective named Paul Winston had interviewed her and taken her statement about the specifics of how the two intruders had broken into the house and tried to kidnap her. He explained that they'd been involved in killing five others and told her she was fortunate to have the small army of rescuers that had foiled their plans. It would take some time before the reality of how close she'd come to a terrifying and cruel fate sank in.

Paramedics examined her, telling her that they wanted her to spend the night at the hospital. Paige had abrasions and rope burns where they had tied her. They examined her throat, telling her she needed to have it x-rayed and checked out by a doctor because of the woman pulling on it and choking her. Despite the protestations from Morgan and Sam, she stubbornly refused.

She avoided any look at the body of her cruel female captor, now covered as men from the medical examiner's office lifted her onto a gurney. Her mother's expensive terrazzo floor was covered with pools of blood. The woman leading the crew had ordered endless photos as others now attempted to soak up the pooled blood and clean the frightening reminder of the terrifying few minutes of her captivity.

She had rushed to Morgan who suddenly wore the look of the warrior again. Her captivity had awakened the old instincts that had made him so successful. Paige could see it in his steel-gray eyes. She could not have been happier...though she would have chosen a less violent way to give his flagging confidence re-birth.

She had approached Sam and held him tightly, thanking him and his friend.

"Well, to tell you the truth, Miss Paige. We were here 'cause your father wanted us to keep an eye on things," Sam admitted with embarrassment. "Think he was afraid that you had something in mind with Morgan's real father. But Lord knows, no one ever figured on anything like this."

****

"Morgan," she whispered as she stood, reluctantly releasing him. She turned so they faced Ezra Wilson, who drank coffee and sat disconsolately on the sofa in the study. His hands shook as coffee dribbled over the top of the generous earthenware mug. Lizbeth, who lived close by, had been summoned. She offered coffee and soft drinks to the large contingent of police and CSI techs as she clucked around, patting Paige and shaking her head and neck every time she was close.

"Come on..." Paige said taking Morgan's hand.

They walked, arms around each other, until they stood in front of Ezra. It took a moment. He seemed lost in thought, but Paige coughed discreetly. He turned his eyes upward to find them.

Paige let go of Morgan and closed the two feet to Ezra, holding out her hands. "Thank you for my life," she managed as tears overflowed and ran down her cheeks.

He stood and took her hands then surrounded her with his arms. "It was a group effort, Paige." He tightened his embrace as tears filled his eyes. "And your man here"—he nodded at Morgan—"got it started."

She backed away, still holding his hands in hers. Paige was amazed at the emotion being shown by this man who had been an inmate at the state's maximum security prison for a decade and a half.

"Yep, it was, but if you hadn't been here they would have taken me." She laughed self-consciously. "My dad asked Sam to be here. I suspect it may have been because of you." Paige shook her head. "Funny how things turn out."

Suddenly she felt Morgan's arms around her.

He reached out with his hands and grasped hers and Ezra's. "Thanks…Dad."

"Hey, son. You were the one who threw that metal thing."

"But I knew you had my back, and I just knew you wouldn't let anything happen to Paige." Morgan tightened his grip on their hands.

"No, son." He shifted his gaze to find her eyes. "I would never let anything happen to Paige."

They all backed away, standing mute. Paige had no idea what to say. She hoped desperately that Morgan could find forgiveness in his heart.

"Well, look," Ezra began. "I'll be leaving you in the morning if Paige can give me a ride to the bus station. Let you two kids enjoy the long weekend."

"What?" Morgan said in a confrontational way. "No way. You're not getting away that easy. Paige makes the best French toast and pancakes you've ever tasted, and I'm a whiz with the scrambled eggs, but we need some help with the bacon."

Ezra showed a smile, sniffled again, and offered, "I think I can handle that."

Chapter 55

Around noon the next day, the front door flew open and Candy rushed in, tears in her eyes. "Paige!"

Seeing her coming out of the kitchen, she ran to her sister and took her in her arms so tightly she heard Paige gasp. "How many times are you going to pull these stunts?" Candy demanded as she shook with sobs. "The jumping accident, the car crash, and now practically getting...getting kidnapped. Do I have to stand next to you all the time to keep you safe?"

Paige managed to pull away and found Candy's eyes. "I think you ought to give it a try," she answered with a laugh as tears rolled down her cheeks, too.

"When Daddy called me, I couldn't believe this was really happening. Poor Daddy. He feels so guilty." Candy shook her head. "Like these lunatics breaking in was somehow his fault."

"I know. When he called he must have said 'I'm sorry' twenty times in five minutes."

"Where are they, by the way?" Candy asked, scanning the house. "I thought for sure they'd be here by now."

"Weather. A major sleet storm has everything grounded in the Capitol," Paige explained.

Candy stood just watching Paige, thinking how much the baby sister who'd secretly arrived one night when she was only a toddler had come to mean so much to her. Only her parents, Robbie, and one other person knew that Paige was not a Fuller by birth. But Candy remembered treating her and fawning over her like a doll. Candy had never adored anything or anyone the way she did Paige.

But when her sister had used the word guilt, Candy wondered if it was true confessions time. Her father was not the only one who was haunted by something. On the five-hour drive from New York City, Candy thought it was time to tell Paige the truth. She had come so close to losing her adopted baby sister three times in the last two years. What she had to tell Paige needed to be said.

She approached Paige and took her by the shoulders. "Paige I have something I have to tell you."

"Okay. What?" Paige asked with a hesitant expression. "Just as long as it's not bad news or some revelation that will bring me down. I've had enough angst to last me a lifetime."

As she studied Paige, facing her looking tentative and unsure she knew. It might clear her own conscience. Paige was so kind and so caring. Telling her after all these years might finally give Candy some closure. What would it do to Paige?

Laughter carried from the kitchen. She heard Sam, Morgan, Lizbeth, and at least one other man. Perhaps the cliché was right and confession was good for the soul but would it only bring on more heartache? Candy sighed deeply and looked into her sister's eyes, knowing the answer. She hesitated then blurted out, "Ben's asked me to marry him."

"Oh my God. That is so exciting!" Paige looked around and took her sister aside, adding, "I haven't told anyone yet, but Morgan's asked me, too."

Paige giggled and surrounded Candy with her arms.

"What do you say we make it a double ceremony…save Daddy and Vera some money?" Candy whispered.

"Sounds like a plan." Paige beamed as she turned Candy and took her hand. "I want you to meet Ezra."

Candy swallowed and felt both relief and a strange sense of disappointment. She had waited so long. Now she realized it had been too long…

When Robbie had jumped in the stream to save Paige, no one knew that Candy had jumped in too—to help him. He managed to throw Paige to the bank but as he did, Candy tripped and fell face down in the water. She struggled and screamed trying desperately to get some footing, but though the water was shallow, she kept slipping on the moss-covered rocks. Robbie pulled her up and placed her on the riverbank next to Paige who lay crying, coughing up water.

As he was about to call for help, Candy spotted her favorite doll—one she had brought to their impromptu picnic—floating away.

"Emma," she cried out, pointing to her toy.

"It's okay. I'll get her," Robbie promised Candy as he turned and headed back into the shallow stream. It was then that he slipped on a rock and fell, hitting his head. Robbie lay face down as the swift current pulled him away. When her father and Sam found them, Paige blurted out that he had fallen after rescuing her. Candy said nothing. It had held her captive for more than a decade…

She wanted to be rid of the guilt. And while the

revelation might clear her conscience and give Candy closure, it would devastate Paige and could well alienate her and turn a loving relationship into something bitter. To know that after years of sadness and regret the big sister who adored her had kept silent about the most tragic event in her life would serve no purpose. Perhaps it was her desire to keep Paige from being hurt, perhaps it was part cowardice. Whatever the truth, as she entered the warm fragrant kitchen, Candy knew it was a secret she would keep to herself.

****

If Paige needed one final thing to cement her confidence, she found it late one hot August afternoon. As she scurried around the mall looking for things to decorate her dorm room at Brown, she spotted a tall figure standing in front of Starbucks sipping on a coffee.

She hesitated, staring at the girl she thought of as her nemesis. When Monique Burke lifted her gaze and saw Paige she froze. Paige could have turned and walked away. But she'd spent too many hours fantasizing about confronting Monique. Time to finish this. Paige took a deep breath and swallowed, then walked with a purpose toward the girl who continued staring at her.

"Hello, Monique," Paige said as she stopped.

At first Monique wore a confused expression, apparently unable to decide what Paige's motive was. Was this to be a long overdue confrontation? The final chapter in their lifelong feud? She fidgeted with her free hand, dumping her coffee in the trash barrel next to her while never taking her eyes off Paige.

"Hi, Paige," she said quietly. "I heard about what

happened at your house. It must have been awful." Monique shook her head disconsolately, whispering, "Sorry. I…I should have called you."

Paige kept staring. "It made for a great story to tell at parties," she said after a long pause. "But it was so terrifying when it was happening," she added as she shivered at the frightening memory.

Monique sighed. Her shoulders had been tense and stiff, but as Paige watched, they slumped. Monique bit her lip and opened her mouth to speak as she closed the two feet between them. "Paige, I," she began quietly. "I've always wanted to…to say that I'm sorry about the…accident. I mean I…" her words trailed off.

Paige watched Monique's face turn pale as her eyes welled up with tears that slipped down her cheeks. Her rival's gaze shifted to the tile floor. Was this a confession… Monique's clumsy attempt at an apology? It was too long ago and it was over. Suddenly Paige realized as she studied the girl she'd envied and feared for so long, that all she felt was pity.

"I hear you're going to Boston College this fall," Paige said after taking a deep breath. The tension was broken. "I'm going to Brown."

"So I've heard." Monique nodded. "That's great. You'll do real well. I hear they have a great riding program."

"Yep. Derek Talbot's the coach."

"Wow, that's awesome." Monique sounded genuinely impressed.

"Well, gotta go get some stuff for my dorm room," Paige said.

"Me, too," Monique said with a swallow, adding meekly, "Would you…you mind if I tagged along?"

Paige hesitated then nodded. "Not at all. I'd love some company."

Two hours later, they said good-bye in the parking lot. "Good luck, Monique," Paige said offering her hand.

Monique stopped for a minute, then approached Paige and embraced her. "You too, Paige. See you soon." And while she couldn't be sure, Paige thought she saw a tear as Monique ran off.

Paige walked slowly to her car shaking her head as a smile crossed her face. When trying to help Morgan's mother, Paige had read that getting angry, resentful, or losing your temper when dealing with those you fear or dislike gives them power over you. Having practiced it with Monique, Paige agreed.

Paige had finally exorcised her worst demon and like the frail child who finally knocks the chip off the bully's shoulder only to have the bully back down, she reveled in her triumph and control. When she returned home that night, she smiled as she picked up the small book that had seen her through so many highs and lows.

Dear Diary,

I haven't been with you for a while. Today I saw again that love and compassion is so much more powerful than hate or fear. Thank you...for always being there for me during those difficult, mixed up years. I will always treasure our friendship!

Paige

She smiled and reverently placed the worn leather volume in the secret hideaway of her desk as she let her hand gently work across its cover and closed the tiny lock that kept it secure.

Chapter 56

December 2002

Morgan recognized that every story does not have a happy ending. It took time and effort, and though difficult and clumsy at times, he and Ezra eventually found the ability to grow close. Probably in great part because Paige had become so attached to Ezra. She had the amazing ability to see the good in people, and he loved her more for it.

Despite his involvement in Paige's rescue and her affection for him, the Fullers maintained a discreet distance from Ezra. They expressed their gratitude and were courteous on the rare occasions when Ezra was present but never showed him any warmth. Understandable perhaps since he had once represented all the things which Josiah Fuller had taken a stand against.

Paige and Morgan divided their time between Mattapoisett and Cambridge. She favoring the former, he the latter based on simple geography. Just before Valentine's Day, Morgan had met a charming woman named Karen O'Malley. Karen's loyalty and affection coupled with Paige's helped Morgan gain a grudging respect for his father. If two caring and generous women could find something in Ezra to admire, he must be worthy of love.

Morgan had made a valiant effort after Paige's kidnapping, but one of the clouds that shadowed his silver lining was his inability to play competitive football again. The damage to his hip and knee was too great. He'd lost the ability to turn instantly and magically weave his way through a myriad of defenders. And the upshot of his departure from Crimson football meant newfound recognition and praise for Ben.

But Morgan had not lost the ability to help others strive for the elusive skill that had set him apart. And though he held no official status, he was a welcome and regular contributor on the Crimson practice field. As the 2002 season drew to a close, his head coach asked Morgan if he'd ever thought of coaching, reminding him that their backfield coach was leaving the year Morgan was due to graduate.

One thing he hadn't lost was the ability to mount one of the Fullers' horses and spend lazy afternoons overlooking Buzzards Bay. And Paige had taken Morgan up on his idea about bringing inner city kids to the country. And with her father's help (especially since it made all the newspapers in his district), they garnered funding so they could have weekly clinics and outings at the stable where she worked. Two years ago, Morgan had never imagined himself as an equestrian instructor, but as he helped teach ten-year-olds how to properly mount a horse he smiled. If life had taught him anything, it was a solid belief in Malcolm's favorite saying. "If you want God to laugh, tell him your plans!"

And though he seemed relieved of the burden of the troubling nightmares from his youth, there were the long dark moments when he would see something, hear a piece of music, or inhale a familiar scent, and he would think of his adoptive parents and all they'd done for him. He suspected these times would never pass.

One thing that Morgan never found an answer to: Sam's involvement and deep devotion to Paige. But as he spent days in the bedroom with the pictures that had puzzled him on that first weekend, he thought he might have found a conclusion. Paige was absent from that first family photo taken when Candy was just a toddler. She appeared in the one taken perhaps a year later, and she bore little resemblance to the tall, blond, statuesque Fuller clan. Was it possible that she was somehow connected to Sam, and the Fullers had adopted her like the Cahills had him? If so, the only ones he could ask comfortably would be his parents, and they would never have the chance to answer.

****

Every story doesn't have a happy ending. Morgan would wonder about other things from that first summer. After seeing her at a local shopping center, he wondered about Monique Burke. Vixen or victim? And of course there was that curious trip to Australia that never came to pass. Was his relationship with Paige really the cause of its cancellation? It seemed unlikely. And why the appearance of Sam's helpers that summer? Had they kept Paige close to home and employed the strong silent types because they were afraid for her?

But in the end he came to understand that life isn't a simple, zero-sum game. Complex and fraught with mistakes, detours, crossroads, and questions, all we can do is learn from it and our errors and move ahead, hoping to someday find the answers, knowing we may never get that chance.

But he had Paige and she had him. That would never change…and that, when all was summed up, was all that really mattered. Like the beautiful butterfly that emerged on their first sultry afternoon together, each had helped the other reclaim their life, and somewhere along the way helped another desperate lost soul shed his cocoon and live again.